T0151401

Queeries

Queeries An Anthology of Gay Male Prose

EDITED BY DENNIS DENISOFF

Arsenal Pulp Press

Vancouver, Canada

ARSENAL PULP PRESS
100-1062 Homer Street
Vancouver, BC V6B 2W9

The publisher gratefully acknowledges the assistance of the Canada Council and the Cultural Services Branch, B.C. Ministry of Tourism and Ministry Responsible for Culture.

Art Direction by Alex Hass
Cover Photo by Daniel Collins
Printed and bound in Canada by Kromar Printing

CANADIAN CATALOGUING IN PUBLICATION DATA
Main entry under title:
Queeries
ISBN 0-88978-271-7
1. Canadian fiction (English —20th century).*
2. Gay men's writings, Canadian (English).*
I. Denisoff, Dennis, 1961-
PS8323.H64Q43 1993   C813'.5408'0353
PR9197.33.H64Q43 1993   C93-091675-1

Contents

Acknowledgements

While the names of most of the individuals who made this anthology possible already appear in the Table of Contents, I would like to take this opportunity to thank the authors not only for their willing submission, but also for their insights, suggestions, and on-going correspondences. Both the clarification of the project and the process of selection were made much easier by the help and commentary of Dennis Cooper, M. Morgan Holmes and Robert K. Martin. The support and advice of Henry Abelove, Daniel Collins, Daniel Gawthrop, Kevin Killian, Don Larventz, Jim Nason, Steve Minuk and Felice Picano are also greatly appreciated. Besides the obvious benefits of having a supportive publisher from the start, I would like to thank the staff at Arsenal Pulp Press, particularly Brian Lam and Wendy Atkinson, for their flexibility and adaptability. Thanks also to all the community papers across Canada that supported *Queeries* and fostered the overwhelming response to the call for submissions. Finally, I would like to acknowledge my gratitude to the Canada Council for its financial support of this project.

Introduction: The Fruits of Queeriosity

This anthology of contemporary Canadian gay prose is a product of many individuals' serious curiosity regarding homosexual queerness. As *Queeries* passed through the stages of conception and production, the titular concern became, well, queeriouser and queeriouser. Not only did the number of participants in the project increase as more people became curious, but, with the passing of time, most of those associated with this project became more interested in the sociopolitical potency of queerness. It is not the issue of queerness, then, that became more *serious* as the project developed (to address another implied tangent of the neologism), but the project participants' awareness of this seriousness.

The concept of queerness, as a principal element in current sociopolitical manoeuvering regarding issues of gay and lesbian rights, is still only emergent, and it counters any attempts at fixed definitions. Since the articulation of either a conclusive definition or collectivizing characteristics of homosexual queerness is neither possible nor desirable at this time, I would instead like to consider some of the principal issues at play in queerness, as it is currently used, and to suggest a few of the ways in which the concept is addressed by the works collected here.

In his discussion of the strategic infiltration of dominant nineteenth-century language by homosexual discourse, Michel Foucault notes that

homosexuality began to speak in its own behalf, to demand that its legitimacy or "naturality" be acknowledged, often in the same vocabulary, using the same categories by which it was medically disqualified. There is not, on the one side, a discourse of power, and opposite it, another discourse that runs counter to it. Discourses are tactical elements or blocks operating in the field of force relations. (101-02)

The tactic of infiltration and contamination that Foucault discusses here can be seen to operate most obviously in terms central to gay society, such as 'camp,' 'dyke' and 'queen.' The same manoeuvering is also behind the contemporary usage of 'queer.' During most of the twentieth century, 'queer' was a term of disparagement used to suggest homosexuality or effeminacy. The word was adopted as an act of political effrontery by various people who have been oppressed because of their sexual preferences and, through this act of subversion, 'queer' has come to signify their collective political concerns. Such a use of the term is primarily practical; as Gabriel Rotello, former editor of the now-defunct New York weekly *Outweek*, explains, "When you're trying to describe this community, and you have to list gays, lesbians, bisexuals, drag queens, transsexuals (post-op and pre), it gets unwieldy. Queer says it all." As Rotello implies, the list of types of individuals who can be classified, or who classify themselves, as queer is never complete because an image of infinite plurality remains a major constituent of the term.

It is the seemingly paradoxical desire amongst queers for both pluralism and universalism that gives the concept its protean quality—a quality that, while disconcerting for some because of its apparent lack of grounding, is ultimately necessary if it is to play an ongoing formative role in the process of sociopolitical revision. This amorphousness, furthermore, ensures that the term's definitions are constantly critiqued and revised. Lisa Duggan, in her analysis of the concepts of identity and community in relation to queer politics, notes that

> the continuing work of queer politics and theory is to open up possibilities for coalition across barriers of class, race, and gender, and to somehow satisfy the paradoxical necessity of recognizing differences, while producing (provisional) unity. Can we avoid the dead end of various nationalisms and separatisms, without producing a bankrupt universalism? (26)

In Duggan's quotation, it may have been more appropriate to italicize, rather than bracket, the word 'provisional,' because it is the protean quality of queerness that ensures that any sense of unity, however useful, does not become fixed.

As Rotello's list of queers suggests, queerness is no longer associated with any specific type of sexual orientation. While sexual preference remains a fundamental element of queerness, 'queer' also connotes both political self-assertiveness and a dissension from heteronormativity and its support for rigid sexual (and therefore sociopolitical) classification, with "the rhetoric of difference replac[ing] the more assimilationist liberal emphasis on similarity to other groups" (Duggan 15). Michael Warner notes, in an analysis of 'queer' in contemporary gay political discourse, that the term "rejects a minoritizing logic of toleration or simple political interest-representation in favor of a more thorough resistance to regimes of the normal" (16). All discourse is political, but in the 1980s the word 'queer' began to model a bolder gown than it previously wore. Queerness now consciously proclaims political activism with regard to the assumption that a sexual normativity can be defined and maintained.

From its conception, *Queeries* has been intended primarily as a dynamic forum perpetuating discussions and analyses of the queer politics that are inscribed in contemporary gay male writing. Needless to say, the twenty-seven works included in this collection do not cover the spectrum of possible interpretations and representations of gay male queerness, even though diversity was one of the criteria used in the selection process. Nor are the twenty-five authors represented here by any means the only excellent gay male prose writers in Canada. Due to limits on space and funds, far more submissions worthy of publication had to be rejected than accepted. *Queeries* is best described as a sampler intended to be more disruptive than conclusive. While each of the chosen pieces stands as a well-written and provocative work on its own, the friction between the various works is equally stimulating. How does George K. Ilsley's depiction of a psychotic fusion of sex and love in "Talismen," for example, relate to the lush, romantic representation in Mark Kershaw's Whitmanesque "We Two Boys Together," and what do the discordant results of such a comparison say about queerness as a collectivizing trait? How does Jeff Kirby's criticism of snap queen wit, in his monologue "Grazy," relate to the camp, and often catty, tone used by various authors, including Kirby himself? I would suggest that what Kirby does, in this piece, is not condemn the type in general, but counter the dilution of its political potency (a dilution brought about by the persona's saturation of gay culture) through his foregrounding of the political function that the persona has generally fulfilled in the past.

It is worth noting that, like "Grazy," many of the submissions to *Queeries* were either monologues or plays. Performance and costuming, camp and drag, remain crucial elements of gay male literature, reflecting not only a major stream in the history of gay politics but also the contemporary relevance of past gay political acts and strategies. A common criticism of gay political action prior to Stonewall, even prior to the 1980s, has been that it lacked a direct and confident approach. While this argument is itself contentious, it should also be noted that overt militancy need not be the only method of attack, as is shown by various works in this collection, such as Mike Murphy's depiction of nonaction, in "Something Makes a Difference," and David Watmough's subtle comparison of heterosexual and homosexual versions of domesticity in "Wedding Dress for a Greek Groom."

In his 1982 book *The Homosexualization of America; The Americanization of the Homosexual*, Dennis Altman states that

> the crucial question to be asked about the new gay culture in its broadest sense is whether the various developments of the past decade have created a genuine gay community, one held together not just by external hostility and commercial venues, but by self-created institutions and images. In this process matters of politics, psychology, and aesthetics blur together. (155)

Even though it is now more than ten years since Altman made this statement, a similar consideration, and a similar awareness of the inherent contingency of politics, psychology and aesthetics, served as the inspiration for this anthology. There was never any doubt that the question of the existence of a "genuine gay community" could only be answered for the passing moment at best, but the potential, enduring insights into the concepts of gay culture and queerness that the contemplation of this issue would likely produce was equally enticing, if not more so.

Altman is aware that the rapid process of commodification in late capitalist society has made it difficult to differentiate between the originator(s) and the adoptees of any image. Whether it be chaps, Caesar cuts, or pacifiers, collectivizing symbols begin to spill out of the gay male community before the community is itself fully saturated. It would appear, however, that while members of the non-queer community have often been quick to adopt various queer surface-level aesthetics, they have, generally speaking, been slower at supporting sociopolitical issues that find popular support from members of the queer community. Two such issues that were common topics amongst the submissions for *Queeries* are AIDS and the relation between pain and pleasure. Approximately half of the submissions to the anthology addressed the issue of AIDS, often as a factor in the structuring of community, while about one third of the submissions dealt primarily with pain/abuse and pleasure/gratification of various types: homosexual, heterosexual, familial and others. The writers offered especially close analyses of ambivalent consent and the overlap of pain and pleasure, both on a physical and a psychological level.

If *Queeries* has exposed any new, particularly rich vein of aesthetic and thematic interest in contemporary gay male writing, it is what I call grunge prose, in which the depiction of sexual ambivalence is used as a tactic of sociopolitical criticism. In this collection, Lawrence Braithwaite's "Spunk: Special Kiddy Porn Issue," Sky Gilbert's "Calvin Kine and Johnny Bad," and Ian Stephens's "Wounds: Valentine's Day," contain the most obvious examples of grunge. In this anthology, the theme of sexual ambivalence often appears in literary efforts to conceptualize AIDS; however, as Stan Persky points out, "these days, even when the pestilence goes unspoken, we let it underlie everything" (9). Douglas Crimp comments, in an essay on queer political tactics and AIDS research, that the gay community is currently experiencing a "waning not only of our optimism but also of a period of limited but concrete successes for the AIDS activist movement" (4). This waning, Crimp goes on to note, has resulted in "a new kind of indifference, an indifference that has been called the 'normalization of AIDS' . . . AIDS is no longer an emergency. It's merely a permanent disaster" (5). Grunge prose is one product of this frustration and indifference.

Grunge writing recoils from the act of philosophizing and, therefore, actual discussions of AIDS and AIDS-related issues are not a mainstay of this body of literature. More often, the texts focus on depictions of either sexual indifference or violent forms of sexual experimentation. These two themes are actually complementary, both implying the author's sense of living in a period of sexual decadence. While sexual indifference reflects a sense of social decay and a loss of faith in the progress of the current social system, sexual experimentation suggests a striving for new sensual experiences that will shift the individual's purposefulness out of the secular realm and into a realm defined as ideal by negation—ideal because it denies the value systems of contemporary society. However, the fact that few of the submissions to *Queeries* (and none of the grunge writing of such popular authors as Kathy Acker, Dennis Cooper or Kevin Killian) depict idealized or utopian contemporary societies hints at the active intentions, rather than resignation, of the authors. Though grunge prose generally appears to be nihilistic on the surface, its tactics are actually commensurable with seemingly more optimistic representations. While the accentuation of sexual indifference over sexual experimentation suggests that nihilism, rather than antagonism, is the dominant attitude amongst gay male grunge writers in Canada today, the fact that a grunge text is itself the product of a creative act contradicts the author's implied nihilism. Grunge, therefore, is an aggressive interrogation and critique of the social constructs that oppress and misrepresent homosexuals and the gay community in general.

The pose of aggression does not mean, however, that grunge is more political or more sincere than works in which less obvious literary tactics are used in the process of interrogation. Grunge is not a dominant force in gay prose writing in general, with texts that focus overtly on gay-positive attitudes and the strength of community dominating both in publication and in audience reception. Some examples of pieces in *Queeries* that use this approach to gay issues in novel and enlightening ways include Peter Dickinson's "Home," which queries the concept of family in contemporary society, Joshua Berkovič's "Father Figure," which compares and contrasts the oppression of homosexuals and the oppression of Jews, and Raymond Woolfrey's "Pages from My Window: Red Geraniums," which analyzes the influence of AIDS on the formation of community. Playing with sympathy and conventional moral values, these texts ultimately force readers, whether they are antagonistic toward gay lifestyles or not, to realize the familiar premises on which many homosexuals base their existence.

While grunge denies its own ironic existence, as a creation produced from a seemingly nihilistic impetus, narratives that are overtly optimistic about the sincerity and strength of gay communities generally require only a mild form of irony, if any at all, to make their statements. Much gay writing, however, does use irony as a tactic of inclusion and cultural definition. In *Queeries*, examples of works in which irony plays a crucial role include Gordon D. Bradley's "Brennan's Eyes," which depicts a commonplace and somewhat run-down reality through the naïve romanticism of a gay, adolescent narrator, and Wayne Yung's "Brad: December 19, 1992," which uses irony to manipulate the readers' assumptions about the relation between sexual desire and its commodification. These works differ from the more optimistic pieces mentioned previously not only in the pivotal role that the irony plays, but also in its bitter potency.

In this brief introduction, I have referred to less than half of the pieces in the anthology, and have mentioned only a few of the queer tactics at play in the works. While the pieces collected in this volume display a variety of formal and thematic manoeuvres, the works are all united in their interrogation of various sociopolitical assumptions that marginalize the gay community and isolate homosexuals as individuals. The contemporary definitions of homosexual queerness are constructed on the same desire to question. It is my hope that *Queeries* succeeds in presenting a wide range of literary tactics that are part of the current sociopolitical strategy of queerness, while also perpetuating a sense of diversity and contingency amongst all members of the queer network.

—*Dennis Denisoff*
Spring 1993

Works Cited

Altman, Dennis. *The Homosexualization of America; The Americanization of the Homosexual.* New York: St. Martin's, 1992.

Crimp, Douglas. "Right On, Girlfriend!" *Social Text.* 33 (1992): 2-18.

Duggan, Lisa. "Making it Perfectly Queer." *Socialist Review.* 2.1 (1992): 11-31.

Foucault, Michel. *The History of Sexuality.* vol 1. New York: Vintage, 1980.

Persky, Stan. *Buddy's.* 1989. Vancouver: New Star, 1991.

Rotello, Gabriel. " 'Gay' Fades as Militants Pick 'Queer'." *The New York Times.* April 6, 1991.

Warner, Michael. "Introduction: Fear of a Queer Planet." *Social Text.* 29 (1991): 3-17.

Joshua Berkovič Father Figure

GWM, 5'10", 165, br hair
g eyes, 21, 7" cut, smooth
skin, seeks father figure
for good times, possible
relationship. No pain.
Box 2984.

Harry assessed the ad again while surveying from his station. The patrons were creating worlds at their separate tables: building histories in their whispered tête-à-têtes, reviving memories and aspirations between bites of food, illustrating situations and geographies with salt shakers, half-empty wine glasses, and drawing invisible lines on tablecloths with omnipotent fingers. First there was the word, gently radiating beyond each banquette to reach Harry's ears in disjointed phrases; then there was the food, which fuelled the fiction of their lives.

Harry, benevolent god, overlooked this universe and assessed which systems should be propelled with a dessert menu, and which should be annihilated by the arrival of the food bill. He oversaw it all while imagining a smooth-skinned young man, nude in his embrace.

The maître d', a scowling shadow in black tuxedo, sat two men at Harry's only empty table, reminding Harry of their hierarchical and ultimate power.

"Your waiter will arrive presently to serve you," the maître d' ordained, walking away, erect.

Harry filled the water glass of the older gentleman first. This rotund man was immersed in the menu; Harry divined a gourmand and a large tip. The younger man whispered "thank you" as his glass was filled, then dropped his eyes back to the plats principal. Harry glanced at him briefly.

"It's a paper for my history class," Harry heard from a distance, "on homosexuals in the concentration camps."

Harry wasn't sure if it was the dissonance of "homosexual" and "concentration camp" that invaded his universe, or whether his attention, like a finely-tuned and patient astronomical telescope, was set to pick up sounds from only that gentle voice. He reminded himself as he calmly set down a demitasse and a crème caramel on a nearby table that topics for school papers did not imply orientation.

"You couldn't find a better subject?"

"You mean Jews in the camps?"

"Well, you *are* Jewish."

"I'm also gay."

"Please, not so loud," said the father, looking around quickly.

"Dad, no one's listening. Anyway, everybody writes about the Jews, like no one else died, or mattered—"

"Don't talk stupid! Of course they mattered." Now it was the young boy who looked up, checking to see if his father's voice was imposing on others. "But when someone tries to annihilate an entire population, it is more significant than murdering ten percent of Europe's socialists, or thirty percent of Europe's gypsies."

"If the percentage of Europe's Jews and homosexuals killed were reversed, would you feel any less pain for your losses? Do you think there would be as many sympathetic books and made-for-TV movies about the gay holocaust as there are now for Jews?"

Harry refilled their water glasses. The young man drank from his immediately, this time not acknowledging Harry. A passionate young man, Harry thought. He wondered if that intensity carried into the bedroom, whether the man's hands would quiver crawling through Harry's chest hair, his face flush as Harry consumed his neck, or, after coming, whether his hands would fumble to regain composure, as now, waiting for his glass to be refilled.

Harry could feel his imagination manipulating his shorts. He wondered if the older man noticed the swelling. Worse, he worried that the son didn't.

Endive and radicchio salad: $4.95; potage à la crécy: $3.25; and do I want a 'son'? Would it be some ploy to live off a sugar-daddy until he runs off with the VCR? Médaillons rossini: $14.65. I can feel his eyes on me . . . yes, he just looked down. Could I have any intelligent conversation with the kid, or would I start, like, thrashing to headbanger shit?

"Actually, it wasn't a tragedy. To be tragic one has to have control over one's life, to try to be great, and fail through a flaw. What was the flaw or the greatness of being a Jew? That they wanted to be treated like equals, have human rights. They weren't great, so they couldn't be tragic. And they had no control: they were victims. Victims belong in melodramas—"

"Auschwitz was not a soap opera."

Omelette parmentier: $8.95; asperges béarnaise: $4.00.

"The homosexuals were in the same position as the Jews: victims. Except they got treated worse."

"Worse? How do you rate torture?"

"Maybe . . . when even the other people tortured feel they're innocent, but that you deserve it."

Don't I want an equal? If I always have to act a role, how long before it gets boring? Pichon-longueville: $60.00. What if I'm not his type? Does he want an older man who's stable and mature, or some pot-bellied, cigar-chomping caricature strutting around in stained boxer shorts, swilling beer? Attraction or psychoneurosis? The kid will never cruise me with his father here, and he doesn't have the bucks to eat here alone. Maybe an ad:

WE couldn't talk. You:
young, cute, green eyes,
brown hair, with father.
I: served you rack of
lamb . . .

"Life was hell for all of us, David. If we looked out for our kind . . . why not? Who else would take care of us? I remember seeing the pink triangles. They took care of each other, too. And we were dirty Jews to them, like we were to the others."

"Everyone hating each other, just like the Nazis wanted. Dad, you were interchangeable. Anyone who wants to kill one minority won't wait too long before getting another. If you got together, you don't think you could have done something? How many lives saved?"

"We all spoke different languages, were weak, terrified of being separated from family. . . . "

Tax, federal and provincial. Service. White-chocolate truffles . . . uh, I'll give them one extra, Harry thought, and let them fight over it.

"So how could the holocaust be a tragedy?"

"Because every murder is a tragedy."

"No. Every murder is a pity. They kill someone, or let them die, they show how little people are valued. It's a waste, our lives."

"So now who's melodramatic?"

"How can you be great and, at the same time, worthless?"

"We survived. We rebuilt our lives, and we won't let it happen again."

"Who had control over your survival? Mengele. Doctors decided who would live and die. Doctors under government orders. You were all either guinea pigs in medical experiments or part of the slave-labour force. Expendable. You survived through luck."

How many other men responded to the ad already? I'm not going to include a picture until I know what he's looking for. I'd die if the ad turned out to be from David. He's waving to me! Oh . . . the bill. Yeah, with Daddy's credit card.

"I hope you enjoyed your meal. Please come again."

"I hope to," David said, smiling, but without looking up.

Putting a hand gently on the older man's back, David guided him out the door, the gesture piercing Harry.

I don't look anything like him. I'm not fat, or balding. I've got a beard; he doesn't. I'm not Jewish. I could never afford to bring David here.

The maître d' lifted the little silver tray that held the credit-card receipt and an uneaten truffle, popped the chocolate into his mouth, and prodded Harry with the tray.

Orbiting his tables, Harry refilled wine glasses while his patrons recreated worlds in their own images.

Brandishing flowers, David's mother busied herself with the arrangement while her husband, obligated to male bravery, dragged a chair towards the bed. David stood silently and resolutely by his lover's bedside.

"Are you in pain?" she asked.

"No. I get morphine. I feel pretty good. I used to worry, before, when I'd start to have conversations, and then realize I was alone. Now I just enjoy the conversations. Are you really here?"

"How's your blood count?"

"They stopped checking it. At this point, the numbers don't mean anything anymore."

Say anything. Anything that sounds normal.

"It's terrible outside," she said. "It's raining, windy. It's miserable. And slippery . . . I knew I shouldn't have worn heels."

"It's just terrible."

"Yeah, it looks bad."

"It's just terrible."

Don't look at him.

"But you have a nice view."

"I can't really see it from the bed, but I know the view. You can see our house from here. David, point out our house to your parents."

My son living with another man; why can't I stop that from bothering me?

"Very nice."

"It's a nice house. David showed it to us before we came here. Nice. Clean. Quiet."

Their house. Yet he only lived there two weeks before he was admitted, or rather before he chose to admit himself. So David wouldn't wake at night to find the man beside him dead.

"There wasn't much choice," she said, rearranging the flowers in the chrome vase. She read the cards propped in the other bouquets: WE'LL VISIT YOU WHEN YOU'RE BACK HOME. THINKING OF YOU. GET WELL SOON. She was glad she tossed her card in the refuse bin by the elevator. "Do you like lilacs?"

"My favourite."

She stared at the machine pumping placebos into his veins, the monitor flashing sets of numbers as mystical as the cabala. She recalled her father hunched over the zohar, recalled the transformation of the man from tateh to zaddik. The change was imperceptible, but so astounding the result: like a poison gas that would take her father away from her; like words that divided people; like numbers that had to be destroyed. Science, like religion, both attracted and repulsed her.

"Patty, these are David's parents. I requested Patty."

"The other nurses are jealous of me. We all adore David. Ah, lilacs!"

"I need to be alone with Patty for a few minutes."

The nurse pulled the curtain around the bed. David's mother saw his chart lying open as they waited, and she read it just as she had searched her father's zohar. But there was no need to read all the details, to divine the abbreviations, or to assess the numbers; she only needed to see the mundane order of clinical facts to detach herself from the man, to restrain the visceral screams in her throat.

WEIGHT: 106
PRESSURE: 80/100
TEMPERATURE: 41

"I'd like to go to the toilet," David's mother overheard him say.

"Would you rather have a bedpan?" the nurse asked.

"I can make it to the bathroom. Please let me try."

Yesterday, according to the chart, he could walk, providing he was supported. His feet, lacking sensation, moved by rote, leaden, jerking.

Now she could see below the curtains, as Patty guided his legs to the floor. He pulled himself up, only to collapse. Knees buckling, his body resisted the ambitious dignity of independence. He fell on the commode. Patty wheeled him into the bathroom, his expression sunken in his skull.

"David told me that Jewish people cover the mirrors of someone in mourning, so they won't stare into their pain; I wish someone would have covered my mirrors years ago."

David's father moved the chair closer and everyone waited for what he would say but, after several interminable seconds, he only sighed.

They had discussed in the car what could not be discussed at the hospital: wills, funeral arrangements, income-tax reports. She guessed it didn't leave him much else.

"I'm glad you came. I wanted to say goodbye to you. I need to let go, I guess."

David's father took his hand, at first pretending to examine the bruise where the intravenous tube entered the emaciated arm, finally just squeezing the hand between both of his.

David sat beside the bed, reading, too used to hospitals. Let them have time to be alone, she thought, to say goodbye, or will sleep glide gently into death? Will David, glancing up, see the calm face, and know? No, she thought, they don't die as quickly or quietly as on TV.

David's father stood up. "We should head back before it gets dark. It's just terrible outside. Can we get you something before we go? What do you want?"

"How about another thirty years with David?"

David rushed out of the room.

"I really tried to take care of David."

"We know. Thank you."

She reached for the photograph on his night table—he and David mountain-climbing up north, near where they first lived. At 7,000 feet, in mountain gear and perched on a cliff, they were identifiably a couple. He was much taller than David, muscular, hairy, hints of a belly. He had his arm protectively around their son.

David's mother had met him only after he and David had moved back for his treatments. When she first saw him, skeletal and walking with a cane, she thought of the last time she had seen her father.

She couldn't sleep that night, finally deciding to wake her husband to talk about it.

But David's father hadn't been sleeping either. Each time he closed his eyes, he saw David's friend in the camp, answering to his name.

Stuart Blackley Summer–Weight

F O R   D A V I D   A N D   P A U L

Balancing his cup firmly in mid-air while dishes rained down from every direction, Gerry lurched over the tiers of glaring white china set out for coffee after Michael's memorial service. As he tried to render himself erect, and very still, he met a dazzling set of teeth at eye level that he mistook for more porcelain coming at him. "Walk much?" they enquired.

He sensed that the man next to him was structurally gorgeous, with a vague, chalky contour due to Gerry's rather impaired vision. To regain his sonic bearings, he choked out an introduction.

"Yes, we've met," the familiar voice replied.

"Sorry, I'm not very good with faces," said Gerry, adjusting his huge, futile pair of glasses.

"I remember you were very good with your hands, though."

"I take it this was not a formal introduction. Sorry if I'm hazy about the details."

"Are those new glasses? I didn't recognize you at first."

"I used to wear condoms . . . contacts . . . before."

Something like a freight train passed between them in absolute silence.

"I'm sorry I startled you back there. My pathetic attempt at humour."

The damage was already in progress.

"Are they still putting out the fire?"

"They may have to airdrop chemicals. Why don't we leave them to clean up, and go explore these hallowed, cum-stained halls?"

Gerry remembered well the ritual of studying Immanuel Kant's *Foundation to the Metaphysics of Morals* in the library of this college, of setting a goal of a few pages or even paragraphs, and when his head was ready to explode, attempting to apply the famous dicta—to act only according to that maxim by which you can at the same time will that it should become a universal law, and to treat man always as an end, never as a means only—by going for a long walk down these same halls or chatting with some fellow student, perhaps the jock who, lounging across from you, wore big socks and his gym shorts hiked up in a studied doze, and, after finding just such an empty music room as this, sucking his cock until he hammered out his orgasm.

"What did you study here?" Gerry asked.

"Men in heat, mostly, but I did get an engineering degree. Not here. At Western. This was my summer vacation, all the hours I spent here."

"Did I ever know your name?"

"No. Alvin Steins." They found each others' hands. "Though I used to make a point of giving my real name, however unlikely the encounter."

"I must have been very unlikely."

"You were amazing. But very quiet." A pleasing, embarrassed silence followed. "Sorry if I'm gushing. You had to be there."

Gerry felt a little sentimental about these two distant acquaintances who had shared genitals but, under the circumstances, there was also something mortifying about Alvin's easy recall. He searched the ghost sex of his past but couldn't find anything resembling Alvin, except the nubbly texture of garden statuary.

"Do you know David or Michael?" Gerry fished.

"Neither. I was someone's date. It appears I've been dumped."

"Aren't memorial services too sad."

They wandered outside to a balcony overhung by a canopy of dreary Gothic lace. In the middle distance they watched the anonymous haircuts of the student soccer teams bob over the unruffled nap of lawn.

"This is the last of days like this for awhile," Alvin observed. As he watched, a sinew of a Skin was plucked by an extreme move, provoking a grunt that emanated from deep inside the player's torso, a moment that seemed purely musical to him. Gerry, who was more aware of the sickening effect of staring close up at a Seurat, registered the red jerseys flickering across the screen of grass beyond them as more like a mesmerizing pattern of surface wounds.

After a spell, Gerry began to squirm amid the arrangement of circulating undergraduates. "I need a cigarette. Too much fresh air." He steadied his hand on Alvin's shoulder, and felt the dry, sleek surface.

"Rubber," Alvin said. "It's a poncho."

Suddenly, without warning, Gerry felt his past returning to him in a floating, slow-motion surge, as well as the immediate need to vomit. He pushed past Alvin into the corridor and, in his panic, lost his bearings among the freshmen and widows from the memorial service. He could place Alvin exactly here, two years ago this summer, could see the honeyed light searching every pore of the limestone hallway, emptied now by memory, the clarity of memory.

In the toilet along the well-worn path, everything was graph-paper white and sweaty with the usual humidity. Despite the subtle nauseating smell of urine, and the usual feeling in the pit of his stomach, Gerry began to get the old sexual hunger again, sucking his oxygen like chronic asthma. A perfect shoe, plain oxford poised only two feet from his own, pointed to instant relief from the adjoining cubicle, but Gerry knew this never happened in real life. He hesitated, and a note arrived from the shoe: *Eat me*. Well . . . one look won't hurt. Gerry crossed to the urinals opposite, casually peed, and glanced backwards. Incredible! The crack of the jamb revealed fragments of day-glo skin, and apparently an extra limb. An eye trapped Gerry in its searchlight.

They discreetly trailed each other to a small, finely appointed Victorian study, empty as a museum exhibit, on the rarely used third floor. Getting caught was always a gamble, but the dribble of summer students made the campus seem almost deserted, and sex in here as safe as a tomb: cautious fondling, the removal of every shred of clothing except shoes, and Gerry getting fucked standing against the oak panelling, followed without word or thought, only a little scuffle on the hardwood floor.

Despite the mine-field of acquaintances on campus, Gerry had never felt so reckless. His face skated over the man's spectacularly smooth, hard ass and, thumbing open the crack of his cheeks like a heavy dictionary, he pierced his tongue inside. Every pore in Gerry's face was filled with the swelling ass until he couldn't breathe for trying to chew his way through the flesh. Before he knew what had happened, he had his entire hand inside the man. The tentative probing that was safely within Gerry's repertoire was ravened up by this strange, eager mouth. The man was vulnerable to the smallest motor function of Gerry's wrist, yet his thrashing about seemed to threaten to pull Gerry into an uncontrollable sexual machinery.

Then the man did an extraordinarily calm thing. Bending completely over, he pulled both Gerry's legs under him in one movement, dropped to his knees, and came down on him, still clenching Gerry's hand deep inside him with his buttocks. Gerry was nearly levitating. He thrust up his cock like a baby's fist deep inside the man's throat and, when he came, he came like a gun going off.

Or it was the sound of a door slamming nearby. In the final blur, as the undressing rewound in fast motion, Gerry retained only the images of their shredded condom lying next to his face on the floor, and the man's superb rubber poncho spattered with his cum.

Gerry was eventually found by his pals throttling a balustrade with whitened knuckles, recovering from his bout with the past. They surrounded him like a gaggle of shop mechanics conferring over a rare automobile with a tendency to swerve into oncoming traffic.

"We leave you for five minutes and the entire West Wing is on fire!" Gerry had no resistance against the onslaught of his friends' best intentions. They stood about awkwardly, their youth collectively erased by the memorial service. Some had even lost their tans, momentarily.

"I liked the Yeats. I didn't get the political allegory, but it was nice . . . "

"The Cole Porter was great."

Gerry woke up, and repeated:

We know their dream; enough
To know they dreamed and are dead:
And what if excess of love
Bewildered them till they died?

After debating the degree of blame, if any, this implied, they agreed that the suit Paul made for David was itself a real poem. Paul had found some ink blue summerweight gabardine that hung like a light rain. He first used it to make his own suit for his lover Daryl's memorial service the summer before, and it had become a tradition, while supplies lasted.

"If I hear one more tale of unemployment, failed love or clinical depression, I'll implode. Can we please get out of here before I'm cornered by my ex and his latest case history?"

"There's still enough sun to get incinerated on the patio at Boots."

Just as suddenly as they had appeared, they were gone. They had taken to ministering to Gerry silently, like the angel hierarchies, and only the ruffle of wings or the squeak of weegums indicated that they were off fetching the car or retrieving the coats.

David and Paul, who were both tall, seemed to shift into view from out of the past like stage scenery of the Forest of Dunsinane. Or, Gerry thought, as things had turned out, our history has come to meet us and here we are, still standing. To be still standing was something.

"I'd given up on you," he told them. "What a nightmare."

"So we've heard."

Both tilted unconsciously away from Gerry, as if they might accidentally slop their store of tears. For visual relief during the ceremony, Gerry had set his eyes on Paul, who anxiously watched the lines of David's garment as it performed its important duties, and amused himself with Paul's little exasperated sighs, or sudden humble silence at the unsuspected moral dimension of his choice of cut and fabric. The three of them met now, in their mid-twenties, at the exact same point of exhaustion.

"The service was beautiful, though," Gerry added, which in retrospect did seem like the only lucid interval.

Various friends had read a series of poems, virtually an autobiography of Michael's taste, followed by David Roche's beautifully bruised version of "For All We Know." Michael had selected the works soon before he died, as if for an ideal reader but, when David came forward, it was the halting punctuation of his grief that spoke most eloquently.

Gerry himself had unravelled before his bewildered audience. "It occurred to me that the sensitive one was probably gay . . . Pierce, or whatever . . . 'Easter, 1916,' I mean. The Yeats. And he went to his death with that lout married to Maude Gonne . . . and the others, who were probably louts when they weren't transfigured by all that terrible beauty. He probably died for Ireland, famous or infamous, with a secret he would have kept all the way to the gallows. Especially from the heroic buddies he was going to hang with." About all of this they had had no response, but each for a moment thought that Michael would have at least known who Pierce was, if that was his name, and whether or not he had been gay.

"Could you believe that Richard sent a wreath after all of his shit?" Gerry asked.

"Chrysanthemums . . . such a serviceable flower," Paul intoned, evolving his six-foot-four frame into a merciless Maggie Smith.

Their laughter was almost alarming in their weakened state, but they held each other up like convulsive Graces. When Paul went to search for their missing transportation, no doubt cruising the neighbourhood, Gerry could finally tell David about the unnerving encounter with Alvin and the 'fisting thing' from his sordid past.

"Relax. Are you trying to invent new routes of transmission?"

"The condom was in pieces."

"Well, that's possible. But you told me ages ago that he didn't come inside you."

"But what about lesions or tears?"

"It's pointless obsessing over who did what when to whom. It's a done deal."

"But I'm going blind."

"I know." David placed an arm like a support beam on his shoulder. "I've heard about Alvin. He gets tested with every shift of the breeze. So, there's one less exchange to worry about."

Gerry held him away, as if assessing his bulk, which was considerable. David no longer seemed caught in the slipstream of his lover's last party. He was coming in from the periphery of his life.

As they hung around waiting, the circuitry of Hart House brought them back to a balcony that Gerry couldn't recognize until he came upon his coffee cup where he'd left it. They looked out over what might have easily been an empty parking lot, the polished grass now darkened by the coming night. They looked out nonetheless. The great whispering sheet of space invited them seductively into its safety net, but they deferred somehow, blissfully anchored. Twilight drained the cup Gerry held heavy and almost invisible in his hand, and his memory rippled stone, stone, the stone to trouble the living stream.

Gordon D. Bradley Brennan's Eyes

Brennan's eyes are worlds unto themselves: they churn and fold with green and gold and bronze; they ripple like warm, hidden lakes; traders bring back mahogany and cinnamon from within them. His eyelids rise and fall periodically, like curtains marking the end of one act or the start of the next.

I have a crush on this guy at school named Brennan. 'Crush' is a teenaged word. It implies compression or destruction. I feel both: I am compressed and futile when I try to talk with him—I am numb and useless; destruction is an over-dramatic way of saying my life hasn't been the same since him.

Brennan and I never talk. Either he's too shy or he has nothing to say to me. I prefer to believe he's shy.

We're leaving the one class we share, where Brennan has received a critical grilling tonight. I'd like to reassure him or to cheer him up. I have also been looking for an excuse to talk to him, which is difficult because really, logically, there is no reason why we should talk. I have quite enough friends, and zero is quite enough friends right now. Social inertia should logically win out, and I should just acknowledge (or even politely ignore) him. But Brennan is beautiful: he broods like a Byronic hero (dark and carrying heavy lead weights in his eyes), his gestures are perfectly choreographed. Brennan is simultaneously everything and nothing to me. He also strikes me as tender, which is why I am following him down the stairs. He is putting something into his pack, and he seems shocked that I have called his name (it's power to call someone by name).

"Here," I say. "This is a story that I wrote. I'd like you to read it. If you have time and if you'd be able to. . . . "

"Okay," he goes. "Cool."

I talk to a girl at school and she tells me that where she's from the greatest gift you can give someone is a story. The tradition of storytelling and the magic of altering place/time/event is foremost. I would like to entertain Brennan. I'd like to captivate and fascinate him, to amuse and occupy him. A tall order for an amateur. I walk home and the smells freeze in the winter air. Exhaust and french fry grease seem to linger, a smeared pawprint. At home someone's grilling sausages, and you can smell the burnt pigs trotting about on cloven hooves. My tiny room with its single bed seems a sanctuary.

I have a ghost TV. All of the plugs in my boarding house are grounded to the same place; everyone's TV meets somewhere electrically. Besides getting free cable and pay TV, I also get to see whatever the neighbour on my left is watching on his VCR. Last night I saw an awesome Bruce Lee retrospective. Tonight he is playing a gay porno film called *Lagoon Lust:* the water is aqua; the wet Speedos are tangerine or black; the men are firm, tanned and have hairless bodies. I am not in the mood tonight—I have a headache. I have considered switching hands so that I'd feel like a stranger.

The philosophical distances separating my brain, my heart and my body. I'm trying to reconcile the three. I am not sure how my heart feels or what it is saying; its language is coarse and unexpected. Its native speech sways me with immediacy and truth. If I could figure out what my heart really wants, perhaps I could enact the getting of it.

I leave the sound on the TV and adjourn to my small table, which is all of four feet from my bed. I take two Actifed and a Gravol. I sit at my desk to write this shit about Brennan's eyes. The sounds of soulless humping, of greased and sweaty flesh, fill the room, which is otherwise dead silent except for my angst. I wonder if it's possible to have sex vicariously—other people humping each other like animals, others coming. I have a cigarette and go to sleep under Brennan's eyes.

A saffron sunrise under God's most excellent eyes. I realize I have been worshipping Brennan for about a month now, from afar. I am obsessed with inventing scenarios for us. I have endowed him with personality traits that he might never imagine. In short, I have destroyed a man. Maybe not destroyed. I haven't altered him or done anything to him. I haven't really even spoken with him.

This morning I take a bath because I have the time. I run the water way too hot, as a form of self-flagellation. I speak to myself: *get in you fucker—I dare you.*

I get in and I am quietly yelping, sweating, my face red. Steam is rising nastily all around me.

All of your problems could be solved. Just add cold water.

"All of them?" I respond, sensing this is too good to be true.

The more pressing ones.
"What about Brennan?"
What about him?
So I don't add cold water. I ignore the heat, and in my dreams I take Brennan on a road trip to Montréal. He does the driving to the Québec border. I get the boring part. It's all boring actually. I decide to omit the driving—the satin tape effect of highway driving crosses easily enough into my dreams on its own.

Once we are in Montréal, the rainy city beckons us: the cast-iron spiral staircases, the pouty Québécois. We have ordered a blowdryer, an iron, a can opener and a corkscrew from room service—just to keep them on their toes. There are seventy-two channels on our hotel TV which we watch while drinking red wine. Brennan smells like Dial soap from the shower, and his hair is raked back in jags. His lips are slightly stained from the wine, which tastes of oak and tannin, afternoons in Portugal, dates, figs and plums.

I grab the shitbox Japanese camera (which has an autotimer so that we can both be in the pictures) and we walk through the rain up Boulevard St-Laurent. There are aluminum pots and pans in the window of a hardware store, Kosher delicatessens smelling of smoked meat and latkes with sour cream, taverns with charcoal-smeared artsy types. I love this city. We take pictures.

We stop for a game of pool at Bar St-Laurent. Some whores and junkies watch us. We drink Miller High Life, which comes in quart bottles so big that your hand feels like Barbie's. Brennan plays some tunes on the jukebox and I go to the washroom. There is this tall lanky man standing in the doorway with a joint in his hand.

"Es-tu venu pour un piss ou un toke?" he asks.

"Out of my way, man," I say. "I don't speak French."

Later we get some curried chicken from a takeout, a baguette and more red wine. Or maybe the concierge brings us champagne. This is where my bathwater gets cold.

I am not in Montréal and Brennan is not here. I am in a lukewarm bath at home. In my room I turn on the TV. The neighbour is watching a tape of last year's *Miss Universe Pageant.* How can they call it this when they have no contestants from other planets?

Later tonight I will come home from work and the neighbour will be watching *Construction Honchos in the Dust.* The concrete will be grey, the jeans faded and packed tightly, and the men will be firm, tanned and have hairless bodies. I will go to sleep to the ring of a series of loveless humps. More humps than a fucking camel farm.

I see Brennan at school and he likes my story. Maybe he says he loves it—I can't remember. This is gratifying, and I want to ask a thousand questions: did it make pictures for you; did you get shivers like I did; does it speak to you? I ask no questions. Brennan mentions my language is dense and cloying in places—not wholesome enough.

The following week I bring him another story and some blackstrap molasses/whole wheat bread. If Brennan says the story isn't magic, I'll bring him a piece of beach glass that depicts ten million angels dancing on the head of a pin. (Brennan's beautiful eyes cross my text, left to right and slowly down.)

When I was small we used to watch the Magic Tom show on TV. This was an older magician who made things come out of people's ears. At the end of his show, he would always take an empty cardboard cylinder speckled with stars, do some magic things, and the tube would be full of candies. These were then tossed into the young audience.

When Magic Tom came to town, my brother and sister and I had to see him or our lives would obviously end. I nearly peed myself when I was chosen as his helper. I don't so much remember the candy. What I do remember is: I stand close to the magician under the stagelights. Whenever I smell that certain mix of Noxzema, pancake makeup and loneliness, Magic Tom is right in front of me. I smell that smell today; Brennan has the magician smell.

It's 9:30 p.m., and I just get to the liquor store in time for red wine. At home I write. I have become very productive since Brennan has been reading my stories. But I am numb. There is a drop of cold water hanging on a rainpipe in February. It freezes, and another joins it, extending it. A realization hardens, crystal clear: an icicle is forming in my brain: drops of reason freezing. My fingers and toes are cold.

The fake Brennan and I live in an igloo of prose that I've built for us. It is walled and safe, but chill. The fake Brennan's with me; the real one isn't. The real one doesn't exist the way I see him, is not an accessory to my dreams, would never believe how I feel. We have scarcely spoken.

The neighbour is watching *Ivy League Studs*. The dorm showers are white-tiled, the towels are thirsty, plush cotton, and the men have firm, tanned and hairless bodies. My ears fill with the echoes of heartless humps.

This is the Hour of Lead—
Remember, if outlived,
As Freezing persons, recollect the Snow—
First—Chill—then Stupor—then the letting go—
     —*Emily Dickinson, no. 341*

Lawrence Braithwaite
Spunk: Special Kiddy Porn Issue

F O R   M E N   T H A T
A P P R E C I A T E   T H E M

Oct 12, 1965 VIDEO PACK 26

[Intrude from overhead above] they are smaller than normal. Aged 6yrs, they play;

—Gooood, good—

They play. Daddy's on the ladder above them. He handles the camera and begins to zoom in slowly.

—O.k., Joey starts takin' his shirt off. Stephen's, yeah, take it off—

The boy looks up at Daddy:

—No, No, I told you not to look at me—

Mr Mozart never took his eyes off the monitor.

—You like tv, Joey—

Joey takes his brother's clothes off, then his.

—Now the shorts and then you can do the same—

And so on.

—I love it. You're pleasing daddy kiss him down there again, o.k., we're not going for the money shots yet—

—I'll explain . . . —

Joey is hairless. He sits slumped in an armchair, happy for the camera.

—Beautiful—

Stephen is, too.

—Great, great—

They kiss and Joey kisses Stephen nowhere near his lips. Stephen has his legs spread.

But it was time for mommy to come home and for daddy to edit.

MONEY SHOT // NARRATIVE FUNCTION // SIGNALLING THE CLIMAX OF A GENITAL EVENT. THE MOST IMPORTANT ELEMENT . . . EVERYTHING IN THE NARRATIVE SHOULD BE SACRIFICED AT ITS EXPENSE.

Ziplow/Williams

Secret sex
education //
commercial and home
made //
film and video—the
taking of a photograph
is in itself an act of
sexual abuse.
The making of video is
a healthy expression
involving consenting or
eventually consenting
objects.

Braithwaite/Tate./T013

35:26 min sec

Dad always took care of the spunk shots

Some
of the
men I
work
with
mastur
bate
whilst
looking
throug
h
Mother
care or
childre
n's
catalog
ues . . . th
ey find

photo-
graphs
—even
of
toddler
s—very
arousin
g.

erot
ica
toys
gam
es
dra
win
gs
fant
asy
wri
ting

seri
ous
aca
dem
ic
text
s
abo
ut
pae
dop
hili
a

The Familyman
+
The Homosexual
=
Pornography

Wyre/
Braithwaite

S
av
e
th
e
C
hil
dr
e
n
N
o
w
,
Pl
e
as
e

Homemade

—I feel really hot Joey—
—Yeah me too. wannagofor—
a swim—
—Yeah sure thadbegreat—

JoeyandStephenMozartpickedupavideocama
fterworkingallsummeronpeopleslawns.The
yhadenoughleftovertobuythelatestbookonho
meediting.Daddytaughtthemalotbuthishand
wasn'tsteadyenoughandhislightingandpoints
ofviewwerelimited.Daddy'slightingdidn'tca
pturethemilkywhitesilknessoftheirsoftskin

The camera shoots a middle shot of two boys jogging toward the pool.
Their backsides all untanned, pinky, round, firm and bouncy.

They dive in:

the camera picks up
the underwater fondle and
suck scene, but Joey
inhales water.

—It's o.k. we'll move to the cutaways—

It took hours to get the meatshots right. Stephen was working with close-ups and clear-plate glasses.

HE DIDDLES THE SWEATY LAD.
HE SOON HAS HIS DONG DOWN
HIS THROAT.
HE IS MOUNTING HIS GIGANTIC
COCK.

The
conventional
wisdom among
many
investigators
has been to
distinguish
between the
glossy
commercial
child
pornography
... produced in
Europe, and the
home-produced
porn of the
U.S.A.

In commercial child
pornography films, some
attempt is made at
imitating adult
pornography—several
performers, lights, music and
titles.
Typical homemade films involve
a single child being taken to
a hotel room where the
abuser waits with a video
camera.

Tate

Braithwaite/Jupp
... a huge-hootered blond who shoots a chunky load while being finger fucked.

It must have visual proof of the
involuntary
confession of pleasure that peni-
tration
obscures.
The stakes of visibility have been
escalated to include the precise
moment of orgasm.
Williams

THIS WILL BE CALLED JOE AND HIS BROTHER

60:32 min sec

They	The vcr	It was pride
were	went	day somew
sitting	off.	here.
on the	And	
couch	they	
viewing	stared	
the	ahead,	
day's	then	
rushes.	flipped	
	on the	
	tv.	

—Stephen, do you think the reason we're queer is because dad took pictures of us—

—yeah—

Joey and Stephen decided to get political. They found out where a demo was being held and dressed up and went.

Seven years later, they died for seconds, came to life and shot more videos wearing leather harnesses and breaking homophobic cds.

They saw a show with queer people in it; they were black and happy: they sang a lot—like the songs Joey and Stephen would hear in the gender exclusive clubs and later at warehouse parties.

—Stephen, have we slept with any of them—

—No, I don't think so—

—Catch the image off the monitor—

Joey and Stephen packed a shotgun into a gym bag and rode around town, with the floppy disk and the printed video image taped to their dashboard, looking for a blackqueer.

Chad Scott was coming from a university commerce and engineering party, where he went as a Zulu. He had borrowed his sister's wig and she had blackened out his face and made him a perfect fur loincloth g-string. Joey and Stephen had found their man . . .

—A blackguy—

—where—

—There, look at the image. He fits it perfect—

—Yeah, he's stopping at the corner—

All at once . . . the attitude towards me changed, and they turned into overbearing liberals. We were no longer equals. They made it clear that i was totally under their power, and that I had two choices: i could put myself under their protection, and do everything they said, or they would turn me in and i would go to the slammer.

Braithwaite/Scott/Berdan

But in the blink of an eye, whites look up to and revere the black body, lost in awe and envy as the black subject is idolized as the embodiment of the whites' ideal.

Mercer

H
o
w
C
o
ul
di
t
b
e

COMMERCIAL

23 Mar 1991 Video Pack 210

In order to blacken the black up more, Joey held the gun to Chad's head as Stephen painted white lips around the black's mouth.

—This will make a great loop—

The stag film shows . . . its almost exclusively male audiences, discontinuous moments of genital activity, the new narrative pornos organize this activity into complete and fully rounded dramas . . . of arousal, excitement, climax, and satisfaction.

Braithwaite/Williams

Loops can be seen in private booths in adult arcades

Williams

The lighting was dim to darken the atmosphere—make it look more street.

Plot:

Blackonwhite, a handsome lean black guy
meets two very rough-looking, very white
guys, and fucks them, sucks them, and
fucks them again.
Then a shotgun is put into the black's
mouth and he sucks on it . . .

CLOSE-UP OF HIS TANGY BUTT
CUT BACK TO THEIR COCKS

as they deliver the goods in his face.

Commonly
the children are
required to
have sex with
other
youngsters as
well as
adults . . .
Frequently they
are made to
urinate on each
other or on their
abusers. Almost
invariably their
faces, chests or
genitalia are
coated
in semen when
the
adult men
ejaculate
over them.

Tate

Deliver the
goods: slang
term for the
moment in hard-
core film—the
representation of
sexual pleasure.

Williams

90:33 min sec

Stephen shuts the video camera off and starts to wipe off his brother and himself. Joey raises his arms in joy, still holding the shotgun, as his brother cleans him.

They flip Chad a 50 and see him out the door.

Stephen and Joey had found a way to outdo their daddy. They got a grant for the "blackonwhite" video and wrote papers; later they opened up a media centre in the city. All the politicians discussed them and some even used their work for ad campaigns.

They were queer because of dad. They were loved because of their talent and because they looked good too. They had become political.

14 Jul 1992 VIDEO PACK 310
Camera held at chest level:
[screen reads]
Demo tonight

Quick fade //

00:32 min sec

—I like that, Stephen; what do you think—
—It's cool, yeah, sure. You horny? We could watch a Lance video—
—The pool one and the hitchhiker one: I'll be Leo—

Daniel Cunningham The Gaunt Man

Sometimes, in the inky blackness of the night, when my only companion is a half-empty bottle of whisky, I remember many things. I remember Alex. I recall the last time I saw him.

It was Tuesday. The sound of the morning paper hitting the front door woke me. I wish I hadn't opened the door, I wish I hadn't read the paper. The headlines screamed AIDS HOLOCAUST; the details were equally lurid. In Toronto, three men barricaded the doors of a house, doused it with gasoline, then torched the place. Inside were seven men, all with AIDS. No one survived.

My stomach growled, breaking the silence. Could it be that endless nights of drinking, drugs and fornication were finally taking their toll? Or did this cheery bit of news have anything to do with it? Maybe I was hungry? I opened the fridge, then quickly slammed it shut. No goddamned food!

I sat around all morning drinking coffee which, given the condition of my stomach, was not the wisest thing to do. Then I took a bath. The hot water soothed my aching body and washed away all traces of the previous night's debauch. While I soaked, recalling my many transgressions, the telephone rang. I let it ring; nothing was going to interrupt this confession. The caller was persistent, however, so, annoyed and dripping wet, I finally answered it.

I was surprised to find it was Alex; he hardly ever called. As he spoke, I closed my eyes and imagined him standing before me. I did this often when I thought of Alex, though I must confess I would have preferred it if imagination had nothing to do with it. He had broad shoulders, a tapered waist and a washboard stomach upon which any gay man would want to rest his head.

Alex had been in the Merchant Marine. He had travelled all over the world. He had been to places I had seen only in pictures, had done things I had read about only in books. I wanted Alex to tell me stories of seas, and ships, and sailors, like in Conrad, Melville and London, but he never did. We rarely talked. He didn't tell me why he left the Merchant Marine; he didn't tell anyone. He just arrived in Edmonton about three years ago—no reason given.

In fact, Alex never really said much of anything to anybody. He was very uncomfortable with people. The only time I ever saw him at a party, he arrived late and left early. He sat alone in a corner, apart from the crowd, shrouded in shadows. When I approached him and started to speak, he avoided my eyes. "Can't talk," he mumbled. Then he left. Now, here he was on the phone, wanting to talk. I dried quickly, dressed and went right over.

The door was unlocked, and the blinds drawn, shutting out the light from the street above. On the table by the door was an unfolded piece of paper containing the name and number of a friend of mine, Benny. I had placed it there almost a year ago. I had told Alex to give him a call, but he never did. It hadn't been moved.

Alex was sitting in an armchair in the far corner of the room. This morning's paper was spread out on the floor before him. On the side table was a half-empty bottle of whisky. Alex liked the taste of whisky. "A man's drink," he had once said. He offered me some, which I accepted, then he pointed towards the sofa. After I sat down, he began his tale. "The Congo is a magnificent river, the highway to the heartland." Alex had been there, in 1980.

It was the end of a hectic day—low tide, late arrival, corrupt authorities. Alex had just finished unloading some crates, hours behind schedule. He was hot and his shirt clung to him like another layer of skin. He was thinking of a cold shower when he tripped and fell over what appeared to be a pile of garbage. It wasn't garbage, however. When Alex looked back, there was a man at his feet. He was lying on his side, curled up, but Alex could tell he was tall, and extremely thin.

The man's skin was wrinkled, hanging in loose folds that collected at his joints. All of these were swollen, especially his knees and elbows. His lips were swollen too, and his eyes were set deep in such oversized pockets that Alex thought they might fall out. Flies buzzed around the man's head. One landed on his cheek and, when he tried to brush it aside, his arm jerked upward like a marionette's.

The man was not alone. Three others stood off to the side, a huddled mass of skin and bones. They wore little and their meagre possessions lay at their feet. They said nothing.

As Alex stood up, he heard horns blaring in the distance and, looking in the direction of the sound, saw four vehicles racing along the waterfront towards the dock.

The first two were jeeps, the latter two trucks. They came to an abrupt halt about one hundred feet away. Before the dust could settle, the tailgate of each truck fell open and armed soldiers jumped out.

"What the hell's going on?" It was Søren, the first mate.

"Damned if I know," Alex said.

One soldier, who had been sitting in the first jeep, swaggered towards them. He had pockmarks on his cheeks, the rank of a lieutenant, and spoke in a language that neither Alex nor Søren could understand. When he was about ten feet from them, he raised the barrel of his gun, and motioned them aside. They obeyed. He continued on until he was standing directly in front of the gaunt man. The lieutenant's eyes narrowed and he clenched his teeth. His finger tightened around the trigger of his gun.

The gaunt man rose and began to speak. Alex didn't have to know what he was saying to know what he was doing. He was pleading, but for what? The gaunt man gestured towards his three companions and brought his bony hands together, as if in prayer. Then he stepped forward. The lieutenant shouted and immediately stepped back. When the gaunt man took another step forward, the lieutenant raised his gun. He was going to fire. Alex sprang towards the pair but the lieutenant spun around and, with his gun, struck Alex across the head. Søren rushed towards Alex but stopped short. Now the lieutenant was aiming at him.

The confrontation did not go unnoticed; the dock was at a standstill. From an office in an adjacent building, Captain Jarvis had also watched the scene unfold. He had left the office as soon as the lieutenant started giving directions with a firearm so he hadn't actually seen the lieutenant strike Alex. The gash over Alex's left eye was proof enough.

Cautiously, Captain Jarvis approached the lieutenant, inquiring in English as to what was going on. He got no reply. He tried French—still no reply—and then a bastardized version of Lingala, the only native language he knew.

The lieutenant sneered but said nothing. Did he understand Captain Jarvis? No one really knew for sure. It wouldn't have made a difference anyway; the lieutenant was not concerned with questions. He had a job to do and nothing was going to prevent him from doing it.

The captain examined Alex's wound, bloody but superficial, and then suggested they leave. Alex disagreed. "We can't abandon these people."

"Why not? They're nothing to us. For all we know they could be criminals."

"Fuck, Captain, look at them! They don't look like criminals to me."

"Nor to me," added Søren.

"It's none of our business," snapped the captain.

The lieutenant raised his voice, ending the argument. He then ordered four soldiers back to the trucks. Turning to another soldier, who was obviously second in command, he continued barking orders.

"What's he saying, Captain?" asked Alex.

"I'm not sure."

"What's happening?"

"Shut up!"

The lieutnenant was raving now, the blood vessels in his neck becoming engorged. "Something about a disease. . . . "

"A disease?"

"A thin disease."

"You mean these people are sick?" Alex was astounded. He was also angry—God, how he hated this place. They all did, even Captain Jarvis. Here, they were the confused foreigners, trying in vain to understand a culture that defied explanation. They had no power. They were forced to bribe officials just to get a decent day's work done. Nothing worked like it was supposed to, and nothing made any sense.

Suddenly the lieutenant turned, fixing his gaze on Alex, Søren and Captain Jarvis, speaking so quickly that the captain could not understand a word. With the barrel of his gun he pointed towards a dinghy tied to the dock. This needed no translation.

Alex wanted to stay, but he knew that the lieutenant would kill him if he tried to interfere—kill him, Søren, even the captain.

So this is Africa, Alex thought. Such a godforsaken place. Such barbaric people. He reassured himself that this could never happen in the civilized world, that in Canada it would be the disease that was eradicated, and not the people. Alex knew what was going to happen next; he just wasn't prepared to see it.

The soldiers poured gasoline on the four men. The lieutenant stepped back, pointed a flare gun and fired. The explosion set the sky ablaze. As the flames began to consume their flesh, three of the men bolted for the river. The soldiers immediately mowed them down. The fourth man, the gaunt man, just stood in silence, awaiting death. When he fell to the ground, the soldiers riddled him with bullets too.

The dinghy drifted downstream.

Alex stopped speaking and I poured myself another drink; I should have finished the bottle. I asked him if he wanted me to stay. He shook his head.

"Are you sure?"

He said nothing.

When I got up to go, he mumbled under his breath, "This isn't supposed to happen here." As I closed the door, his pitiful voice, repeating the sentence over and over, echoed through the hallway.

I walked the streets for hours, not wanting to go home. When I finally did get back, the phone was ringing. I couldn't talk to anyone, so I unplugged it. I lay on my bed and watched the sunlight move across the ceiling to the far wall, marking the end of the day. I watched the light begin to fade, to fail. While the darkness surrounded me, Alex's voice continued to ring in my ears.

Later that night, I saw Benny. He was sitting alone in a bar, sobbing softly, drinking heavily.

"Do something," the bartender pleaded to me. "He's driving away business."

I sat down next to Benny. "What's the matter?" I asked.

"Where have you been?" he demanded. "I've been phoning you all afternoon."

I could have given the truth, but didn't. After all, Alex had told his story to me, not to Benny, not to anybody else. So I lied and told him I had spent the afternoon drinking and fucking.

"You'll never change, will you?" he snapped.

I didn't reply.

"The police called me this afternoon. They found my number at Alex's."

"What were they doing there?"

"You don't know, then?"

"Know what?"

I have never forgotten what Benny told me in that bar, though I've often tried. That afternoon, Alex had gone to Paul Kane Park, doused himself with gasoline, and struck a match.

David Dakar
The Guardian of Domestic Tranquility

First of all, I believe in the freedom to consume. I'm not one of these socialist jerks who—no, no, wait:

First of all, it was an election year. Which is not such a good thing, at least not in a democratic country. The main problem with people who think of themselves as democrats is that they're not acquainted with losing. Losing is part of democracy—it's at least half of democracy. Until you can learn to accept losing, it's all wishful thinking. But even winning in a democracy is a lot of wishful thinking. The only changes that occur around here are currency devaluations and more expensive clothes for the emperor. The real revolution of rising expectations rests on magic—winning the lottery, the express return to honest values, more ozone, all of that. Which, despite my enormous social conscience, isn't necessarily what I'd wish for if a genie came my way.

If luck were in my court, if I were rubbing an old lamp one day and a genie emerged and offered me one wish, I'd wish for visual histories of virtually everyone in the western hemisphere. Imagine: a library of European biographical newsreels. Oh god, I know that sounds terribly ethnocentric but think of the bribery-slash-blackmail value. Think of the self-interest fulfillment. Better yet, just make that visual histories of post-industrial revolution elites of European ancestry. No, forget that idea, here's the best scenario: one day, extra-terrestrials (Martians, they're really Martians, just that real science has now merged with popular science so we have this overlap of technical terms in the new age paranormal) come down to Earth and the first person they meet is me. They meet me and are able to transfer to me telepathically all the possible knowledge and human gifts known to man. To mankind. To peoplekind (I'm trying not to be gender-specific). Anyway, there I am, a concert pianist, a physicist, a charismatic evangelist. It's all I can do to lampshade the genius within. Alas (what an archaic term, but unfortunately unreplaced in time by modern lingo—lingo, there's another), enlightenment doesn't come easy. Sleep therapy, metaphysics, hypnotism, mean-spirited unemotional intellectual cliques—nothing provides policy coverage. Nobody will do it for you. You actually have to get up and enlighten yourself. It's a basic truth I've tried hard to avoid.

Even self-enlightened individuals have a hard time bearing their adult responsibilities. Take fatherhood, for example. Bad example. Besides, I'm not interested in genetically forcing myself on another person. Well, we're all just overgrown fertilized eggs anyway. And I know what a monster I was as a kid and therefore the horror that is my sperm. The horror that is my sperm. In pre-twentieth century times, sperm was one of the few constant, free things the average prole could depend on. Thanks to science, taxation, technology and disease, sperm is now just so much organic metaphor. My advice—avoid the cost of sharing sperm. Which is not an anti-sex sentiment, but rather another twentieth-century wish. I mean, everything has either been invented, outlawed, beaten beyond boredom or milked to near-extinction. At least sharing wishes comes tax-free.

Of course, the best things to share are the expensive things: leather jackets, audio-visual aids (the more hi-tech, the better), things of cost but not quality (e.g. beer, pornography, etc.), things of unendurable oppression (e.g. politics, taxes and so forth), and of course those most embarrassing moments of our true nature that drive us to alcohol and adult fantasy material. When I, as a consenting adult, am driven to the sexual video image, I find myself with this dilemma: do I surrender to the pitifully one-dimensional caricature of fantasy sex, or do I deconstruct the preoccupation with dildos? Worse than that, I've never been able to figure out when you're supposed to come while watching pornography—at the end, when the big stars come? Or are you supposed to just excite yourself until you come at will? This has always been my own personal moot point. My own personal moot point. Brazen porn, however, on the cutting edge, tends to have orgasm scenes mid-session. And of course, the sucking that comes before the fucking may not come at all and nowadays who knows when they'll throw in a sex toy, like a dildo (word origin unknown, should any semioticians be scanning the text). (Really now, can we call a piece of latex modelled after Jeff Stryker's erect penis a 'toy'? I mean, do Wham-O! frisbees and Midge dolls even compare?)

I was accused of having visual aids some years ago, by a country singer who sang an underground hit about baby Jesus, and I've never denied it. What's to deny? I know the style and the age and the gangbang scenarios as second nature; I know when directors have gone out on a limb and when their pseudonym falseness compares with the greats; and of course I know those stars. The porno star system is only the Hollywood star system magnified a million times over, so 'superstars' are born and retired in three-flick, double-orgy careers. Hollywood Hedon, the Palm Beach Penis, Astor Asslets in the pleasures of forbidden paradises. Are they such a personal thing, these movies, that in fact you shouldn't come at all—just watch in amazement that this sort of caricature exists to excite us? Being a liberal, I'm not against pornography. I'm not against very much in fact—it's a liberal curse. Maybe the whole pornographic genre can be traced back to a single booth picture house with quarter slots and a man with a mop outside. Like the one-horse cowboy, we'll call it the one-armed wanker.

I've always wanted to make a porno. For a first feature, to be called *Greased Lightning*, I'd duplicate the cruising fifties—boy hoods and rumble seats. With my directorial status established, I'd embark on my *pièce de resistance—Good Looking Assholes*. In the requisite sequel I'd feature all sorts of egomaniacal queers with bulging gym bodies (but who couldn't converse with a cow) in *Mean Queens: Good Looking Assholes Too*. Unfortunately, this is all a dream because my passport says I'm a Canadian. In Canada, public use of the word 'asshole' is considered deleterious to those who, although assholes themselves, find freedom of speech a hazard to family values.

Speaking of freedom, I was in the public washroom one day when a man with audaciously tasteless footwear and, as it turned out, terribly dark, straight black hair that just gently caressed his face sat down in the stall next to mine. It was a bit early. I mean, this was one of those washrooms where there's one or two people hanging about the door making sure it's a safe environment for sex. I'm not promiscuous, but I do enjoy the odd visit to the pubic toilet. I too used to concern myself with these issues. Then I read *Why Die* by Dr. Seth and it changed my views. He said that degenerative disease was just the subordination of individual values to constrictive, misguided, appropriated, moral hogwash. He said that lending your physical self to the hateful discourse of spiteful, narrow-minded social truants was certain death, which was in itself a twelve-step programme toward accepting yourself as worthless. Gosh, all of this sounds awfully mechanical and cold, and I really want to bring some warmth and feeling to this story. And of course to relate the facts. I guess I have to weigh the moral equations—is morality, in fact, like development? Can there be sustained morality or under-morality? Are those who are most 'moral' among us actually morally deprived? There really isn't any way to quantify such subjective, qualitative social features, so why we spend so much time arguing about them, I don't know. That's all there is to the world. Get used to it, people. I don't lose any sleep over it. Wait, this story isn't about deprivation—it's about the black-haired, rather good-looking but obviously imbalanced man in the next stall.

I've worked in public service and I can tell you a lot about mentally imbalanced people. First, all of those isolated investment bankers who rush between their gleaming Jaguars, underground garages, towering office blocks and over-designed bistros may be unaware (but not immune) to the teems of unreliable and unpredictable cretins treading city streets. The media always makes a big deal about the mass murderer, the child rapist, or the morally reprehensible washroom at the bus terminal. But it's the drones from a fractured society, mesmerized by patriarchal histories and running on automatic by conspiracy politics and monotonous, uninformative television broadcasts, who are the worry. The foundation for future revolutions and misdeeds. They're the ones who turn to planting bombs at chic salons and condominium clusters. Nevertheless, *I'm only trying to relate the facts:*

A quite good-looking but apparently 'not all there' black-haired young man sat down in the stall next to me. I didn't do anything at first—toilet etiquette. Also, I had just started a health kick, no alcohol for two weeks, and I just wasn't up to an active role. Third, I was terribly hungover (hence my resolution of sobriety), following attendance at a wine-tasting salon the previous evening, where I got completely tanked from the Oregon Pinot Noir some sommelier would-be was forcing down my throat. (I hate the way some people say 'Pee-not,' when it should really come out 'Pee-no.' I hate Oregon too—ever since that 1992 referendum on legalized homosexual hate. Institutional hatred is so institutionalized now.) Anyway, I've never let a hangover keep me from what they call in San Francisco 'funch.' Mid-afternoon is a good time for funch. And don't think I just run around town pulling my pants down, and sitting in any old stall. No sir, I select toilet venues and I inspect the stalls. I, like most people, choose 'end' stalls—the privacy and 'detachment' from the others is so appealing. After choosing a stall, I like to ensure the lock works and that no hinges are loose on the door. I always check the toilet paper. *Never enter a toilet stall that doesn't have toilet paper.* God, that's important. That's a tenet to live by. Once entered, and secure, use liberal amounts of it to clean seat and seat area. Once this area is cleared, dump toilet paper and flush. When the flush has died down, tear off yet more paper in appropriate lengths to construct toilet paper panels along the left buttock, the right buttock, and the rear proper. Once the cleaning and cushions have been conducted, sit. Sit gently and hold penis carefully in and away from rim of public toilet seat. *Keep penis distant from rim*—God, that's important. That's a tenet to live by. Once seated in this position, you are prepared to a point in which defecation may occur without undue anxiety. While this may sound like such a task, once you repeat it to memory, then practice some times when in public (or at home), you will develop a standardized pattern and may even add swish little details to make the whole procedure a more agreeable experience. A friend of mine once told me that he was never out in public without a container of Wet Ones in his knapsack, that he depended on that 'just cleaned freshness' after any anal activity. So you see, there is room for ingenuity and technique.

While this is all Defecation Procedure, and not Promiscuous Sex Procedure, I always follow the former. It's a useful rule. You never know when you're going to have to sit on a toilet seat, so always prepare. Once I was comfortably seated in the specially-prepared cubicle, rubbing the furrows on my brow to soothe my aching hangover and defiantly denying this pain should interfere with my regulated sexual activity, I heard a sound.

There was a scuffle on the other side—perhaps the black-haired male was engaging in some sort of activity with someone in his adjacent cubicle. Careful to leave my paper cushion intact, I knelt down and peeped into his stall. He was staring candidly into space, tapping his fingers on the stainless steel paper dispenser. "Hello," I said; it seemed like the thing to say. Then I carefully returned to my passive position.

Passive and active. Such are what relationships appear to be made of. Really, they're about attachment and detachment. Attachment is the ideal, the fantasy, what you get when you poke someone's gut in a bar to see how hard it is; detachment is the reality, the day to day, everything Harvey Fierstein hid in the 'morning after' scene in *Torch Song Trilogy* (i.e., his looks, his breath, his body odour, etc.). Oh, Jesus, I'm referring to Harvey Fierstein while kneeling on the floor in a public lavatory!

So anyway, I was there, thinking about what it would be like to be stoned, just dazed there on my seat, instead of being possessed by urban ills, city viruses and little artistic anecdotes. And as I was thinking it came to me that being stoned, being out of it so that you're unstable, it so happens that little-known characteristics come peering eerily through you, like so much plaster-work with cracks and leaks, that eventually the transluscence of your being becomes just so much crazy space. (I should be a poet, don't you think? In fact I'm a hairdresser. There may be no God but there's certainly fate. I'm so well-versed in just talking on about anything.) Well, I was thinking on this Ken Keysian image when I saw the head of the black-haired boy start to peer under my stall—and this distracted me considerably.

My immediate thought was that he appreciated my initial pass. My initial pass! Like first I would make a pass and then I'd try to get a date, and while we were dating I'd get to a few bases, and then we would start going steady. Ready steady.

I said, "Hi, I'm Radomiro."

Now, 'Radomiro' is a bit of an embellishment, and I usually don't relate all four syllables of this name to people right off the bat. It's true I have Italian roots—I'm ten percent Italian and I cook a mean carbonara—but my name is Andrew, really. I'm ninety percent middle-class white Protestant. But everyone called me Andy or Drew and I just couldn't stand it. And when I first moved to London and started assisting at Sumi, well, I naturally assumed an alias. First, I assumed Brat, because it was so brash and boyish and typified that early-eighties obstinance that was characterized in such things as wearing Doc Martens years before they were popular, or being the first one to actually have the gall to return to wide ties—in sloppy two-piece suits, I might add. And what about all that spending of money on rags with labels—blatant spending on labels—what was it with labels that drove us so crazy that by the end of the decade we were too insecure except in plain white tees with bold black letters writ large in as banal and perceptively dim words as those which represented our fashion tastes, our musical tastes, our (minimal) social consciences— and all preferably one syllable? I was so much of this era. I had the Chanel logo; I had the logo only, white on black. I always considered it so much smarter than the Chanel proper. I had the WHAM! I mean, can you believe that? "I had the WHAM!" I mean, saying such a naked truth takes guts. There are queers, you know, who have given WHAM! albums a Viking burial. You guys really have what it takes to get me to say this stuff. Oh, the eighties, I was thinking—a frequent thought of mine, like Fred Flintstone anticipating the 5 p.m. crow—when the black-haired boy looked up and, in a rather hushed and embarrassed tone, said, "Excuse me, do you have any extra toilet tissue?"

"Do I?" I said. "Do I have any extra toilet tissue?" Just the thought of sharing toilet paper caused me to fade. Nothing too dramatic, but some noticeable beads of perspiration began to drip down my forehead. I've always been afraid of fading in public, and go to great lengths to avoid such a scene. You know what your publicist does, when you're famous and you start to fade, to boost your popularity back up? What he does is prescribe a disease from the stress of being famous. Take it from me—I've known some 'famous ill people' in the best of health. In the seventies, cocaine addiction typified the stars—they were so caught up in their hectic social schedules and demanding careers—I mean, being on the set at 5 a.m., that's living hell. Then, in the eighties, bulimia and anorexia superseded drugs. Drugs were bad, thin was in. There I was, in the eighties, among the hip and idiotic, the nearly-made-it people, wasting away from all the pressure, all pretending they could keep up and have as much fun as the next made-it person. You know, I was brought up to lead a different life, but it took me a long time to realize it. And this is the part that gets sentimental, and will really make you sad, and if you're reading this in bed I suggest you just tuck in for the night because you're going to have 'Love Is . . . ' nightmares all night long if you read what I'm about to say.

(By the way, if you're too young or too selective with your memory to remember 'Love Is . . . ,' let me remind you. It was a syndicated cartoon strip in America that featured two generic naked trolls that cuddled and coddled in various positions with captions that always read "Love is . . . " Love is cheesecake on your birthday. Love is learning arithmetic. Love is curling my fingers around the hairs of your forearm. There was a whole line of 'Love Is . . .' clothing and household goods you could, at one time, buy. Then came 'Hello Kitty.' But 'Hello Kitty' is another story.)

The flamboyant sentimental part promised earlier: my first ex-lover was my first love. He had olive skin and dark eyes and a funny accent that came out of a childhood in the Mauritius after his father was transferred there when he, my ex, was just two. We met accidentally on public transit on a cold and windy autumn night. I don't know who spoke first or if we spoke at all but I know he moved along the bench until he was beside me and then he slipped his hand into mine and we slid them both into the flannel pocket of his parka. We decided to get off at the stop by the park that runs along the shoreline. Then when we were standing there in the cold, he asked me if I wanted to walk along the waterfront. Well, it was cold and windy and quite frankly I wasn't interested, but his eyes had a persuasive glint that was unavoidable and irresistible. There was a big bright moon slowly rising on the eastern horizon and we walked towards it, sometimes stumbling over rocks and pebbles, but in a sort of quiet bliss. I asked him a few questions and he asked me a few. It wasn't until we ran into a private fence, forcing us to turn away from the shore and head into the city, that we really began to talk. I guess we had been walking along not talking which is a very unusual thing to do when you first meet someone. I find that, unless I know someone terribly well, it's uncomfortable being silent with someone. Anyway, I stopped to empty my shoe of sand and while I was emptying it he took hold of my foot, a little cold in the night air, and began massaging it, pulling my toes and rounding his knuckles against the arch. It had such an instantly relaxing sensation on my body that I sort of jumped six steps on the twelve-step relationship programme and, when we started walking again, began telling him stories of my life.

I'm sure my life sounded like this: likes to take long walks in the moonlight, cuddle, enjoys good conversation, is outgoing, wishes to meet same. Of course I wasn't a washroom bitch back then but of course I made my way about. And of course I didn't describe myself as someone who knew how to make their way about. I lied. Lying is the foundation of all good friendships anyway—contrary to what therapists may tell you. I mean, if therapists came out and tried to be as honest as they profess, as though honesty holds the cure to all woe, they'd have to confess to the power of lying. Which would of course drive them out of business. One great thing about lies is their simple yet effective power. Even if you say, oh, "the sky is red," and everyone knows it isn't, they're still going to discuss it and argue about it and, even if they all agree it's blue, they're obligated to deny your lie. Lying provokes much more interesting discussion than truth-telling. Say some trick tells me he suffered five broken ribs from a broomstick when he was nine years old because the neighbourhood kids thought he was a fag: say someone told me that. Then I say "Sorry," which is trite and typical. A Pavlovian response. Or else I tell a similar story, which appears as though I'm trying to diminish the pertinence of his. In these kinds of situations, it's much better to lie. Much better to lie. Oh, I might say, for example, "I had a friend beat up bad by a broom handle and he's never recovered. I don't think there's any way to recover from trauma in our youth. Do you?" As though I know anything about trauma in our youth. As though I'm the Robert Coles of the toilet circuit. After I told my lies, he told me his. Maybe his lies were truth?

His name was Henri, which is not so much a name to remember but sometimes a person defines their name in such a way that they could be called Jack Sprat and still have grace, charm and a butt to die for.

He told me that it was Passover and he had been visiting friends of his who were celebrating, and he told me he wasn't Jewish but he was circumcised because the family doctor persuaded his father to do it because it was a late-sixties hygienic thing to do (and of course I secretly felt sorry for his lost foreskin and then I began wondering what hospitals do with all that cut-off foreskin anyway), and Henri also asked me if I was Jewish or if I was circumcised and I said I wasn't on both counts and that I could never figure out whether it was Passover or Yom Kippur or Hanukkah and I didn't really know what each holiday meant. Henri described each Jewish holiday and its meaning to me. When he got to the end I just looked at him and said, "Gee, you must have had a Jewish lover," and he responded, "No, I just spent one summer working in the Catskills." Which is how he came to have so many Jewish friends, and, I wondered, how many Jewish boys . . .

We had been walking for some time when we suddenly arrived at a little café called the Pious Miranda and we decided to go in. It turned out we had much in common because I had trained at LAMDA in London and he had gone to Uta Hagen's hole in New York. They kicked me out of course because my cock wasn't big enough—you have to have a really big cock for acting—although judging from my experience in public toilets my cock isn't so small, unless compared with an actor's ego. Christ, how some of those would-be actors could fit themselves through a stage entrance, I'll never know. I made my ex-actor's ego palatable for romantic discourse. How I gave so much to my roles, my improvisations, my inner self. And of course how as an ex-actor I started cutting hair, freelance, as well as volunteering time for community theatre groups, and, as usual, I embellished my stories a good deal until I had become a love slave for Stephen Sondheim and was once asked by Harold Prince to direct an off-Broadway play. Or some such theatrical hogwash.

Henri told me that he had done The Naked Improv, along with a lot of other lesser-known theatrical events. He said he was really against the trappings of a clothed society, and that these trappings increased with prudishness and perversion, evident to the extreme in the very clothed northern hemisphere. He jokingly said that if he were to write a self-help book it would be called *Why Dress?* and we both laughed at that. Sharing a laugh when you first meet someone is a gratifying experi-

44

ence. He said he quit the improv because, and I think he quoted Boyd McDonald, he felt that nudity has great value only in a clothed society. I knew at once that if he had the nerve to do the The Naked Improv, he must have a great body.

After Henri told me about the improv club I began to wonder about his body. No matter what he said or did, I couldn't pay attention. When he scratched his face, then groomed his sideburns down afterwards, tugging the hairs gently, I began to think about his hair distribution. I imagined him with dark, defined lower body hair that abruptly ceased when it reached his midriff. I pictured distinct, long-stranded hairs on his feet and big toes, and the same but much thicker on his calves and inner thighs. I pictured his pubes as dark and concentrated, triangular—not messy and sporadic like my own. I saw a hefty armpit clump, curiously emerging onto his biceps and triceps. I saw his chest hair as light, and nondescript, and framed between his well-defined breasts. (I imagined his nipples as dark, splotchy, and dangling slightly off the muscle in a droopy way.) I consider hair distribution quite important. I myself am rather hairless which, at least in the media, has a certain modern appeal. Actually, hair is quite sexy and its sexiness is largely determined by its distribution. Too much hair or not enough in a certain area can turn me off a person. One of the advantages of washroom sex is that I discover relatively little about a person's hair distribution and hence am rarely disappointed. As my infatuation with Henri grew, my expectations grew too, not just in regards to hair. When he ordered a café au lait, I thought about the way sperm would shoot out of his cock. Did he have directional skill—could he in fact ice a cake or two? Did it simply splatter out in large, heavy white drabs, or did it spray, in translucent beads, across the room? If we did end up having sex, was all his come going to come out in a condom? (Condoms have really ruined the art of coming.) When he took his tongue and wiped it across his lips, catching some foamy milk on his upper lip, I wondered what sort of blow job he would give, if indeed he gave blow jobs. Was he a mouth-totaller? Did he gorge on the appendage? Or did he simply tickle, taunt and run his tongue around the rim, the way those big hunks in Kristen Bjorn films do? Did he use one or two hands on the shaft? When he held his coffee cup and his thumb stuck out I stared at its length and width and the cut of his nail. I pretended his thumb was a cast of his cock. I wondered was his cut cock, when erect, long and narrow or short and thick, or was it bent slightly up or to the right or left, and was it tubular or rather conical, and did it have any distinguishable marks on it? Were his balls big and baggy, or unobtrusively hidden by an upstaged penis? Later, when Henri crossed his legs and gave a little wince as though stifling a fart, I wondered about the location of his sphincter. Was it a good five centimetres away from the base of his ball sac, or was it much nearer, precisely between his legs? Some people's sphincters tend to be four o'clock, others six, some eight and even nine. It makes a difference. Was it one of those sphincters that had puckered, bulbous flesh around the rim, like an abstract formation in a lava lamp, or was it neat, contour-less and tight, like an inverse volcano, creased inward? As you can see, I became absorbed by personal thoughts and missed the intimate details of how as a child he was beaten by neighbourhood thugs (friends I think he later called them—schoolfriends, pals, chums) for being queer and had four ribs broken from a broomstick wielded mercilessly to the tune of "Take that, faggot." And all this when he was only nine, I might add. I should have been paying closer attention, getting the full details of the story—but Christ, if Laurence Olivier had been paying attention in *Rebecca*, there wouldn't have been a dramatic climax, would there? We wouldn't have seen Judith Anderson consumed by flames. Happy endings aren't consumed by sentimentality, of which great stories are made.

The sentimental part is that, later, we ourselves were consumed by flames, for a brief period. And it was lovely, until the flames went out. I discovered his hair distribution, the layout of his genitalia, his sexual preferences and techniques, the firmness of his body, the location of wayward moles and scars, strange protuberances on his ankles and feet, his look and body tension in orgasm and the scale/proportion of sperm produced in three consecutive ejaculations. He had a very big cock. And I'm not going to tell you anything else. Why? First of all, because I'm not the size queen you probably think I am. Second, because the sex was wonderful and fulfilling. First, it was slow and romantic and drawn out. Later it was fast and furious and sweaty. We talked. We drank some herbal beverage. We lay in each other's arms. It became daylight, we hadn't slept, and we had sex yet again. It was bliss in another dimension. Then disaster.

First, Henri began talking about René, and I said, "René who?" Henri looked at me, having only about seven hours previously related to me the terribly intimate story of having René lead a group of boys against him when he was only nine, and the devastating psychological implications this has had on his adult life. I said I was sorry, I forgot. I remembered the story but I forgot the name. I'm not very good with names. At this point all was still well. However, just moments later, and only for a split second, I forgot Henri's name and called him Mark. This was a mistake. Even though Mark could have been spelled M-a-r-c, which is quite French and hence could have been a connection, Henri took offence. I realized my error without being able to capitalize on it. Terrible thing, I guess, to have three orgasms in just a few hours with such a great guy and to call him by the wrong name at the end. Henri was insulted. He became very quiet and suggested we both get some sleep and, since we were at my place, he preferred to take a cab home. He preferred to sleep alone. He left me his phone number. This is the saddest story of my adult life. I hope I didn't make you cry.

Henri showed himself to the door. When I heard it click shut, I jumped out of bed, ran down the hall naked, and stared out the peephole just in time to see the shape of his firm, round butt bending down to steal my Sunday newspaper, and his large, hairless hands reach for the elevator button. He was really cute, that Henri was, even clothed and from behind. He was really handsome.

I went back to bed to mope. On my way I discovered he had left his underwear. How could he have left his underwear? Who leaves their underwear? Did he do it on purpose? It was a good pair of underwear, too. Light grey Armani jockeys. I picked them up and looked inside. I don't know why—did I expect to find something inside? There were a few pubes and later, after I'd slept, I took the pubes out and put them in an envelope and put them in my copy of Forster's *Maurice*. And then I think I mislaid that copy, probably in a public toilet.

I should have said, Wait, I'm sorry, please don't leave. I should have said the reason I forgot about the story you told me that meant so much to me was that I was falling in love with you. But I never tell people I'm falling in love with that I'm falling in love with them. I just don't. Anyway, half the time I don't know I'm falling in love so I can't come out and say it anyway. I should have said the reason I said Mark instead of Henri was that I was looking at the scar across your back which looks like you were clawed by a wild animal. But that sounds Freudian, and I don't believe in Freud. Or at least I don't put any store in his ideas. And Henri didn't have a scar across his back. So I just lay in bed, naked and uncovered, watching my cock recede into my body with the thought that I had met such a wonderful person and screwed it up so quickly. He left me his phone number, which meant I was supposed to call, which meant I was supposed to apologize, and apologies are so difficult (and of course I didn't know it wasn't his number at the time). In those last few moments together, I got to see Henri insulted and upset. It's the one part of that evening I'd rather not remember. Honestly, gay men are so sensitive.

I've never seen Henri since. Not even in a public washroom. Once, about two years ago, out of the blue, I got a postcard from Melbourne, Australia. Henri had formed a theatre troupe called Captives of Scarcity and they were performing a dance-slash-performance piece called 'Relative Deprivation.' He quoted a review which read, "splendidly anarchic, socially realized and of a dramatic depth uncommonly political"; it sounded dreadful. I realized Henri had become an entirely different person than the compassionate romantic I had met that cool autumn night. He sounded politically assertive and attached to ideals that are just so much hogwash. But, regardless, I still have my sentimental memories. Henri is my number one sentimental memory.

I tore off some squares of tissue for the handsome man in the next stall. The rolls were hard to pull and the squares kept tearing off in small bunches. Eventually I handed him a large wad.

"My name is Amherst," he said.

"Nice to meet you, Amherst," I said.

"Thanks for the toilet paper," he said.

"You're welcome," I said.

Then he receded into his stall and proceeded to let nature take its course. The toilets were quiet so I thought I'd better move. Someone in another stall began tapping his toe—but when I looked under on my way out, and saw it was Joseph, the senior citizen with orthopedic boots, I just checked myself in the mirror and left. I decided to look for a good book.

Peter Dickinson Home

Consider this. It is that buying time between darkness and unreality, between remembering and forgetting, that unmapped hour of consciousness just after the clubs have closed and just before your mind does the same. You are sitting on a bus, alone at the back, on your way home. Somewhere someone is listening to something. And you think: I've been to the end of the world and back on this road. Winding. Snaking. Of this you are sure. All else: forests of memory, whizzing by peripherally, anonymously. Trapped as you are in the hereness and nowness of Hyundais and high beams, you yearn for the thereness and thenness of another time and place. And you know: like the Trans-Canada, the ribbon of asphalt you're travelling, the highway of the mind runs west to east.

It is T-minus three months, two weeks and five days until my twenty-seventh birthday. I am fossilizing before my very eyes. Wasn't Mozart on the market before he was twelve? And what have I done with my life so far? Just the other day I attempted a clinical assessment. Staring at my reflection in the cracked mirror of a Vancouver washroom, I asked myself who exactly I was pretending to be in these faded blue jeans, these red high-tops, this worn leather jacket borrowed from Mike, this mop of unruly brown hair. This is what I came up with:

Name: Christopher Robbins (what can I say, my parents were fond of A.A. Milne).

Age: 26¾

Sex: Much too late.

Nationality: I prefer to think of myself as a citizen of the world, especially in these dark times.

Occupation: Retired world traveller, occasional hustler, general derelict bum.

Political Affiliations: Most desperate and all lost causes.

Aspirations in Life: To foreswear my homosexuality, and to successfully bed and wed Madonna, Cher, Mitsou and any other female pop star with only one name. Not much to work with, I admit. But at least it's a start.

Of course, I was always better at hindsight than foresight. For me it was not so much a question of how do I get there from here, but rather how did I get here from there? The answers were never much to my liking.

Take Mike, for example. Six weeks ago he died an anonymous death in an anonymous Toronto hospital room. And here I am already in a new city, trying my best *not* to remain anonymous, cruising the streets and clubs, indulging in random, casual sex.

There is a buying time. A buying of darkness, practiced emotions, excised dreams, cherished regrets. And a selling of lost souls.

I sold mine long ago for a pair of calf-skin gloves and a cashmere muffler. In exchange for a hand job behind a dumpster in an alley off Jarvis. From there it wasn't a big stretch to here. By the time I met Mike I figured I'd had close to a thousand dicks up my ass and given a couple thousand blow jobs.

I was never much good at hustling; I always wanted to be somewhere else. Not the best sort of thing in a businesss where your customers demand highly personalized attention. Mike was the one exception.

I was standing on the corner of Church and Wellesley, one cupped hand emerging from the shadow of an overhead awning and a dulcet tone in my voice. All I wanted was enough money for a cup of coffee. But the man from whom I asked this favour insisted on taking me to lunch. That's how I met Mike.

He took me to the Church Street Café. I felt out of place in my tight Levis (which were conveniently ripped under both cheeks) and muscle shirt. I hadn't shaved in four days. Mike, himself under-dressed, was at least trendy. In fact, he looked downright sexy, his tall spare frame well suited to jeans and sports jacket. His hair, which hung in tangled black ringlets to his shoulders, added to the picture. Mike, I was to discover, spent his whole life looking the part. None of the other customers, most of whom were male, seemed to mind. We even received a handful of approving stares.

Mike ordered for both of us: chef's salad, oysters in a white wine sauce, orange sherbet. He ate heartily. I, however, feeling suddenly melancholy, could not get past the bread basket. We sipped chilled Chablis.

We were sitting on the outdoor patio. The air felt languid as we exchanged anecdotes about ourselves, drank platitudes from china cups, indulged in protracted

nuance. And drowning, drowning in air, I offered myself to the appetites of etiquette, cleared my throat, only to blush at my boldness and sigh at my despair. He
smiled at me from across the table. Such a lovely smile. So disarming.

Between coffee and cheque, I assumed a suitably provocative posture, reached discreetly underneath the table and squeezed Mike's thigh. As he turned toward me his
eyes were only partially obliging, betraying his shameless misery. His loneliness.

"Not just yet," he whispered.

A silence descended over our table like a thick cloud, blocking out the sun. Mike
suggested a walk. Setting down the salt shaker I had been examining so intently, I
agreed.

As we left the restaurant, I thought: I love this man. Please, dear God, don't let us
sleep together.

And we didn't. Sleep together, that is. Or rather the sleeping part we did quite often.
In fact, for a time it got so I couldn't fall asleep without some part of Mike's body
touching my own. In the seven years we spent together I got to know his body very
well. Night after night my fingers and tongue were insatiably curious, tracing every
crevice, each line: his full lips, the cleft in his chin, the laugh lines around his already
ancient eyes, the quarter-inch scar under his left nipple, his hard stomach, the soft
dark trail of hair that led from his belly-button to his lovely cock.

It never really bothered me that our lovemaking remained unconsummated. After
three-and-a-half years of hustling, sex had become far too commodified a practice
anyway. For me, anal penetration was less a gesture of intimacy than a way of making a quick buck. It was an explanation Mike found hard to accept. He couldn't seem
to understand a profession in purely economic terms. Only recently out, he sought
to rationalize my turning tricks as a way of flaunting my sexuality in the face of
social convention.

"Jesus Christ, any queen can do that," I responded when Mike first ran his
hypothesis by me. "All she needs is a good dress and a sturdy pair of heels."

At any rate, I gave up hustling soon after I met Mike. Oh sure, there was the occasional pick-up here and there, if we were out dancing, for example, and I was being
cruised by a particularly hot number. But that was just a healthy release of tension.
No money changed hands. And Mike never seemed to mind.

As for Mike's sex life, I think his celibacy was a carefully negotiated mediation
between his long-suppressed homosexual desires and his very real heterosexual marriage. Poor Mike, I think he only had sex twice in his life. The first time someone
got pregnant. The second time someone died.

By the evening of the day he bought me lunch, I had learned the following about

Mike: he was twenty-six, a part-time actor and sometime husband. Born in Brantford, Ontario, he played pee-wee hockey with one of Wayne Gretzky's brothers. He had lived in Toronto for the past eight years. He was enrolled in the Master's program in theatre at York University and had a summer job playing Polkaroo at Ontario Place. He had a tattoo of Blake's 'God' on his right shoulder and one of a black panther on his left inner thigh. His wife's name was Helen. They had a seven-year-old son named Kevin.

"We were high school sweethearts," Mike explained. "Or so everyone thought. By the time I realized I preferred boys, Helen was already pregnant. A stupid grad night mistake. Not that we've ever regretted having Kevin. He's the best thing that's happened to me. Helen and I are still together because of him. It's a strange relationship, but somehow it works. Helen lets me have my space. And, strange as it might seem, she loves me, she really loves me."

Within two months, I had moved in with Mike and Helen and little Kevin. It was a further twist on an already unusual arrangement, one that Helen was not entirely pleased with, but which she nevertheless agreed to put up with when Mike threatened to walk.

Helen, as I soon discovered, had her own life very much in order. She had earned a Bachelor's degree in psychology and a Master's in social work, all while raising a child. In between counselling families of autistic children all day and volunteering at a women's shelter two evenings a week, she taught Kevin his times-tables and rehearsed scripts with Mike. And without any visible signs of strain, except for the constant chewing of her bottom lip.

The night it was announced that I was to become a permanent fixture at the breakfast table, she and Mike had a terrific row. Kevin and I were playing checkers on the living-room floor, both of us finding it difficult to concentrate with the screams emanating from the adjoining bedroom. When the shouting ended, it was Helen who rejoined us. She watched silently as Kevin beat me for the third straight game and then she announced that it was his bedtime. When Kevin protested, she said that there would be plenty more chances to play checkers with me because I would be living with them from now on. Then she turned to me and said, "Just remember, Chris, I may have been kicked out of my bedroom, but this is still my home. We all share in the cooking around here. And I don't pick up anyone's dirty laundry."

Over the next couple of years, Helen and I grew accustomed to, if not altogether fond of, each other. Between the two of us, we ran a fairly efficient household, taking turns playing nagging fish-wife to hopelessly disorganized Mike. Still, there was a distance between us. It was not so much that Helen resented a nineteen-year-old ex-hustler usurping her place of affection next to her husband and son. It was more like she feared I would suddenly leave and break either one of their hearts.

By the end of our second year together, we had become what we all—or at least I—feared the most: a family. It took a near-tragedy to drive this point home.

Helen and I were both in the kitchen when the phone call came. There had been an accident. The boys were playing hockey in the street. There was hardly ever any traffic after supper. Kevin had gone to retrieve a runaway ball.

"Where is he?" Helen interrupted. "Is he all right?"

The ambulance had just left, on its way to Sick Kids, the driver saying something about a fractured skull.

Helen hung up the phone, leaving a trail of dish soap where her hand had reached from sink to receiver. I looked up from the mess of pamphlets and papers I had spread out before me on the table. I was studying for my first trial week on the AIDS Committee of Toronto Helpline. Helen just stood there dripping soap suds onto the kitchen floor. I handed her a towel and went in search of my keys.

Mike was at a rehearsal at the Poor Alex, his directorial debut. We tried the box office number but it just rang and rang. We toyed with the idea of going by the theatre but it was out of the way, and we didn't have a car. We decided to leave a note instead.

When we got to Sick Kids we were told that Kevin was still in Intensive Care. In addition to a fractured skull, he had broken ribs and a severely bruised left leg. But they had managed to stop the bleeding and, aside from the broken ribs, there were no internal injuries. It looked like he would be all right. By the time Mike arrived, Kevin had been moved to his own room. Helen and I were haggard and bleary-eyed when Mike burst through the door.

"How is he? Is he all right?" Mike asked, holding the door for someone I recognized vaguely as an actor named Joshua from his company.

Helen was the first to respond. "He's still unconscious. But the doctors say he's going to pull through just fine."

Mike looked at me, apparently unwilling to believe the information Helen had just relayed to him.

"He's going to be O.K.," I reassured him. "He'll have to stay here awhile for observation but—"

"Why didn't you come and get me? He could have died, for Christ's sake. And all you did was leave me that fucking note."

I had never seen him so upset. Helen started to cry again.

"Take it easy, Mike. It's not Helen's fault. One of us should have come to the theatre. We just weren't thinking straight."

"Shut up, just shut the fuck up. My son could have died. My son. I'm his father, for fuck's sake. I'm his father. Me. Not you."

And with that Mike left the room just as abruptly as he had entered it, taking Joshua with him. Helen and I looked at each other but said nothing. We went back to our lonely vigil. All I could think was that in his fury Mike had forgotten to kiss his son.

I always found it cruelly ironic that given my former lifestyle Mike should be the one diagnosed as HIV-positive.

I had been working at the AIDS hospice for over a year before I developed enough courage to take the test myself. Mike was the one who finally convinced me. He said we would take it together. Imagine the horror then when one of the test results came back positive. And it was Mike's, not mine. Sitting in the doctor's office holding Mike's hand, I counted back the eighteen months to his encounter with Joshua the night of Kevin's accident.

The months of training and counselling were not enough to counter the psychological devastation of hearing that the person you loved was infected. I knew that HIV alone did not lead to AIDS. Any number of co-factors were involved. Mike was still asymptomatic. And he could stay that way for quite some time. But sooner or later his T-4 cell count would drop and anti-retroviral treatment would have to begin. That day came sooner rather than later. Mike began taking daily doses of AZT, ddI and a host of other medications. He was a willing guinea pig. He had long reconciled with Helen and me and was curiously resigned to his contraction of the AIDS virus. He somehow viewed it as appropriate penance, not so much for breaking his vow of chastity as for breaking what he subsequently perceived to be a sacred family bond. Mike could be strangely religious for an out-of-work actor.

Helen listened patiently at the kitchen table as I explained Mike's condition to her, what side-effects the drugs might cause, the routine that all of us would have to get used to. And I watched, silently amazed, as she conveyed this information to Kevin in terms a ten-year-old could potentially understand. "Daddy has a virus," she told him. "It's like the flu bug, only different. It's in his bloodstream. He's not very sick right now, and he's taking medicine to make him better, but he could get worse. So we all have to help out to make him feel well again. Just like we did for you after your accident . . . Of course you can still kiss Daddy. You must give him lots of kisses and hugs to keep his spirits up."

During the course of his illness I never once saw Helen reproach Mike, accuse him of abandoning her and leaving her a single mother. But, every now and then, I would come across her crying in front of the bathroom mirror or silently rocking Kevin in the dark. I never could put my arm around her, or wipe away her tears. Just like she couldn't do the same for me when she found me huddled on the kitchen floor at 2 a.m. the night Mike was first hospitalized. It was as if we were afraid of admitting just how much we were both hurting, just how much we loved Mike, lest one of us love him more.

For the next four years, the three of us watched the man we loved wither away to nothing. Two years after the original diagnosis, he came down with his first bout of pneumocystis carinii pneumonia and dropped suddenly from 160 to 113 pounds. And that was only the beginning. He subsequently contracted and successfully fought off MAI and cryptococcal meningitis. He suffered from chronic diarrhea. Thrush made it difficult for him to swallow and Kaposi's sarcoma left purple lesions on his arms and legs. Six months before he died, he developed CMV retinitis and went blind. We used to take long walks together outside the hospital during that last autumn and early winter, despite the fact that neuropathy in his legs made each step difficult for him, and that no matter how many coats we piled on him, he never could get warm.

"It's all right," Mike would say when Helen protested. "At least if I can feel the cold I know I'm still alive."

Mike would ask me to describe virtually everything to him as we walked: the colour of the Christmas lights wrapped around the trees along University Avenue, the slogans on the signs of the anti-abortion protesters outside the birth control clinic on Bay Street, the pattern the snow made as it dusted sidewalks, settled on scarves. Knowing Mike had a penchant for the dramatic, I always tried to make my descriptions as poetic as possible. He seemed to appreciate my efforts.

"A pity I never knew about your eye for detail before," he'd say. "I could have used a good set designer for my play."

This always shut me up. If there was one thing that put a stop to my inane chatter during those final weeks it was the sound of Mike's own voice. He spoke so rarely; every breath was difficult for him. His words barely rose above a whisper and were delivered, amid long pauses and wheezes, so close to my ear that I could feel the warmth of his breath on my face, smell the slightly musty mixture of marijuana and raspberry jello on his tongue.

"I'm going to die, Chris. Helen and Kevin will be alone. Promise me you won't leave them as well."

I could never bring myself to answer. Only silence, that same thick cloud, followed by a lengthy description of the latest Benetton ad to grace a billboard overlooking the skating rink at College Park, or the perilous flight of a stranded blue jay crippled because of ice forming on its wings.

I wanted to bolt and run. Luckily Helen was there beside me. And Kevin. I was inevitably caught in the middle, holding each of their hands. As we walked past the reception desk, the waiting area, down long white corridors toward Mike's tiny room, people stopped and smiled sympathetically. Nurses carrying charts, orderlies with breakfast trays and bedpans, hunched patients trailing IVs. And why not? We were a family, after all. A perfectly normal family off to bid one of its members goodbye. I don't know which part of this equation caused me the most panic.

The next time I walked into the hospital was the last. The doctor had phoned and said that we had better hurry. The week before, Mike had contracted toxoplasmosis. One lung had already collapsed and he was hooked up to a respirator.

The call came at midnight. Kevin was asleep. For reasons that I could understand, but could not entirely forgive, Helen decided it was best not to wake him. I was to go to the hospital on my own. Just before I left, I stopped at the front door and returned to the hall closet, exchanging the coat I was wearing, an old threadbare parka, for Mike's leather jacket. It was far too big, of course. And much too thin. But it felt right.

By the time I got to the hospital, Mike had slipped into a coma. He never regained consciousness. I sat beside his bed holding his cold hand for two hours after the doctors declared him officially dead, until a sympathetic nurse said that they must remove the body—they needed the bed.

I phoned Helen.

"He's dead," I said as matter-of-factly as I could.

"I see," she responded, equally coldly.

We were still competing, you see. Even in death the question had to be asked: who loved Mike the most? It could only be answered in terms of who grieved the most. We both opted for measured stoicism rather than full-blown hysteria.

"You must tell Kevin, Helen. And don't wait until morning. Wake him up as soon as you get off the phone with me and tell him that his father is dead."

"I will," she said.

"Oh, and Helen?"

"Yes, Chris?"

"Tell him goodbye from me as well. I'm leaving."

I hung up the phone and immediately began checking the pockets of my jeans. They yielded a used kleenex, three condoms, a pack of gum, sixty-five dollars and some change. Restoring all items but the kleenex, I exited the hospital onto Elizabeth Street and headed for the bus depot.

The sixty-five dollars got me as far as Thunder Bay and breakfast. A blow job in the

Thunder Bay depot washroom got me a ride to Winnipeg. A pick-up in Winnipeg drove me as far as Regina. And so on. I slept my way across Canada in a mere four days.

I woke up at a truck stop just outside Vancouver with a massive hangover and a two hundred-pound man dry-humping me in the back of his cab. When he finished, he rolled off of me and said that with an ass like mine I could give the boys on Homer Street a run for their money. I asked him where Homer Street was. He tossed twenty bucks in my lap and said he'd drive me there himself.

Going back to hustling was fine. So long as I didn't think about it. So long as I didn't think about anything. Not Mike, not Kevin, not even Helen. Those first few weeks in Vancouver were a blur. I barely remember getting from one day to the next. I spent Christmas puking my guts out on the floor of an apartment that belonged to the coat-check person at one of the clubs. New Year's Eve, I was leading a conga line down Davie Street, high on ecstasy.

It was a john named Leo who found the photograph. He was rummaging through Mike's jacket for some matches and pulled what looked like a crumpled old piece of paper out of one of the pockets.

"Who are they?" he asked, tossing it to where I lay on the bed searching for my underwear.

It was a black-and-white snapshot of Mike, Helen and Kevin that I had taken on one of our many visits to Centre Island. Helen and Kevin were mugging for the camera. Mike was standing off to one side, watching their antics. Somehow he had been thrown out of the depth of field, his face blurry, his shirt sleeve fading into the white border of the photograph.

Appropriate enough, I guess, considering that in the six weeks since his death Mike had already become a shadowy figure. I couldn't seem to remember what he looked like, his face hazy and pale in my mind, forever frozen against an expanse of whiteness: the border of the photograph, the walls of our apartment, the neatly pressed sheets of his hospital bed, the still-dead winter air he so loved to walk in near the end. This crude image was all that remained of him. Everything else was just a series of indistinct lines and unconnected memories looming over me like the pretend smoke exhaled by children on cold days, a kind of omnipresent, ghost-like mist.

Memory is made up of small things, hard things, things that have a shape, and a weight, things you can hold on to with your hands.

I looked from Mike's blurry figure back to the smiling faces of Helen and Kevin. They were holding hands. I stared at them for a long time, thinking about the anatomy of memory. The anatomy of this photograph. And my place in it, holding each of their hands.

I glanced up at the john named Leo. Having found the matches, he was now trying to stuff his oversized frame into a pair of polyster pants. It's like I told you: I sold my soul long ago. But, with a bit of luck, I might still be able to buy it back.

"These people," I said, waving the photograph at him, "these people are my family."

Consider this. You're closer now. You've traded Greyhound bus for rental car, 401ing home through layered dreams and darkness. It's 5 a.m. and you're wide awake, attentive, anticipating every bump and turn, easing car and shoulder and mind into longer curves, longer curves. Over roads, through hills, impasses of granite rock, decades of remembrance and neglect, you move. Glide. Tongue rolling over mounds of chocolate, searching for the maraschino centre, its juice, its blood, collecting in your throat, coagulating, loud falls the rain, anaesthetizing air dense with morning frost and wet leaves, all brown and crumpled. Floating, falling, colouring a firmament of golden fire a shade brighter than despair. Not to blind, or burn, merely to warm frost-bitten faces and sensitive souls. The highway of the mind ends here: home.

Charles Dobie Like A Dream

Toronto, last summer. Peter refuses to get out of bed; he has stuffed three pillows around his head, determined to hide from the morning sun and birds. I can stand the sticky heat no longer, so I get dressed, feed the cat, and go outside in search of milk and newspapers.

A house down the street is having their monthly yard sale, so I wander over. Record albums spill from a ragged cardboard box onto the lawn; the top album makes me pause—something about the title. Probably just more yuppie shit, I think, but what the hell, it's only a quarter. Half an hour later, I'm sitting on the living room floor, stunned at the tears running down my face, listening to the whales.

Anchored in Tasu Sound, Queen Charlotte Islands, 1962. I've locked myself into the sonar control room. I'm trembling, weak with shame and anger. Bastards! I'd like to kill them!

I flop into the operator's swivel chair; its grungy familiarity helps to calm me. There is a muted roar from the loudspeakers on the bulkhead, and I realize the equipment is powered on. I glance at the compasses, run my fingers over the switches on the control panel, and fantasize that I'm about to sink a submarine.

There's a tentative tapping at the door, then a shave-n-haircut rap. It has to be Casey. He's never seen me really upset like this, but I unlock the door and let him in. I turn quickly and sit down, trying not to let him see my face.

He sits in the chair beside me. As usual, we don't say much. He pretends to be interested in the switches and dials, and caresses them gingerly, one by one. He is my age: almost twenty. Two years of gorging Navy food and wrestling with the 4-inch gun has barreled his chest, and he stinks deliciously of rum. His faded blue work shirt is speckled with ancient paint; the sleeves are rolled above his elbows, revealing brown arms scarred with flaky white trails from his constant scratching. His hands are those of a mechanic: rough and powerful, the left thumbnail a black souvenir of steel hitting flesh.

Casey turns suddenly to punch my shoulder. "So, how ya doin'?"

I shrug. "Okay."

"No, I mean really. How ya feelin'?"

"The shits."

"You got the shits?"

Laughter tugs at my throat, and I gag on a porridge of tears and cigarettes. "No!" "The bloody card game was your idea in the first place, you know."

"So?"

"So? So? So why'd you run out on everyone like that? Tired of all the high-class conversation or somethin'?"

"Or somethin'."

"Yeah? Well? Hey, c'mon man, out with it!"

I'm soaked with sweat, fighting panic. I ponder the meaning of trust, then suddenly don't care. I marvel at the calmness of my words: "I guess once you've heard one fag joke, you've heard 'em all."

Casey turns slowly back to re-examine the switches. Then: "Smoke?" He waves an Export A.

"I said, once you've heard one fag joke, you've heard 'em all!" My voice is an ugly shout.

He feigns amazement: "That what you said?"

"It's not funny!"

"But the guys always talk like that. Shit, man, even you've told lots worse jokes than that one before—hey, remember the one about the two . . . "

"I don't wanna fuckin' hear about it!"

"Yeah." He sighs loudly, absently scratching his arms; left, then right, left, then right. Suddenly he scratches his head furiously with both hands in frustration. "Look, about what happened yesterday . . . I mean, with the picture and everything . . . like . . . I'm sorry, I was always going to tell you, but. . . . "

I slam the console with my fist and turn my head away from him, trying not to bawl like a baby.

He touches my shoulder. "Hey, c'mon, man, what you need is to blow off some steam. You're much too fuckin' tense. Hey, we'll go get shit-faced when we hit Vancouver, or somethin'."

"Thanks, doctor. That's all the world needs: two more sloppy drunks."

Silence. The ship rolls and strains against the anchor cable as it tries to follow the tide out to sea. A steel door crashes, muffled by silence. Casey clears his throat: "It's all my fault, you know." His voice falters, grows husky: "I lead you on . . . like . . . like I kinda knew but didn't, if you know what I mean."

"You knew?"

"No. I dunno. I mean . . . it's like I wanted to see what would happen, I guess. Like . . . when I think of . . . I guess if I ever . . . I guess it would be someone like you. *Fuck!* I'm sorry, I really am." He gently squeezes my right arm just above my wrist, but after ten seconds of his heat he removes his hand, and I die.

Then we jump, wide-eyed, startled by a weird, sobbing wail from the loudspeakers. There is another. Then a chorus. I grab two cold, greasy sonar headsets and plug them into the console. The headsets are ancient, pre-plastic, original Second World War issue, corroded and filthy from generations of sweat and panic.

I show Casey his volume control, then flip a worn brass toggle switch, and five decks below, hydraulic pumps ram the huge sonar transducer through its seal in the bottom of the ship. Soon the roar in our earphones changes to a cacophony of shrimp-clickings, crab-poppings and porpoise-whistlings, and Casey's face becomes that of a child who has for the first time seen the stars. I curse my camera stowed away in my locker.

Then the whales! I drown in their sound. I seem to drown forever. My sadness is nothing in the face of that primordial sorrow. When they finally release me, it is to the clatter of the crew from the evening watch climbing the steel ladder to the wheelhouse as we prepare to lift anchor. And I find myself utterly alone, lost in a web of cigarette smoke which floats like a dream in the still, stale air.

Casey slept next to me. We had upper bunks, our noses six inches from the steam pipes and cables, our conversation hidden by the wail of an electric motor.

We took an instant liking to each other, though we had little in common. He was a gunner and I was a sonarman, so we rarely worked together, and tradition dictated we be socially aloof: gunners had hard heads, hard muscles and hard pricks; sonarmen read books and were polite.

When he first joined the ship, I couldn't stop looking at him; I tried not to stare but I couldn't help myself. If our eyes met, he would flash a quick grin and a wink, leaving me flushed with confusion, hoping desperately that no one had noticed.

He was a compulsive grinner and winker, with laugh lines around his eyes even though he was barely twenty. He was a crotch-rubber, a muscle-flexer, a joint-cracker. A hair-twisting, teeth-grinding, skin-scratching bundle of energy.

But in spite of the grin, he was a loner. He wasn't shy—far from it, he was the first to join a group—but once established, he would stand back, tossing tidbits of jokes, jibes, salty one-liners, like bacon to puppies, amused but absent-minded, his thoughts elsewhere. This was different than lust, I told myself. I wanted to know him, to hear his secrets. I wondered if our secrets were the same.

As our ship prepared for summer training, he was re-assigned to my messdeck, and suddenly he was sleeping beside me, only a foot away. Every night! Our bunks were bolted to the same steel beam; I could touch him if I dared. I hardly slept the first week. I lay gazing at him through almost-closed eyes, terrified he might awaken and discover me watching.

One night, in the midst of an impossible dream, I jerked awake at some sound to find him watching me. I was shocked: he was crying. He didn't turn away or wipe his face, he just let the tears roll unhindered.

"You okay?" I breathed into the whining semi-dark.

He reached over, grabbed my hand and held it tightly, silently. Then gradually his hand relaxed as he slept.

In the morning, it was as if it had never happened. Perhaps he thought he had been dreaming. Perhaps he had. Or I.

So Casey began to consume my life. I thought of him constantly. I watched him every chance I could, sat with him at meals, stood extra duty just to be with him, coincidentally took my showers when he did—I became his shadow. And always, I hoped I could reach beyond that hearty, grinning, arm-punching camaraderie. I hoped I wasn't just another puppy.

It was after the night he cried that I noticed the scratching—I mean really noticed it. Before the kindling of my hopes, his scratching had been faint static in the background of an otherwise perfect recording. Now it became music too.

He had chronically dry skin, a genetic condition which made his skin as thick and rough as sandpaper; he had permanent goosebumps all over him. The ship's medic carried a supply of olive oil especially for him and Casey slathered it on, sometimes two or three times a day in the summer when it was hot and the air was full of salt.

So with studied casualness, I became his official back-rubber.

It never ceased to amaze me, his strange, rough skin: it was so stiff and hard I don't know how it bent without cracking. The oil soaked into his back like it was a beach, right at the water's edge, where the waves leave a gloss of wetness to show where they've been, the gloss gently puckering into coarse, pale sand. His skin was like that. For a while it would be almost smooth, soft and supple before flaking again; rough and gritty and itchy. Like sand.

I embraced my new duties with such fervour that we became part of the ship's sexual theatre. He would stand before me totally naked while I rubbed the oil into his shoulders and back as far down as I dared.

I worshipped every muscle and bone in his back. I marvelled at the gravelly contours of his skin, the secret separations of his muscles, his tense, animal grunts of enjoyment. I savoured his smell. I learned where to squeeze and where not, how much pressure tickled and how much produced a moan of ecstasy.

If there was an audience (and there usually was an audience, since almost fifty men slept in our messdeck in an area the size of a one-bedroom apartment) then his moans would be particularly loud, with gasps and throaty pleas of "Harder, *harder!*" and "Oh, yeah, *do* it, do it *harder*, oh yeah! *Oh!*," the watchers responding with cheers and slurpy wet kisses. But on the rare times when the messdeck was deserted, when everyone was ashore on a Sunday afternoon, or watching a movie in the cafeteria while the ship was on winter manoeuvres, when we were totally alone with just the possibility of someone flying down the hatchway ladder at any moment, on those rare times I rubbed the oil into Casey's back with the most tender strength I could muster.

The rarest of those times was the last time. It was February. They were showing Psycho in the cafeteria. We swayed slowly together, countering the roll of the ship as I worked on his back—almost like dancing. I basked in his heat, my chest on fire from accidentally rubbing against him.

"You ever been in love?" he asked quietly.

"Yes," I replied.

"Me too. Not easy, is it?"

"No. No, it's not."

"Here, I'll show you." He opened his locker; the hinges of the aluminum door shrieked and popped in protest. His uniforms hung razor-creased, immaculate; not at all like mine. He carefully lifted a small colour photograph out of a pocket concealed in his wallet. He twisted his arm behind him, the photo in his hand, holding it away from his glowing, gravelly skin, away from the oil. "What do you think?" he asked.

I refused to focus my eyes. The photograph smelled of leather and sweat. "Beautiful. You're lucky."

"Yeah. She's meeting the ship in Vancouver. Maybe you could take our picture, this one's not so good."

"I've got lots of film," I said. "I'll take as many as you want." He flinched; my hands had suddenly turned cold.

That night as he slept, I watched him as if for the first time. I talked to him, my words instantly sucked into the electric motor. I told him that I loved him. I told him I would never love anyone again. I told him that I hated him, that he had betrayed me, and that I would never let anyone betray me again. I begged him to let me touch him, to hold him, to kiss him just once. I thought of all that might have been, and lost myself to fantasy.

I imagined wrapping my arms tightly around him, trying to become him. He wakes with a smile, embraces me and crushes my face to his rough, sweaty chest. His salt in my mouth is more thrilling than any salt on any wind in any storm which has merely blown from China. Then our clothes miraculously disappear and he pulls my head lower. And lower. Then I struggle for breath. There is fur in my mouth. Someone is laughing. I open my eyes; they are brimming with tears.

Peter is kneeling beside me, holding my hand and grinning delightedly. "God, you should see yourself! Laughing and crying and carrying on in the most *scandalous* way!" He scoops Casey off my chest and hugs him. "You guys havin' a wild session together, eh, Case? Two old flea-bags sleepin' on the living room floor!"

Peter Dubé Cold Front

FOR DOUG McCOLEMAN, WITH MY LOVE

Maybe it doesn't matter if you never met him, because you saw him once and that's enough. It could have been a movie. Maybe you saw it alone.

He was there, a fabrication of light and celluloid, insubstantial and just about eternal, larger than life and better dressed. You sat there, erect in the dark and by yourself.

Maybe you had mixed feelings about his feelings but changed your mind later and decided that you liked the picture. It was a long, gorgeously photographed love story set in a city you had once visited.

He was a young man, a journalist perhaps, staying in this city and she an even younger woman, let's say twenty-one, just for form, recently orphaned and left an inheritance, travelling. They meet at a concert, look at each other, casually at first, smile. The plot twists just enough for them to be introduced by a mutual friend at the bar during intermission. They talk, nervously and intelligently, mostly about the city they are both in, and the feeling of removal from it they both share. There is the appropriate undercurrent of tension, sexual and social. You can tell by the rapid blinking of their eyes, enlarged to dozens of times their natural size on the screen, and by the irregular pauses in their talk.

Although it is the same tired boy-meets-girl story once again, you find just enough ambiguity in him to let yourself into the narrative and enjoy.

They, the he and the she, meet together regularly—coffee, museums, dinners—and grow familiar. One day they are walking through an elaborate park; everything is laid out perfectly, shrubs, trees, flower beds, ponds and fountains, situated and shaped to convey some meaning. Even the shadows of the tree's limbs as they cross the water are perfectly composed and articulate. All of this could, of course, be in the photography. It is here that they make their spontaneous declaration of love for one another.

Outside, in the lobby, there were men wandering in and out of the washroom, eyes fixed only on the barren wall before them.

There, in the dark, you recognize that there is a desired emotional response to this moment, know it in yourself—you should be moved. But you can't muster the strength for it. All you see is the way a tree branch in the background crosses the frame of a beautifully moulded window, and there is nothing in their kiss for you anyway.

The film goes on, unwinding on metal reels in a room you cannot see.

They continue to grow closer and closer, spending days and nights in each other's company. You move uneasily in the darkened room. They hold hands, look into each other's moist and luminous eyes as the soundtrack, which seems too rapidly composed, plays on the speakers. The man next to you in the cinema fidgets constantly. The star's face, a vision of almost mathematical perfection, enormous on the far wall, shines in the darkness. Every movement of his eyes provokes another from yours. You follow, flickering and blinking, every gesture.

The sound of rushing water wavers in your memory.

The city seems filled with the two of them. The hours insufficient for their shared histories.

All of the colours in the film suddenly seem too bright. You find yourself on your feet, never noticing how you got there. On your feet and half way up the aisle before the film was done.

Then you are blinking in the glare of sunlight. Colours washed out, faded in your pupils' unreadiness for daylight.

Sky Gilbert Censored

was a dark and stormy night and the middle of winter and I
waiting for him. I would tell you his name okay I will it was
and he was certainly a beautiful boy. With those hard firm
sitting right smack below his nose and those eyes and his
which was straight and young and firm also and I want so much to
it again as I had the night of the orgy which was in the month of
1989. Well, tonight was the big night. My very best dyke pal named
had lent me her apartment for the night. The apartment was on
Street and as I approached I noticed that all the lights on the
were out. Oh no, I thought, would my night of passion be totally
I certainly hoped not. I entered the dark apartment. You really
understand that I was planning a thorough s-and-m scene. The sex
were in the bag beside the bed. I knew because my dyke friend named
always left them there. But it was too dark to see, what if
arrived and the apartment was totally dark. Would it be sexy and
or would it just be awful and awkward? Candles, I thought, so I
out to the store and because there was a blackout that night on
Street the guy at the store charged me $1.00 per candle. I bought
of them which was a rip-off for sure. So I lit the candles and
the wine and was a little drunk and finally it was 9:00 and
cheerfully reached the top of the stairs. I was wearing leather
and my leather jacket too. My pants were ripped. And I had my
ring on too. Tight. He smiled and we talked, drank and smoked
but I tried not to inhale. He asked if I'd ever done any

before. I said no this was my first time which was true. My
was getting harder and harder and just about bursting through my pants.
was very worried though because it was not only dark but very
and it's hard to make love when it's like that only because your
gets small and shrivelled. Finally the lights and the heat did
on and we started our s-and-m scene. He certainly was a wonderful
He had lots of imagination and new really sexy things to say.
told me to remove my pants which I did then he chained me to the
which was really weird and he went off to the corner store to buy
I thought that would take ages so I wiggled free but suddenly he
and yelled at me for being a bad slave. I knew that I was a bad
but I didn't know what my punishment would be. He ordered me to
around. Then he raised his hand and slapped me on my big white
which quickly became red. I think what I liked best was this
who talked dirty and was beautiful. He wouldn't take off his
even though I desperately wanted to see his lithe hairless young
He ordered me into the bedroom and it was time to get the sex
out of the bag. He approved of them. He really liked the tit
because they were 'butterfly' ones. Then I did something very
and he said he would have to punish me again. He got out a big
and whacked me with it. Over and over but then I yelled the safe
which I would tell you now but it's my personal one. But he did
whacking me. I was really feeling like a bad slave and wanted to
his cock. He finally said he would show it to me but I couldn't
it. I was really frustrated and writhing but all this made my
harder. In fact I was aching to come but he told me not to. Then
took off his pants and I got a good very good view of it, of his
which was not yet hard but just sort of waving there big and
Then he put the clamps on me. I screamed and protested my
hurt so much! So he took them off and tried to soothe me and

Sky Gilbert
The Story of Calvin Kine and Johnny Bad

Dedicated to the memory of David Pond
"Godiam—la tazza e il cantico, la notta abbella e il
riso; in questo paradiso ne scopra il nuovo di."

Calvin Kine

Once there was a boy
His name was Calvin
He was brought up by a pair of very nice parents who loved him very much
His home in the suburbs was always clean and bright with flowers in the window
On Sundays, his father used to mow the lawn in summer and shovel the walk in winter
And then he would settle down to watch
The game
Calvin's mother would not let him help his father with these chores
She felt that he was too delicate, and she was right
Calvin had pale pale skin that was smooth and unblemished
At the mere mention of company visiting or sports or fights at the merest suggestion of
any danger or embarrassment Calvin's tender skin would redden and become irritated
His mother made certain that he had many afternoons at home to be creative
When Calvin was thirteen years old, his father insisted that Calvin go to school at
DeLancey College because, he contended, it was there that they would make a man
of him
Calvin obeyed because he always obeyed
His years at school were not happy ones
The chief object of his frustration and in fact intense irritation was the heavy wool
pants that all the boys were forced to wear

The cloth was rough and dry, and it chafed his tender skin

The Protestant clerics who ran the small boys' school were, it seemed to Calvin, amused by his pain

They knew that under the dark brown pants were the pale legs of a boy with sensitive skin, and they often caught him before lights out spreading Vaseline Intensive Care Lotion over his legs in an attempt to endure the pain

And endure it he did

But at his graduation he vowed that never again would he be party to forcing young boys to wear cruelly rough and irritating pants near their tender skin. He did not mention his resolve to anyone, but the purity of his dedication to this ideal (of comfortable non-irritating legwear) gave his gaze an intensity and his brow a furrowed look which made his face appear particularly attractive for the graduation photos

After graduating from high school Calvin went on to art school

At the art school, which was in the mountains, Calvin was able to indulge his artistic impulses to the fullest

There, Calvin met another boy named Roger, who also had artistic impulses

The boys roomed together

Their co-habitation was without incident, except that Calvin found himself longing to be with Roger and also for some strange reason wanting to take baths with him

Roger was also a pale boy, though not as slender as Calvin, and slightly more muscular

Calvin used to sit at the window of his dormitory waiting for Roger to return from his classes

Roger always seemed to be late

Whenever he was late Calvin would find that an inexpressible sadness subsumed him

He wanted to cry but he didn't

He just tucked his knees under him as he sat on his chair looking out the window, and waited

At one point, Calvin suggested that they have a bath together

Roger shrugged his shoulders and said "Okay"

Calvin ran the warm bath, at about 8:00 on Sunday evening, and made sure to fill it with lots of soft fluffy bubbles

The two boys removed their clothing shyly, each staring at the wallpaper which was sea blue

The bathtub was just the right temperature and the two boys enjoyed a chaste time together, the only contact being when Roger asked to have his back scrubbed

Calvin did so at Roger's behest

Afterwards they never spoke of the incident

Calvin went on to design a line of men's clothing which was famous all over the world
The clothing was always comfortable and made especially not to chafe the skin of young boys
His jeans in fact were so famous that they came to be known by his first name alone, as Calvins
The advertisement for Calvin's jeans always contained two men with their shirts off and one woman fully clothed
One man was always looking at the woman and one man was always looking at the other man
The woman in these ads always looked as if she would rather be in another ad
The men in these ads always looked as if they wished the woman was not in these ads
And though no one knew of this the men in the ads always looked like Calvin's university friend, Roger
Somewhere during Calvin's career he fell in love with a lovely young designer who worked as his assistant
Her name was Audrey
Audrey was a very pretty woman who had no breasts at all and was not interested in sexual intercourse
That spring, they were married
It was a fairy tale wedding and all the great and near-great were present
Everyone sighed and said what a lovely couple and Calvin's mother cried
Calvin's father was confused, but happy
He had always preferred women with large breasts
But that seemed a minor point under the circumstances
Calvin and Audrey had very few children, in fact none at all, but they had many parties
They were very happy
Calvin lived to be very very old and it was only near the end that he started having an obsession with having baths with his small nephews, all of whom seemed to have inherited the Calvin sensitive skin
These baths of course were chaste
But irregular
Fortunately, Calvin died before these requests for baths could become embarrassing
Calvin died at the ripe old age of eighty-nine
There were thousands of people at his funeral
They all wore his comfortable affordable jeans
None of them had chafed legs

They did not cry, for none of Calvin's friends were over-emotional
They paid their respects and went home
They spoke of Audrey
"She'll be well taken care of"
They said
And she was
And that's the story of Calvin Kine

Johnny Bad

Once there was a boy named Johnny Bad
Johnny Bad was born on the wrong side of the tracks
When his depraved old grandma saw him in the old shoebox that his mother used as
a cradle she said—
"He's an ugly bugger"
But she was wrong
Johnny's grandma had always been wrong; it was kind of her trademark
Johnny's mother was a diseased prostitute
It was, in fact, amazing that Johnny was born with no birth defects
But in fact, he had one major defect
The doctor noticed it during delivery
Johnny was in possession of one of the largest and in fact most beautiful penises in
human history
Not only was it inordinately long and thick but the glans rose like a flower out of the
strong and veiny stalk
When it was limp it seemed perpetually ready to stir, to rise and do its business
The doctor officiating at the birth of this child of a diseased whore was shocked at
the size of the member
The child will have to be circumsized, he said, and he hacked away mercilessly at the
infant's penile extrusion
Even bereft of its skin, Johnny's shaft was formidable
The baby however wailed at the circumcision and never forgot the incident
Johnny's childhood was without trauma
He lived in a shack with no toilet and slept on a pile of old mattresses which his
mother had found in an alley
His mother between tricks would throw Johnny a crust of mouldy Wonderbread
She said it built strong bodies twelve ways
Johnny grew constantly
His muscles bulged from the age of ten and he could pick up his mother and the

shack and the mattresses all by his lonesome at the age of twelve
At age thirteen Johnny quit school and became a hooker
He moved out on his own and spent a lot of time in alleys and backlots and cars
He always wore a torn leather jacket he had found at the Goodwill and he tattooed
his body with unsightly and crude pictures of phallic symbols and blood
He even had his scrotum tattooed which is a costly, painful and nearly impossible
procedure
Johnny's eager ass and huge dick serviced many and he enjoyed giving and receiving
pleasure
He'd always say "Would you like it rough or easy" but even easy was rougher than
almost anybody would expect
Johnny hung out with a dwarf named Sammy
Sammy was a bodybuilder and used to sing and dance at a local pub
He had a strange disease that was gradually crippling him but Sammy wouldn't give
in
Sammy also had a large member, especially in relation to his own tiny dwarfish size
Sometimes Johnny and Sammy would trick together, and the customers would mar-
vel at how Johnny's thick shaft could ever make it into Sammy's tiny, perfectly
shaped bum
But Johnny's favourite thing was servicing old men
He particularly enjoyed servicing smelly drunks who never washed their sexual
organs
He made an arrangement with them
If Johnny Bad met a drunk he found particularly attractive he would say "Where do
you sleep" and the drunk would tell him and Johnny would say "I'll meet you later"
and then at about 4:00 in the morning, when the drunk was fast asleep and Johnny
was really high, and after he'd already had sex with three or four people, Johnny
would appear at the drunk's hovel, naked, his huge hard-on pulsating, ready for sex
He would wake up the drunk, which was no mean feat, and the drunk would think
that he had died and gone to heaven, or that he was experiencing some strange
vision of ecstasy
Some of the drunks used to call him Johnny Angel
In fact they would have thought they had a fantastic vision of the DTs except that
they all had the same experience with the same angel
Johnny became a legend among the drunks, and he loved them
Late at night, if you were to wander near to the abandoned houses on Jarvis Street
you'd hear the drunks in their sleep, tossing and turning on their filthy beds, moan-
ing oh Johnny . . . Johnny . . . don't stop Johnny . . .
Johnny was also into shooting up large doses of MDA with two lesbians he knew who

had lots of needles because they were both diabetic

He was exceedingly happy for a time

Then when Johnny was about thirty-four years old he heard about AIDS, a severe killer disease that seemed to be linked to certain kinds of sexual intercourse and hard drugs

Johnny got off the MDA and started using condoms

He used to force old men to put the condoms on his huge erection using their mouths only

It was fun for him, and a challenge to the old men

Not long after that Johnny contracted AIDS and died

There were a few old men at his funeral, and the two lesbians who were off the MDA and into cocaine now, and Sammy the dwarf who was in a wheelchair but still dancing (with only his feet) and still singing, and some of his hooker friends

There was a fantastic party afterwards and everybody got really stoned and cried a lot about Johnny who they would never forget because he was Johnny Bad and there would never be anyone like him

Ever again

And that's the story of Johnny Bad

Conclusion

In analyzing the stories of Calvin and Johnny serious questions come to mind

Which was the happiest life?

Which was the life worth living?

Which was the truly moral life?

Who would you most like to have sex with?

And finally the most important question is this:

Many years after Liza Minnelli appeared in the musical *Cabaret,* when she realized she was an alcoholic and spent some time in the Betty Ford Clinic, she decided to clean up her act so she didn't turn out tragic like her mother and she released a new version of the song "Cabaret" in which the part where she sings about the girlfriend known as Elsie, with whom she shared four sordid rooms in Chelsea, who rented by the hour, and who died of pills and liquor, and was the happiest corpse she'd ever seen, well Liza changed that whole part so that it was clear that Elsie had led a bad and digusting life and should have spent some time at the Betty Ford Clinic

Was this a wise idea on Liza's part or just hysterical healthiness?

So

In analyzing the lives of Johnny Bad and Calvin Kine, which was the happiest life?

Well, both appeared to be happy in their own way

However I think a point could be made that Calvin was a little sexually frustrated
Hence the baths with his nephews
But then again Calvin may have been simply asexual, that is not interested in sex at all
He could merely have been interested in baths
Secondly
Which was the life worth living?
Well, let's see
Calvin became famous and helped a lot of people to overcome the serious problem of having chafed legs
Johnny, on the other hand, brought a lot of pleasure to himself and to a lot of drunken old men
Both lives it seems were worth living in their own way
Thirdly
Which was the truly moral life?
This is a hard question
Calvin followed all the rules of course and Johnny didn't
But need we analyze both lives in terms of conventional morality?
What is good, what is bad?
Johnny's life was shorter, but his dick was longer
Calvin's life was cleaner in every way
Is cleanliness a virtue?
And after all, is it really a value not to have chafed legs?
And if Johnny didn't look after the drunken old men, who would?
I pass on this question at the moment
Who would you like most to have sex with?
I think the answer is clear
Johnny Bad of course, because who doesn't like a perfect musculature and a large dick and a gorgeous tight ass
But then again, Calvin did have pale skin and his complete aversion to any sort of sexual contact could have been a turn-on in a weird and perverted way
But you might get tired of all those baths
And finally who would you most like to fall in love with?
Well, obviously Calvin because he led such a charmed life. Then again there are emotional masochists who would sell their wisdom teeth to torture themselves over someone as totally irrationally weird and obsessive and sexual as Johnny Bad
I'd say it's a draw on this one
And as for the question of Liza Minnelli changing the lyrics of the song "Cabaret" after leaving the Betty Ford Clinc, I'd say Liza Minnelli has made some pretty bad

career choices in her lifetime and that was definitely one of them
Leave the song alone
I bet the corpse was happy
In fact if there was a moral to this tale, it would be this
In this crazy mixed-up world of ours there will always be Calvin Kines and Johnny
Bads
But at my funeral there's going to be dancing

George K. Ilsley Talismen

Under the strobe light, the flashing glow, pulsing neon green, catches my eye. The glowing object is framed by a tattered plaid vest and backed by the smooth parallel perfection of delineated pecs—altogether a splendid strip of torso. In a burst of black lights, the object flares phosphorescent, becoming almost completely luminous.

"Look," I say, nudging the guy next to me. "That guy over there is wearing a phosphorescent pacifier."

He doesn't respond, so I nudge him again and shout louder. "He's wearing a phosphorescent pacifier."

The guy is handsome and totally aware of the value of good looks. Faded jeans, filled white t-shirt, an Egyptian medallion on a leather thong. A sentence all in adjectives. The handsome guy glances at me and, unimpressed, pretends my nudging was an accident of overcrowding, pretends my words were drowned out by the bedlam. He turns away to follow a tall guy dressed in faded jeans, sculpted white t-shirt and an Aztec medallion.

I turn back to observe the punk/skinhead fashion/political statement with the pacifier. Except for the serious and sturdy boots which are totally his own, he is composed entirely of remnants and fragments: one imagines slices from the knees of his torn black jeans safety-pinned across the ass of a friend; in return, material for his vest is torn from the chests of young punk buddies, exposing their nipples. The tattered plaid vest, carefully concocted from these soft-smelling scraps of old plaid cotton shirts, is designed with an acute sense of vanity, not at all uncommon in this setting but all the more touching in this handsome case. The vest both conceals and exhibits the torso, displaying a careful awareness of what is so artfully displayed.

Yes—it must be said (I forge on, the courageous observer), What a torso, a torso blessed by a gym membership and discipline . . . or rather, quickly amending my romantic vision, hundreds of push-ups and sit-ups with his buddy in the privacy of their own squat: like Robert DeNiro, only cuter, in *Taxi Driver and Mate*. A torso blessed by crackerjack genes and rampant hormones—a testament to testosterone. Glancing from his broad boots to his broad shoulders, I figure he is a combination of many influences: hormones, genetics, exercise and, of course, packaging.

Framed by the softness of the vest, nestled in the clean sharp cleavage of that torso, that splendid torso, is the item, that talisman—the fetish which first caught my eye.

Neon green, the pacifier hangs from a thick chain, thicker than the chain I use to lock my bike. Keeping the pacifier company, lit by the strobe but unaffected by the black light, is a thinner chain with a crucifix (upside down, of course) and a black leather thong with a silver swastika. I cannot tell in this pulsing light whether the swastika is the original or the turned-around version—the Nazi miscarriage of the original Sanskrit good-luck symbol. It's probably reversible.

Three or four preppy boys noisily approach, bumping through the crowd. Drunk and exuberant and at the same time profoundly shy, they are the kind of totally insecure prep boys who grow up in small isolated towns up north or out west or back east.

The preppy boys spot the skinhead and, amazed and somewhat in awe, cluster around him, as if suddenly confronted by an alien in a zoo. They stand swaying, trying to focus, before reaching out their hands in fascination. The particular object of their attention is, of course, the talisman, the phosphorescent pacifier. The drunkest boy, dark-haired and slightly taller, bends his head suddenly and puts the pacifier in his mouth, making baby-like sucking movements with his jaw. The thick chain hangs from his mouth and drapes around the punk's neck. The prep boys convulse with laughter. The punk remains impassive, accustomed to the attention garnered by freaks. The drunkest boy joins his friends in laughter, and the pacifier flies from his mouth, glistening, and falls back into place on the skinhead's chest, where a line of sweat tentatively explores the sternum.

The prep boys examine all the punk's adornments, fondling the accoutrements like window shoppers; they consider the weight of the thick chain and joke about snow tires, examine the swastika and say *Heil Hitler*, touch with just their fingertips the anarchist pins holding the vest together, and point at the dangling, multi-studded earrings, so unlike the single chaste gold hoops which boys back home, considered *daring*, wear. They touch and hover, they laugh and look; they run the soft worn fabric of the vest between their fingers; they brush against the warm, hard flesh.

Information spills from the boys and onto their neighbours—they have a need to explain, to tell their stories, to let us know the magnitude of this event. They are used to being friendly. They are used to being able to talk to anyone. These drunken prep boys say they are from Sudbury. Tonight is the drunkest prep boy's birthday, and the first time he has ever been in a gay bar, but not his last time, they all laugh.

I turn to the guy next to me. In jeans and a simple tight white t-shirt, he sports a voluptuous gym-body which needs no further adornment. Less is more if there's more to show. I lean over his chest and shout into his face. "It is truly a fetish, that phosphorescent pacifier—do you see the way they treat it? Of course," I shout, louder over the music, "I mean what fetish used to mean before the meaning became worn from rough and careless handling . . . "

The gym-body gives me a generous view of the tapering V-line of his back and demonstrates the agility of his muscular, protuberant buttocks as he insinuates, haltingly, away through the crowd.

Looking around, I realize there is no one else in this room the preppy boys would have—could have—approached and fawned over so freely as they did the punk boy with the shaved head, chains and shitkicking boots. His costume invites, and he receives, as though expected, the attention becoming to an icon—or indeed, an iconoclast.

I silently refuse the beer thrust in my face by a drunken preppy boy from a small northern town.

The prep boys continue standing near the punk, chugging their beers. The punk has accepted a beer (his first tonight) from the birthday boy, and when he looks away the birthday boy looks at him. The punk shifts his weight and his torso dances with his skin.

Yet their energies are so different. The punk is calm and impassive but fuelled by a passionate rejection of conformity and yet, I assume, his passions are well-modulated by humour. The birthday boy, the drunkest prep boy from an isolated northern town, staggers among his friends, laughing, one of a pack, nervous, his shyness demonstrated by his lack of inhibitions.

I fumble in my pockets for a scrap of paper and a pen to write something down. (Later, when I'm about to do laundry and going through the pockets of smoky clothes, I discover this scrap of paper and find it makes little—well, frankly, no sense: "climbing the hills of shyness, fuelled by beer . . . the obstacle of shyness overcome by beer, only to reach the pinnacle where, dizzy from freedom, shyness turns into its polar opposite and the momentum of lost inhibitions greases the steep slope of the descent. . . . ")

The preppy boys, en masse, have to go the bathroom. I am sure one of them makes the joke about "only renting beer." They all laugh loudly.

The birthday boy, dispensing beers as baksheesh, charms his way through the line at the urinals. He returns first and alone. No longer crouching down with the pack, he is slightly taller than the punk, and slightly younger, slightly slimmer, with fine, sharply drawn features.

"Let's get out of here," says the punk, his first words.

They butt in line for their coats. No one complains. It is, by and large, a very polite city.

Their coats are both leather. The punk's is black, cut in straight lines and garnished over the back and shoulders with chrome studs which cluster in patterns like iron filings over a magnet. The birthday boy's is blue and decorated with badges and cloth numbers, like a boy scout-cum-athlete. A good jacket will tell a careful watcher the whole story of a boy's life to date.

"You need a new coat," says the punk.

"I'm nineteen today," says the birthday boy, swaying, as he struggles into his jacket.

They walk through the cold. After a few minutes, the birthday boy pulls on the punk's arm and says, "Hey, where are we going?"

"To bed," says the punk.

"Where?" asks the boy, as if he hadn't heard.

"Home," says the punk.

They walk through the cold. Snow that had fallen earlier, now dirty and churned by city feet, crunches under their boots.

"I have to go to the bathroom," says the boy.

They walk through the cold.

"I really have to piss," says the boy.

"Well," says the punk, with a sweeping gesture indicating the street, city, planet. "There's your toilet."

"Okay," says the boy. He leads them around a corner. "Here's a good bathroom," he says, approaching a fairly clean snowdrift along a line of alley sumac. He fumbles at his fly and pees into the bank, large loopy letters, spelling out the syllables as long as he lasts before tweaking out the last few letters. "Al . . . ex . . . aa . . . nn . . . duh." He shakes himself off. "The great," he says, bending over slightly to return his penis to a warm crevice safe from frostbite.

The punk boy steps up to the snowbank. He too writes in the snow. The prep boy, the middle-class white boy from a small northern town, reads it aloud. "F . . . u, fuck, you. Fuck you," he says. "*Fuck you!*" His words sail off into the city, bouncing off a building or two before being absorbed by the cold and the snow.

The punk finishes the final 'U' and bores a steaming hole deep into the drift. "Low rent beer," he says.

The punk boy lives in a small apartment in a downtown building of a certain age. It is dark. That it is black, lit by candles, does not seem to matter to the prep boy. The punk boy turns up the heat and unzips his jacket. His torso is again exhibited, the sharp cleavage and rippling abs doubly framed by the jacket and the soft worn vest, and the prep boy, looking more often at the exposed flesh than anything else, does not notice in the light a change in the depth of the punk's eyes, or else, noticing the difference, admires them, clear and glittering, in the candlelight. The boy's mind is running over. The punk's torso was the kind flaunted by jock boys in high school, the boys he could never imagine being friends with, the boys who were always friends with boys just like themselves, jock boys who did not talk much and found it strange that he could.

The punk brings two glasses of water. "Take off your jacket," he says. The boy does.

"Drink this," he says, handing him one of the glasses. The boy does.

"Do you have any beer?" the boy asks.

"Maybe."

"Take off your jacket," the boy says.

They look at each other for a minute. Then, at the same moment, they smile.

"Take off your shirt," the punk says.

"I need a beer," the boy says.

"Take off your shirt," the punk says, "and I'll see."

He smiles at the birthday boy, nineteen today, and goes to the fridge. As he turns away, the boy watches, fascinated by the punk's ears, one of which is unbelievably cute and jaunty, the one with only three or four earrings, a nibbly jewel in the setting of a shaved head.

The punk returns with a beer, rubbing it against his bare abdomen. The boy has pulled his long-sleeved striped preppy shirt out of his jeans but is suddenly shy.

The punk offers the beer. The boy reaches out to take it but the punk pulls it back and moves his leg forward, so that the boy's hand touches his thigh. The boy jerks his hand back as if burned. They look at each other and then laugh. The punk offers the beer again. "Both hands," he says gruffly.

The boy reaches out with both hands, slowly.

"Close your eyes," the punk says.

The boy does.

The punk moves forward and with his free hand reaches behind the boy, grasps the bottom of his shirt and pulls it up over the boy's head. The boy shivers as the cool air strikes his torso. The punk touches the beer bottle to the boy's exposed ribs near the nipple and the boy jerks away, laughing, and struggles out of his shirt, throwing it aside. He reaches for the punk but the punk takes a step backwards, and then hands him the beer before moving away. The boy takes a drink and leans back in the chair. His flesh is white and healthy, the torso lean and trim and exquisitely shaped by the benevolence of youth—there is not as yet any sign of the corruption which will envelop him with age.

The punk sits down across the room. The boy takes another drink. "Take off your jacket," he whispers hoarsely, his voice cracking.

The punk slips his hand inside his jacket and touches himself, rubbing his stomach and chest. His knees move suddenly wider apart and then come back, as if accommodating a sudden increase in testicle size.

"Maybe," he says.

The candles flicker, and they are each observed watching the other. After a time, the punk stands up. The boy watches him. The punk puts on a tape, keeping the volume low. They will need to talk in whispers. The music is rhythmic and tribal, traditional yet completely contemporary.

"What's that?" says the boy.

"Dead Can Dance," says the punk, turning from the stereo and slipping off his jacket. He walks over to the boy and stands in front of him. The boy takes a long swig of beer and then reaches out with the bottle, touching the punk with the bottle at the patched crotch of his black jeans. The punk reaches out and pinches the boy's nipple, and the boy pulls away.

"Take off your clothes," says the punk.

"Maybe," says the boy.

"Stand up," says the punk.

The boy stands up in front of the punk. The punk takes the beer out of the boy's hand and drinks from the bottle, finishing it. He throws the beer bottle in to the chair and turns to the boy. He puts his arms around him. He kisses the boy on the side of his soft firm neck, at the border between smooth and scratchy, his hands kneading the warm smoothness of his muscular back. The boy, groaning, returns the embrace, putting his hands up underneath the tattered vest and, instinctively, turns to kiss him.

They kiss.

This is the birthday boy's first real kiss. Of course there have been others—whiskery aunts, the back of his hand for practice, girls primly thanking him good night: that sort of thing. He only dated good girls. He did not know that not everyone found the rituals of proms and dating so meaningless. He just did what everyone else was doing, especially if it involved drinking.

His experiences with other adolescent boys, his friends, did not permit kissing. Such intimacy was reserved for lovers—unthinkable between boys, even (perhaps especially) between boys having sex.

The birthday boy and the punk kiss and neck. They neck and they hug and they grope and growl. The boy is intoxicated by the smells and textures, thrilled by the roughness of unshaven skin which extends from the crown to the chin and trails down to the neck, giving way abruptly to satiny smoothness which spreads in all directions, the smell of the worn, soft, tattered cotton, many times washed . . . the boy moves away, overcome, and does not resist as the punk unbuckles the boy's jeans and jerks them down over his hips.

"Now take them off," the punk says, going to the fridge. The boy stumbles stepping out of his jeans, laughing, falling to the floor. He struggles, continuing to laugh, out of his jeans and underwear.

The punk returns with a beer and looks at the boy laying on the floor looking at him. The boy has a hard-on which lays on his lean hip. The boy, now not laughing, licks his lips.

The punk takes off his vest and throws it on the face of the boy who stopped laughing on the floor. As the boy removes the tattered cotton vest from his face, the punk kneels down next to the boy and straddles his chest, sitting on his stomach. The boy groans and struggles, the punk's weight real but not arduous, and runs his hands and the vest up and down the punk's thighs, the punk, wearing chains and earrings, sitting on top of him.

Taking a big swig of beer, the punk leans forward and pins the boy's hands on the floor over the boy's head. The punk lets some beer dribble from his mouth onto the boy's face. The boy giggles and opens his mouth, moving his head around to try and catch the beer. The punk boy keeps moving slightly so the boy has to move too to try and catch some beer. The punk sits up to take another mouthful of beer and, looking at the boy, swallows it. He belches. The boy reaches out and strokes the torso which reminds him of so many untouchables in high school and so many unreachables in dreams. The punk, taking another mouthful of beer, leans forward over the boy again, hugging the boy's naked delineated ribs with his black jean knees. The boy opens his mouth expectantly and strokes the punk boy, feeling the smoothness of the skin and the latent vigour of the torso, savouring the softness of the hard muscles, feeling the textured hardness of the thighs under the patched black jeans. The boy moves his head from side to side to catch the stream of pale beer dribbling into his mouth.

The punk kisses the open expectant mouth, sharing the remnants of the mouthful of beer. Stopping in mid-kiss, the boy agape, the punk boy moves away and his throng of fetishes dangle over the boy's face. The boy sits up straining, pressing his lean hard torso into the punk's groin. He takes the pacifier into his mouth, sucking it, eyes closed, hands moving blindly and intuitively over the other boy. The punk sits up straight and the soother pops out of the boy's mouth. The boy's hands move to the studded belt, trying to undo it, and stroke the groin of the black jeans.

"Soother," says the boy, remembering a word.

"Phosphorent pacifier," says the punk, standing up to take off his jeans.

"Pee Pee," says the boy, starting to giggle. "Pee Pee," he says again, gasping, choking, laughing out of control.

The boy, nineteen today, laying on the floor in the apartment of a skinhead in the big city, draws his knees up and slowly stops laughing, becoming calm again and expectant. "Pee Pee," he says, his face relaxing.

Mark Kershaw We Two Boys Together

Comrades clinging.

We together, O Peter Doyle.

I cling to *Calamus* and you to find in forests verdant; you, the manly attachment of comrades, friends, lovers. Save me, sing me, solace me. Give me this sweet sacrament of our silence; you upon, within, beyond my lips; and sleep with me reclined on fern and moss.

I have him with me, Peter; his volume of words, volumes of sighs; he who in the streetcar loved you so, a youth in blue; he who loves you so in words and now is gone is mist, is air; he who will love you so in me, we clinging boys together, never leaving, never leaving, in all our perpetuity dreaming.

You are not on this bus I ride, carriage of our strange wedding, to hold me in your hand and stand as you did for him, for me, blue youth. I have not your cotton cloth shirt, and fading sunlight will not illumine curves of cheek that are not here in this, your streetcar, yet free of rail, that rocks a child; the child you were, the boys we are, is what he saw in you, what I see.

One sits ahead that is not you, and looks at me, kind stranger, knows my destiny; his too, no doubt. There he may take you from me, but never shall I let him touch you. If songs of war are what I must sing, then I'll sing him songs of war, my arms on guard around your breast; a tender armour. If to save you I must follow him, bend to him, hear him cry, hear him sing his songs of conquest, then I will, a sacrifice becoming our immortality.

Now our witnesses have gone, he among them. I will let him vanish, grant him privacy, and he will not follow us, follow me as I seek the paths much trodden by difficult desire, to where you are concealed, my dear friend, among the roots and leaves themselves, alone; among the men, the multitude, alone.

O Peter Doyle, I wait for you on this log, cylinder of spirit, as he perhaps had chosen, your hoary comrade lover. You bared your face in the starlight and he held you, boy of responding kisses. This I shall give you, we shall give each other; an example to lovers to take permanent shape.

Patches of light remain, framed by silhouettes of trees. Men, athletic, slink in slow ballet by flourishes touched: here one leaps from the peat to a mossy rock, surveyor of the sweet earth; there two circle, step forward and back, match movement for movement, then follow one after the other into mellow blackness.

I strike a match, am, by my own fire, a shadowed demon mask of passionate cultures. I touch the flame to cigarette, create a beacon in the dusk, glowing sultry and small in this, chapel of our strange wedding. The match fails, trails its death in a blue-white curl. The smoke consoles, resounds in the chambers of the body that does as fully much as my soul.

Who is this that is become my follower? O Peter, you are here before me, carry a beacon, and sign yourself a candidate for my affections. Our signals pass between us; the code of silences. I genuflect before you, O comrade lover, your hands within my hair, mine upon your zipper. My smouldering beacon has found sleep upon the dampness of the peat, perishes, billows white, expels the spirit in threads of grey.

You guard your own, kissed like a rosary, and breathe between your kisses quiet words I cannot hear beyond the poetry of your timbre. Now I have thrust among your clothing and freed you from the prisons of the city of orgies, the clanking world. My own mouth upon you will be like his, he who loved you as a comrade brother and held your hand so gently among the peaceful humidity of leaves.

I reach to push your shirt higher, give more liberty to you so deserving, and my fingers meet the curve of your belly. Not cunning in muscle, not that of a youthful comrade, it is distended as a swollen fruit, laced not with boyish hairs, soft as down, but coarse curls, touched, even in dusk, with grey like ghost-smoke.

He is not you, O Peter, not what I supposed, but far different, the one to whom I must sing my songs of war, my songs of sacrifice. I recoil and behold his swarthy face, he who sang a song of himself as you, my comrade lover, he who now my soul declines to prefer.

I release him and he departs, scorned. It becomes him, he for whom I claim, falsely by my presence, desire, unconditional. How many have passed, how many will follow? To how many have my songs of war and love gone unsung? You sent this last, my Peter, as a test, a proof, and I did not open my throat for him, no passions uttered. Is this my triumph, for you, O Peter?

Still what of all who did not see as he wrote of you, did not see the robust love, the manly love of comrades? Who did not see boys together clinging, loving, never leaving. Who only saw and only see Democracy, the touch of men as futures defined, borders unlined. Who heard not his words as dripping, bleeding drops of longing. As triumph, they despise us, gentle Peter, remake our meaning, and we bury ourselves deeper in the herbage, sanctuary of our strange wedding.

For our triumph, my dear friend, give yourself, for I see now, above all, that we belong folded inseparably together.

I light another beacon for you, for me, and with the flame my face rebirths the mask of passions. Again, the flame dies and flies, ravels around invisible cords of air, turns and wends its way to the stars, those faint lamps winking. And here in vigil I pray for you to see my light, my love.

Now there you are across the roll of earth, blue youth, blue in your cotton shirt and blue in the shaft of sky between the trees. You are how he saw you, now as I see you: masculine muscle at play through, in, and around you; you who held his hand and spoke a little or perhaps not a word. I attend you, permit you to silently select me as your lover, as your long dwelling kiss.

I douse my beacon, for you navigate by your blue light, and in sweet murkiness our roving lives collide, float in the regions of one another's love, and you, the one I was seeking, are at last here, flushed with the universe.

Our dear eyes give and return looks that I shall never forget and pray you remember always. The touch of your hand to mine is pregnant with the energy of the cosmos you carry, runs and flushes me as you are flushed, exquisite body, empowered by the body of surrounding heaven.

Your lips find mine. Your hands know a weaver's talent thus weave around my chest, encircle me in the pensive patience of your warm cotton, the scented gentility of your strength, and I traverse the narrow boundary between love and peculiarity. Yet you are not peculiar, O Peter, only perpetual, never leaving, never leaving.

We to the earth, to where our origins are traced, are drawn. The order of clothing is usurped, is fallen from the bodies, our electric bodies, and lingering, before I fold into and among you, I see your back; a small curve of earth, blue in the light, your light, a light the likes of which I dare nor care not to desert.

Words and reason are not us, Peter. Only you and I, substance of the universe, hold meaning, pervade and are pervaded by the palpable. In these, our bodies that are our souls; in this, our youth that is our mastery of untainted minds; in you of boundless faith, I read the poetry of his past, he who loved you so. I scribe the meter of our present, I who loves you so. I draft the free verse of our future, I who carries him with me who will love you so, we boys together, ascendants of the atmosphere of lovers.

We pass sweet hours, mystic and immortal, with no songs of war sung, only songs of manly attachment that I have gained in you on this earthly rest; bed of our wedding, no longer strange, but revealed in clarity to which I have accorded.

Up through the fronds of trees I gaze to heaven, recall a childhood secret that, from a well bottom by daylight, stars are seen in the blue. O Peter, is this recollection true, too, of the wells of loneliness? Is the perpetuity of those lofty lamps perhaps intangible here in the bottom blackness?

Yet we together have climbed and are closer to the rim of the well than ever I have believed possible in the face of those who see us as corrupters of our own bodies. Here in the night that will not linger long, I love you faithfully and care for your living, you who appeared to him, to me, brought with you the love that comes as naturally as pain.

Sleep now. Sleep, my comrade lover. And when dawn is upon us, and the ferns glow green and the moss is scented with wet, we will part, will fade, and I will sing my last song to you, my one last grateful song of power enjoyed, of the law of ourselves, of feebleness chased away.

Jeff Kirby Grazy

Is everyone twenty-eight years old with a big dick?

On the phone lines you'd think so. Of course, these are the same guys who only want to talk and 'get off' over the line; they don't want to meet for the 'real thing.' That's okay. Both are the real thing. A means of connecting, sharing a story, a climax. I'm delighted to help a guy achieve his fantasy, trade cum. My only concern is when I sense a guy perceives that outlet as his only choice, a substitute for actual human touch. I see too many gay men choose isolation as a means of surviving a lack of intimacy in their lives.

I've reached that age where I no longer pass as a 'young thing,' or, as my friend Bryan used to say after running into old acquaintances, "Isn't she a hundred pounds older?" I'm thirty-four, but this year I *feel* older, out of step with the 'in' crowd. I'd look like Roy Clark in sideburns. Where would I put that tattoo? And piercings?! ("I don't know . . . ") I've never been much of a partier, though I've spent most of my life trying. Truth is, after minimal tolerance, alcohol and drugs waste me, leave me numb, depressed. "Maybe you don't do the right combination," they say. True, a handful of times, it's been fun, celebrating the splendid stupor of life. I've heard once you break the threshold, it takes on an energy all its own, kind of like centrifugal force. My body always seems to upchuck before that happens, though. (Wise body.)

I'm too young to be a 'dinosaur,' and too old for my varsity jacket. I have a lost sense of place and I'm not exactly certain what's out there for me. Gay men my age are still under siege, either surviving or surviving loss (they feel the same to me). Many of these men, including myself, are suffering low- to medium-grade depression, which no 'snap queen' can simply remedy by saying, "Get over it, girl!" Over the past year, I've chosen to isolate myself, for fear of being seen as a 'downer.' My friend Christopher and I have taken the song "Crazy" and changed it to "Grazy," describing ourselves as 'moo-cows' looking for new pastures.

It's quite tempting to party this one out, an occasional wish to fall off the face of the earth. My passion for dance is mainly how I've survived the non-gay world. I enjoy the camaraderie and courtship of gay male rhythm and sweat. I love the male shape, fragrance, energy, *freedom*. The *movement*. Our gay movement. Carving a place for us to simply be in the world. Men who dance with men they desire have always performed a bold, erotic, defiant, and intimate *public* act. As long as our generations continue to find dance in the face of life and death, I know we'll survive anything. (Yes, even 'Techno.')

The music stops. The fluorescents 'tell all.' Boys wait in line for their leather at Boots. Where are they all going? I don't have the energy or interest to do the tubs. Sex takes a lot of work. I would like to sleep with someone, though. It's fucking cold out. I have a fireplace and bed to share. I'm genuinely a loving, caring man. I'm always good for a morning hard-on. And if we both choose, I'm a great fuck. It's an invitation, not an expectation. Do you know what I really like? I like to rest my head on a guy's chest with his arms around me, you know . . . and my face is just close enough to breathe in the sweetness of his exhalations.

I'm a romantic moo-cow, with the appetite of a sex pig, and a lot of puppy left. Sometimes I fear becoming a 'bitter old queen.' We'll survive this time, too, Christopher.

Mike Murphy
Something Makes a Difference

He didn't like nude bodies or abstracts. Instead he painted surrealistic gladiators in fast-drying acrylics. He never considered himself an artist. "In this here town you have to have a degree to be an artist." But he didn't care. He didn't much like what the galleries called art nowadays.

His parents said that the best thing to happen to gays would be to have them all die of AIDS. He couldn't tell them otherwise, couldn't say anything.

It was a combination of everything. He never really thought about what his life would be like, but somewhere, nagging, knew that this wasn't it.

Being laid off made him acutely aware again of how easy it was to lose something. Eighteen years in the industry only to be replaced by some ruddy-faced kid from New Zealand.

Five years ago, ten years younger, he had a friend who moved away. Didn't fit any of the cities he tried. And then he did himself in. Took a gun and just stopped.

As kids they used to shoot the flags off mailboxes.

He had a dog and several cats. His social life consisted of the odd outing with his co-workers. His family never understood his wanting to leave the farm in the first place.

He missed having someone who made a difference. He gained weight and lost the desire to paint pictures of gladiators.

A guy he worked with retired, asked him to start a business selling bulk dog food, chicken wire and the like. At first he said no, didn't like the guy's lazy son, but now he thinks, well, it's something.

Christopher Paw 5 A Day

Each morning after he showered, shaved and dressed for the office, Darren washed the pill down with a hefty glass of orange juice. Cringing at the concept of healthy living as much as at the acidic citrus mouthwash, he immediately poured a coffee from the machine that started brewing each and every weekday morning at 7:15, as programmed.

Black coffee—the Urban Sunrise—the faggot innuendo for everything from avoiding the laundry to a sexual invitation: "Let's go for a coffee." Darren shrugged at the thought. Some of his best coffees had been at 2:15 in the morning, when desperation hour turned into demolition derby—one cruisy stare being knocked out of commission by a drunker, bolder, deadlier set of eyes.

On the TV screen, J.D. Roberts was mouthing words Darren did not want to hear. Darren strategically positioned his thumb and forefinger in the prescribed manner and crushed J.D.'s head. Then he pointed the remote toward the screen and pressed the button that would send the cheery anchor back into the dull grey void of the picture tube.

The daily headache started. He finished off his coffee and practiced his macho hipsway on his way back to the kitchen. He paused to flip another button, sending waves of Sinead O'Connor wafting through the entire three-and-a-half.

Maggie was pissing in the sink again. Her urine washed over the dried remains of yesterday's spaghetti plate, some of it being collected by the glass still cool from the orange juice. The similarity in colour and consistency with the recently ingested juice both upset and intrigued him. She was on the floor and out of the room before punishment could be successfully administered.

Darren popped a Motrin, contemplated the severity of the pain, and popped another. He poured another cup of lukewarm coffee. Automatic machines were not very proficient at keeping the blood of nine-to-fivers piping.

He flipped four or six more Motrins into a tiny, fashionable, antique metal receptacle, fought with the childproof cap on another bottle, and dumped four capsules into the same container. A pill party, he thought. Giggled. Then, ashamed at the stupidity of the idea, snapped the box and his mind shut.

Darren dropped the container into the breast pocket of his off-the-rack-sale suit from Eaton's, straightened the pink and grey paisley tie, slipped into a trenchcoat and began the twenty-minute journey to the office.

8:15

November rain pelted the continual parade of civil servants. Darren always marvelled at the relative calm of rush hour here. He'd lived in Montréal and Toronto, where nervous tension and eager yuppies dominated the commuter phenomenon. Here it was much more relaxed. Less stress.

He got off the bus with the fifteen other secretaries and clerks who shared his route. Outside the building he stopped in the drizzle for a cigarette with Gary, the nightwatchman, just getting off work. Gary had left his wife six months earlier for a twenty-year-old chicken who had subsequently left Gary three months later for a New York sugar daddy. Gary was moving to Vancouver. He had been telling Darren this for the past four weeks. Darren wished he would just get it over with.

On the eighth floor he pushed through the frosted glass doors and greeted Roberta the receptionist. She thought she wanted him. He knew she didn't.

She asked about his weekend. He lied. He always lied about his weekends. He had not yet discovered how to describe driving to Montréal to pay twenty bucks, plus parking tickets, to sit for six hours in a tiny, dimly-lit cubicle, having anonymous sex with almost anyone who would drop his towel. That is, he had not figured out how to describe it so that it didn't sound as sleazy as it was.

Roberta had gone skiing in Collingwood. Did he know there was already snow up there? Darren shrugged at her question. Did he care?

Darren retrieved his messages and wound his way through the partitioned office maze to his own private, federal cell, stopping for coffee along the way.

The morning was spent trudging through the routine paperwork and terminal entries of a second-level clerk.

12:15

Darren snapped open the lid of the metal box and simultaneously swished a capsule and a Motrin down his gullet with a paper cup of stale water from the cooler. Once, he had gotten one stuck at the back of his mouth. The thin gelatin coating had dissolved rapidly and the acrid powder had clung to his tongue and throat like a million tiny parasites. He could still taste the chalky substance when he thought of it. It had killed his appetite that day.

He force-fed himself the tuna sandwich (brown bread), the banana and the yogurt cup he had brought for lunch. He tried to visualize it as pizza and onion rings. It never worked.

14:45

The government works on a twenty-four hour clock.

Marina, from the adjacent cubicle, offered Darren more caffeine and sat in the chair only she used, next to his terminal. They sat sipping their coffee. She smelled the smoke on his breath. He had snuck off to the bathroom again. Working for the government had begun to strike a resounding resemblance to being in high school.

Maria asked if he had heard that the Ontario Supreme Court had just ruled that same-sex-partners constituted conjugal relationships and were therefore entitled to spousal benefits.

Darren snapped open the metal box and washed another capsule down with the coffee. No Motrin this time; his headache had subsided.

It was good news. A little late. James had been dead for two years now. Marina shrugged; better late than never.

The drizzle scurried down the window. Marina left.

On the bus home he thought about the change. Late was better than never, but the enthusiasm of past demonstrations had quelled.

He mentally crushed the heads of the two teenaged girls in front of him.

Ironic that things were happening now, he thought. There was more than a twinge of resentment. Despite the movements and groups and rhetoric and passion and pamphlets and self-proclaimed solidarity, he was still an outcast within his own minority. Lip service was easy to provide, but when faced with the prospect of daily life, too many ran from the lepers. Too many who claimed to understand.

19:00

He popped a blue-and-white capsule and sat down to a liver and spinach dinner, visualizing sushi.

Maybe fags, like the Ontario government, would change too. Maybe in twenty years, when he turned forty-six, the lip service would be replaced with comprehension. Then, maybe, an otherwise interesting and worthwhile man wouldn't run away at the reluctant acknowledgement of four asymptomatic letters.

Perhaps it wouldn't even be reluctant.

Stan Persky It's What's Inside

I woke up one January morning listening to the Vancouver rain wash the snow away, and in the dark a porno ran through my head of Greg fucking Terry, while somebody or something else ran through my mind a jingle for Foster's beer that went:

Where you're from
  It doesn't matter
What you wear
  It doesn't matter
How you move
  It doesn't matter
It doesn't matter
  how you cut your hair

and then here comes the clincher refrain—

It's what's inside (micropause)
  that counts

—closing shot of a frost-beaded bottle of Foster's Light, repeat refrain over a visual dialogue of seven or eight men in semi-western drag, joyously striding/hip-rolling/strolling right towards us. *It's what's inside / that counts*—irresistable wave of oceanic feeling; solidarity with all humankind.

The porno, on the other hand, is a standard humiliation/pleasure fantasy made up of bits and pieces of true life experience idealized, molded, perfected into a utopia while my dick grows hard and my belly warms rubbing against the soft flannel sheet underneath me.

The plot is pretty basic. Terry, a twenty-one-year-old—he phoned me about a week ago to announce this chronological triumph—six-foot tall, rather skinny, long-haired, naked kid, doesn't really want to get fucked in the ass because a) it hurts and makes him feel like he's got to take a shit; b) it will continue to hurt after it's over, or so he imagines; c) and far more important, it's absolutely and ultimately unmanly—the worst thing that a free, white and twenty-one-year-old male can have befall him (i.e., getting fucked is unmanly in some sense that other homosexual acts apparently aren't); and d) even worse, getting fucked in the ass by Greg means that Terry's dilemma of virility—namely, taboos notwithstanding, his obvious pleasure—will be *seen* by his agemates (oh god, anything but that), that is, will be practically a matter of public record.

It's bad enough if I, fatherly and ancient-of-days, stick my dick in him, however privately, since he is in great need of fatherliness even if it means getting fucked to get it, as I've indeed done on several occasions of what we've mutually and jokingly called Terry's "sex education." In fact, so embedded is this characterization in our conversation that, when he phoned from Calgary about a month ago to say he was returning to Vancouver—predictably all fucked up and followed by a paper trail of warrants and scheduled court appearances, the details of which are so dumb as to be barely believable, much less worth reciting—he even sought to entice me by suggesting that upon his arrival (I could easily picture his little leer as he offered himself up to me thus) we could quote further my sex education unquote, followed by the tiniest possible boyish giggle.

So, in the porno, the main psychological pivot is that Terry—naked, coltish, all legs, medium-sized cock, felt up, fondled, sucked, by both me and Greg (the latter a tremendously persuasive cocksucker, by the way)—is, gradually and reluctantly, as I ease a K-Y-lubricated finger into his hole while Greg energetically slurps on his erection, cajoled into being fucked in the ass. Terry gets hotter and hornier by the stroke, so that finally, making it seem as though he's merely seeking to stop being parentally pestered ("C'mon, Ter, let Greg stick it in you"), he gives his assent in the classic utterance, "Awww, shit."

The other element that this turns on—a recurrent feature of my fantasy life— is the sociological construction of the threesome. In reality, Terry and I, over the years, have been in various threesomes, with diverse partners, principally my friend Pat, and a few times with Terry's alleged best friend Jim (I notice that Terry's 'best friend' seems to change with disturbing regularity). Most of these encounters, won-derful as they sound in theory, have been, I'm afraid, semi-successful at best, due to one form of inhibition or other.* Unlike Pat, who actually prefers this form, especially if it includes his best friend and fuck-buddy Fraser (call this sexual preference *para-sexuality*, i.e., sex side-by-side with some third party, irrespective of the latter's gender), Terry, I suspect, merely accedes to the triangular arrangement because he knows from my regularly putting him off on solo proposals that I'm not all that hot for him on his own.

Greg's another story. To date, he's resisted my efforts to entice him into a menage-a-trois, either with Mel, on the grounds of the humungous size of Mel's cock, or with Greg's own best friend Bob, with whom he's inflamed my imagination by his accounts of their love affair a couple of years earlier at age sixteen or seventeen, which included, importantly, mutual assfucking, but which Greg reports they've long since grown out of, having gone on to girlfriends, though they still while away entire days together smoking or snorting dope and playing Nintendo. (By the way, this superfluity of best friends gives all these scenes a nostalgic edge of 1950s TV family sitcoms.)

In any case, the crux of the threesome is the witnessing presence of the third, which renders the activity public in a sense, because it can no longer be played out under the rubric of, "Oh, come on, you and me are the only ones who will ever know," which often justifies some allegedly straight-arrow dude taking it up the ass.

Greg, in all of this, is pretty much a functional figure, your standard-issue All-Canadian boy, nineteen or twenty years old, medium-short blond hair (as compared to Terry's shoulder-length dark tresses), also surprisingly tall, at least six feet, but rather more athletically solid than Terry, and possessed of a dauntingly massive seven or eight inches of hard cock. I see it now milkily translucent, encased in a tube of latex condom. At this point, we might include a couple of cutaway takes of comically exaggerated Poor Pauline pure terror as Terry gets an unexpurgated eyeful of what's about to work its way up his asshole, occasioning second thoughts about what he's agreed to—visible in closeup of Terry's alarmed and dilated brown eyes—although by now it's far too late to offer sincerely strenuous objection.

---

* Often Terry will collude with his agemate to pretend that whatever's happening is merely taking place for my amusement, i.e., isn't really happening to *him*; equally, I ought to admit, if our partner is Pat—someone with whom I have a long and genuinely complex intimacy of body and feeling—I'll conspire with the latter in the fantasy that we're suckering Terry into something. The real moment, when it works—which is rarely; we're always accusing Terry of 'wimping out,' i.e., refusing to let himself frankly enter into the experience—when the beam of light cuts through the prism, is the look Pat and I exchange as Pat is fucking a kneeling Terry while I reach under Pat's ass and through his legs to cup his balls. But that's still a further moment between Pat and myself, not the three of us, when what I'm really curious about is how they handle it afterwards between themselves—the one fact of importance I really don't have.

In the Foster's commercial, to whose jingle my mind at dawn has unconditionally surrendered, there are a dozen and a half or so diabolically stitched-together scenes—wrestlers, dancers, cowboys—stewed in the slightly hoarse understated choral lilt soundtrack, each running about thirty to thirty-five frames. Inevitably, however, there's one image—it's of course variable for different consumer/viewers—which is the hook, that's as addictive as the white powder those lads can never get enough of and on which they will blow their entire welfare cheques.

Let's establish the scenario of this collage which opens with a head shot of a young Asian woman rising from submersion—first drumthumps of soundtrack—out of a sunset-orange surface of ocean, wearing one long, dangling, dripping silver ornament in her left ear—where are we? Bali? In any case, some Paradise—and does her mouth assume a suggestion of meaning as we dissolve to two workers in a blue-filter-lit aviation hangar with long-handled sudsy brushes sponging down the open bay-door underbelly and landing gear tires of a 747 aircraft, and so on, through a dizzying tapestry of one-second tales to which we bring our full cultural repertoire of feelings, memories, significance and continuity.

Meanwhile, under the comforter, in addition to the basic porno situation, I have unrestricted access to a vast archival database, rivalling the great and ancient Library at Alexandria. It consists of actual biographical details, events, encounters, instances, scenes and moments of life with Terry and Greg. For example, as recently as the day before yesterday, in bed with Greg, as he gets himself hard sucking dick (I regard this as a particular virtue in him), I ask, "Are you horny?" Of course that's a rhetorical ploy since I have the incontrovertible evidence of his hard-on in my hand. "Gimme a rubber," he says by way of reply. "How horny?" I tease him. "Horny enough to get it myself," he elegantly answers, stretching himself across my body to reach into the box of Sheiks on the shelf of the nighttable to the right of my bed.

All of which—these biobytes—can now be transposed to the porno itself: Terry sandwiched between the two of us, just having had his dick hardened by Greg's hot mouth, Terry's hand caressing my hard-on as I reach across his smooth, frail torso to feel Greg's rock-solid shaft and ask, "Well, Greg, are you horny?" "Gimme a rubber," he says, by way of reply. "How horny?" I tease him, glancing at Terry (to pick up Terry's recognition that he will ultimately be the ass-end object of that horniness). "Horny enough to get it myself," Greg answers, stretching himself across both Terry's groin and my legs to reach into the box of Sheiks on the nighttable. As he takes out one of the shiny-paper-packaged condoms, I say to Terry, "I guess you're going to get it now," to which he responds with an appropriate comic-strip style gulp.

In the Foster's ad, all of these miniature dramas are offered as intentionally offbeat to demographically target some self-identified degree of sophistication in a particular market share of the 24-29 age group. Now we're getting an oddly tilted shot of a red-haired woman in a black dress (*"What you wear"*) with a collar of animal pelts, the weird kind, you know, complete with claws and little heads (*"It doesn't matter"*), strolling behind the occupied stools of a country & western bar, attracting the attention of a cowboy in a Stetson and jean jacket who half-turns to pick her up with his eyes.

But the visual point, for me at least, of this thirty-second epic, occurs early on in a startling image, shown for a dozen frames at most, just long enough to establish a retinal echo, of two tattooed muscular male arms embracing—the comradely biceps of bikers?—in cut-off-at-the-shoulder jean jackets, one wearing a metal-stud leather bracelet, the tattoos classics of course—big red hearts, waving blue banners through them, bearing the emblazoned word (what else but?) "Mother"—and the point, the blessed point, which some junior copywriting queen in the Global Village Advertising Agency has consciously inserted, for the space of less than half a second in a fucking beer commercial for chrissakes, is the display of open affection, capable of reaching directly into and setting aquiver the harp-like strings of the soul.

Or graft this true-life crucial detail into the porn production. There's a moment in the act of Greg ploughing me, in between the preliminaries and the final humping drive to orgasm, with the entire considerable length of his cock as far inside as it can go, when he reaches under my left thigh to delicately jiggle my balls cupped in his hand, and then pushes it just one micro-millimetre further and holds it there, pressing a prostatal button that reduces me to butt-wriggling helplessness as I say something understandably dumb like, "Oh wow." Now transfer that to the mental home video where Greg and Terry, having negotiated the initial obstacles, are locked in immortal congress. Terry is now fully impaled. I slide my hand under his belly to his genital delta. His five inches of post-adolescent dick are tumescently extended, and his flat butt twitches uncontrollably up into the vector between Greg's thighs. "He's hot," I report to Greg, who wears a satisfied shit-eating grin on his pretty mug. "You want it, don't you?" I demand of Terry.

But what's the message being transmitted by the Foster's Light division of the unnamed ensemble of inter-/trans-multi-national capitalist corporations? Of course, the Commodity Language aims at an infinitely small vocabulary of Flaubertian perfection.

Beer: Fun
Car : Get Rich
Razor: The System Works

Under the conjoined categories of beer/fun—the program instruction is: take one item from Commodity Column A, combine with one item from Ideological Column B—Foster's seems to be preaching a sermon of human acceptance. *"How you look, what you wear*, race-colour-creed, *how you cut your hair, it doesn't matter."* I note in passing the clever wear/hair rhyme. They don't miss a trick, do they? Instead, look to the true essence of the person, *it's what's inside / that counts.* I mean, they could even include *Who you sleep with/ it doesn't matter*, splicing in twenty frames of Greg fucking Terry, like two boys riding a surfboard cresting a Pacific wave, cut to close-up of Greg's lubed milky latex-covered cock inserted halfway into Terry's butt, dissolve sea-foam into beer-foam, and not one viewer/consumer in a million would register an instant of visual disruption.

However, some scholars at the Institute of Advanced Commodity Analysis argue that the message of ostensible acceptance also includes a membranal layer of distanced irony that allows some viewers to regard the pitch cynically and see the oddball characters—bald wrestler, woman in weird muskrat-fringed dress, nerd with shock of orange hair bearing bouquet on first date—simply as geeks with whom they're not required to identify.

Nonetheless, there is consensus—orchestrated by Frankfurt School Critical Theorists—that the message also contains its negation. In point of fact, how you look, what you wear, who you sleep with, how you cut your hair, all matter intensely. Indeed, it's almost all that matters. And is made to matter by the very corporations broadcasting this commercial since it's the veritable fulcrum upon which commodities are predicated. As for what's inside, far from counting, nobody gives a shit about it. The message is that the essence of identity, far from being internal, is comprised of exactly the requisite commodity items displayed here. And now, a word from our sponsor.

What I want, apparently, is the confession. "You want it, don't you?" I demand of Terry. "Oh, yeah," he sighs breathily—the breathiness lifted from an actual porno in my collection. "What do you want?" I sadistically insist, as Greg shoves his cock up Terry that extra-millimetre (though I congratulate myself, rather hypocritically, for not imagining this in terms of rape/coercion—thank god for small mercies—as though that's a token of my basic decency.) "I wanna be fucked," Terry confesses, and the subtext addition might be, "and I want my confession/humiliation witnessed by the world," e.g., by my agemate Greg. Actually, the "humiliation" is a tad more complicated. It's Terry seeing that I've seen Greg seeing it. For example, if Greg later claimed in public that he'd fucked Terry, Terry could otherwise simply deny it and attempt to brazen the scene out. But because of the threesome, Terry knows that Greg can haul me out as a witness. "Just ask Stan," Greg pipes up. "Did I fuck'm good or not?" All eyes turn to me for confirmation, eyes ready to bounce right over to Terry—whatever eyes that count as humiliation for him—and those eyes, by gazing at him, strip him bare.

How's this for a bibliographic footnote? In real life (and I won't even bother to put that phrase in quotes), as juveniles, Greg and Terry served time together in Willingdon Detention, though, as I've ascertained from interviews, they regarded each other with typical mutual adolescent contemptuousness, the thought of making it together never crossing either of their minds. But did they happen to catch a glimpse of one another—water sheeting their gleaming flanks—under the showers, surreptitiously comparing dick-size?

At the heart of this extravaganza, then, is the sight of every beautiful self-identified semi-straight boy (these guys, of course, all have girlfriends and, as they move into their mid-twenties and beyond, wives, separations, in-laws, babies, the works), publicly confessing his ecstasy while eternalized in *flagrante delecto* in the act of homosexual intercourse. The original, for classics buffs among us, is shaggy Hephaistos catching Ares and Aphrodite in his net in mid-fuck.

The multi-entendres of these cultural productions are, at first, straightforward enough. What's inside is the essence of identity: what's inside is the Foster's Light beer in its frost-headed bottle; what's inside—laid-back riff—is what's inside his pants; what's inside is his cock in a human orifice. Ultimately, though, what's really inside is the Foster's commercial and/or the personal porno—inside your mind. Along with the world, temporarily itemized as: plane crash in Scotland, death of Japanese emperor, 750 fresh diagnoses of the plague.

I listened to a car starting up outside in the January morning, and decided not to come, on the strength of a possible phone call later in the day from Mike, another person in my cast. It smoothly took the hill, four-cylinder engine whirring down to an infinitesimal point of sound, leaving the dark morning silent again.

Andy Quan How to Cook Chinese Rice

It's not necessary to have a rice cooker or a wok to cook perfect delicious white rice every time. Here's how.

1. SELECTION
If you want your rice to turn out like it does in Chinese restaurants, you have to use Chinese rice. This is the long grain stuff; the short fat sticky rice is Japanese. Don't buy Uncle Ben's processed rice, or rice with faces of white people on the boxes.

The genesis: I came seven years after my first brother and five years after my second, dragon following monkey and then, the cock. Uranus was on the horizon when I was born, the planet of reversal; also, my house of love was out of alignment with the other planets. Armstrong landed on the moon. The general stress of the sixties ending caused disturbance in the womb. My hypothalamus was larger than my penis; a renegade gene cruised down the family tree from the grand-uncle who moved to New York and was never heard from again. I was born partially clothed, a red silk cloth wrapped around mid-section, patterns of bamboo and cranes stitched in. I arrived with a full head of hair.

2. MEASUREMENT
How many people are you going to serve? Rice tastes best fresh but you can always use it for fried rice if there's leftovers, and rice reheats well in a microwave. Regardless, use ½ of a Chinese rice bowl (or about ½ cup) per person.

In this room I'm listening very quietly as if someone is going to say, "get out, you don't belong with us." But there's only six or seven of us. We're listening to a girl talking about life on the streets of Vancouver.

She says: I remember one time, three of us girls out at the amusement park with Rickie, our pimp, and the ferris wheel rising up in the sky and the sunlight making diamonds out of its metal frame. Us, wrapped in sticky fur coats, looking out at other girls, laughing with their friends. Wishing to be them more than anything else anywhere.

Also: No one on the streets wants to sleep with a black man. It's bad but it's true. Girls are scared. But you know the best? The oriental men. They are always polite, very clean, and you know? They come quickly. That's the kind of customer you want.

3. PUT THE RICE IN A POT
Now, put the rice in a pot that has a tight-fitting lid.

Man in the disco. Empty. Weeknight. Shirt too small. My hand wrapped around sweaty beer, I lean against rail next to dance floor. His white flesh approaching. Glowing fluorescent. Layer of exposed skin above belt like fat-steamed chicken. Eye glint. Bearded grin. "Hey. Me and my friend think you're kind of cute. Maybe you could join us."

No. Flashing lights. I'm waiting. Speakers shake like a vacuum cleaner switched on. For a friend. Like a house being cleaned. Like all the dust in the room swirling into one place. No. Visible only with sunlight pouring through the window. Maybe later. Feel guilty you're not helping. Mother throws reproachful eyes. Man walks away.

Later he follows. Heavy disco beat. Brushes up. "Hey. I had a Vietnamese boyfriend." Bodies sweating, bodies thrashing. No. Asks again. Fat man, his eyes like an outstretched hand. No. Shake my head once. Quick like a flick of a chopstick. Like cocking a gun.

4. THE IMPORTANT PART
Now, rinse the rice in cold water until all of the starch comes off and the water is relatively clear. If you don't do this, then your rice will be starchy, dry perhaps. It will fall apart in single grains. This is how white people usually cook their rice.

When I was ten, I naturally gravitated to the other Chinese boys in our class, two in particular, Winston and James. We talked about computers, hockey cards, mystery books. Not about girls like the cool boys, not about sweaty secret mysteries like the clique of Greek boys with their names of ancient philosophers and emperors.

I drifted apart from them at fourteen, about the same time that Christine Greenstern came up to me with the revelation that all Chinese people were smart, had eyeglasses and were good at math. This must be something genetic. True, we all worked as library monitors, wrote the big math contest, and two of us were still taking piano lessons. All had good marks. I supposed that it was time to go searching.

At eighteen, I climbed the stairs to my first meeting of the university's gay group. I peered around a corner and peeked into a dark room: thin trails of smoke twisting upwards like genies escaping without granting any wishes. About a dozen men sat on three run-down sofas, all of them blond or seeming blond. A stray limp wrist flung about here and there. Few of them say hello.

5. COVER IT UP

Cover the rice with just about an inch of water, 2.5 centimetres or up to the first joint of a normal-sized index finger.

I'm thirteen. I've hidden my ruler in my bedroom drawer. No one is home and the curtains are drawn.

How long is it supposed to be? Where do you measure it from? Will it grow when I do?

Six years later, Philip Rushton, professor at the University of Western Ontario, concludes that I have a relatively small penis.

Two years later, I am kissing with my lover John on his living room sofa. His other lover, Bryan, comes in through the basement, rambles up the stairs, sits down. "I'm so stoned. Whoa," he moans, getting up to leave, "carry on. I'll just go into the bedroom."

He stops in the middle of the room, and invites us in.

"You have a long cock," he remarks, the three of us on the king-sized bed.

I look at him. "Really? I always thought the opposite."

He reaches over. "Yeah, really."

6. CONFIDENCE

Have confidence; cooking, like all other meaningful activities, requires a state of mind where you believe in yourself. Repeat after me: "I can cook rice."

I'm twenty-one and still haven't learned much of anything. But it's the summer of the Gay Games in Vancouver and my heart is bursting like popcorn, outwards with possibility, with the sight of same-sex couples sightseeing, hand-in-hand, as naturally as starfish on tidal rocks, as the mountains against the bright harbour.

I've volunteered, among other things, to help at the bodybuilding competition.

Giggling in anticipation, I eventually get assigned to the steamy weight room in the back of the theatre: short, wide women and men oiling their bodies and pumping muscles with weights. There is nothing to do because too many volunteers were assigned; I'm free to do what I please.

I roam the hallways, greeting people like at a party, eyes wide and energetic. I tell myself that I never had the opportunity to be a goofy hormone-pumped high school guy; I hid my sexuality in asexuality. Hey, I tell myself, this is my chance, and I even have my camera. I pass by a room later in the day where a blond couple is getting packed up to take a lunch break after the morning's pre-judging. I talk to the woman first, that's safer. Then the man, piercing blue eyes and short perfectly spiked blonde hair.

"Hey, where are you from?"

He smiles at me and I'm melting like ice cream. "San Francisco."

"Wow, you guys from California are hot." I wipe imaginary sweat from my brow.

Neil is an accountant back home, spends all the rest of his time training for competitions. He's all natural; he may be muscular but he's not as big as some of the other guys here; they're the steroid ones. He's intelligent and friendly, tells me I've got four years to train for the next Gay Games. I ask, "Hey, can I get a photo with you?"

We give the camera to his partner. I look at him again. "Without the shirt." He rolls his eyes, I make excusing noises, but he obliges and I get my photo: funny Chinese kid with a smug smile, arm over shoulders of a tanned blond mass of taut muscles. I shake his hand and bound off, completely pleased with myself.

There was another intense sort of man, Cain, with prematurely whitish-grey hair, blue-grey eyes; flashy workout clothes, but he didn't look like the other bodybuilders at all, really. When I talk to him, I find out he's only been training for two years; it was his personal goal to get here and compete in the lightweight category. We walk to the weight room together and talk awhile. I notice Neil sitting across the room; I look over at him but he seems angry about something. By the end of the day, I've given my phone number to Cain, who later turns out to be boring *and* self-centered.

That summer night, I'm walking across a bridge with a friend, the stars out like the first practice of a new choir. It hits me then, and I see Neil's face again, annoyed, reflecting off of mirrors and iron bars. I think that anyone else would have known, but caught up in my pubescent asexual sexual state, I hadn't. While I was flirting with him, so obviously that it wasn't obvious to me, he was flirting with me, a skinny Chinese kid who never imagined that someone who looked like all his fantasies could ever be interested in him.

Have you ever been in a fortune cookie factory? The flour mixture falls in small circles, gets cooked on both sides, a tiny paper is placed inside by a flurry of hands. Then, before it cools, it's folded over in one direction, and the ends are brought down in another, gracefully like a crane taking off in flight, the neck crooking down, the wings rising up, drops of water from its legs spreading in concentric circles in the lake. This was my summer, my city, the Gay Games: the rare sights of graceful, beautiful, strange birds soaring into blueness. And also sweetness, the city on one giant pancake being heated up, changing substance, forming into something different from what it was.

I cracked open my cookie. I keep my fortune with that photo I took backstage at the bodybuilding competition. The fortune says: HEY KID, NEVER SELL YOURSELF SHORT.

7. HEAT IT UP

Cook at maximum or near-maximum heat until the water begins to boil. Then turn heat down to medium-high; the water will still be bubbling away at a good rate. Wait until the water has boiled down to the same level as the rice.

The most visible and well-known gay man in my small university town was an older man, an actor, who dressed in drag and sang a song about lemon trees. His weekly column appeared in our university newspaper under 'Gay Voices,' a flowery ongoing series of memoirs about a childhood in an eccentric British household in southern Ontario. All the illustrations for the column were either viny art nouveaux or old newspaper graphics of men and women in flapper costumes and top hats.

All the posters and advertisements for the university's gay and lesbian dances featured stills from either black-and-white Garbo films or lesbian vampire thrillers.

When I complain about this introduction to gay life a few years later, a university acquaintance is angry: "That was camp and camp is not ethnocentric! It's our forgotten history. It was poor black and latino drag queens and bull dykes out there on the frontlines at Stonewall, hauling away at those riot police and kicking over fire hydrants!"

I try to imagine myself at Stonewall, shouts flying over top of me from lips like scythes, salt and anger and resistance flying into open wounds.

I try to imagine myself in black-and-white, languishing in tones of grey, perhaps in a housecoat, maybe in silk pajamas.

I have no reply.

8. STEAM IT UP

Then, put your lid on the pot and turn the heat down to absolute minimum so the hot steam can cook the rice.

Underwear parties sweeping Toronto's underground—the latest, greatest, hottest thing to do. By the time I go to my first one, the trend is dying. What else is new? Before I go, I tie my long black hair back tightly. I try to look masculine and clean-cut.

We shed ourselves from winter gear at the door, try to fit our clothes into flimsy plastic bags. The doormen put the bags in a room full of bags, mark numbers on our hands.

Arrows from the check-in lead us out the back door and through the parking lot to another building. We run against the cold, fly through the door, up the stairs, pay some guy a big cover and enter: a room full of dancing men in Calvin Klein athletic shorts, not even the boxers. Gay men are so cutting edge.

We've just come from the university dance, the 'Homo Hop,' and that's how we look, a bunch of university kids, half a dozen of us, no one confident enough to go bare-chested, and why would we? All these gym bodies trotting around: stacked together, the collective hours at the gym could build railways, erect monuments— great, tall phallic ones like in the mythic cities of Europe.

Scout the place: big to me, but one of the guys says it's nothing—only one floor; one he went to had three floors, all crowded, whirlpool or two, different dance floors. This one has a dark room in the far corner—the lightest one I've ever seen, streetlight moonglow revving through the windows like a brand new Harley. Few men are doing anything; lots are coming around, walking through, waiting, watching. I follow suit, like one in a v-shaped flock of birds heading to the warmest place possible.

The leaders move by instinct and watch no one else for clues. They fall into various types and look surprisingly the same: these ones greyish hair, thick and brawny; these ones short brown hair, smooth and tightly muscled; the others blond and tall and doll-like.

They are with each other, the rest of us all on lower levels of the hierarchy. The light from the window makes all of us overexposed. Muscular back, on his knees, goes in on leather jacket, bare chest. And I don't think they are beautiful because I am not thinking, only seeing, and knowing somewhere they are only images, warmth at my crotch, MTV, Madonna's dancers, porn advertisements at the back of the newspaper.

Later, I see another oriental man, he is short and slight like a bird. Groups have now formed in the room; two men kissing and a train of two or three men behind each of them pushing in close, reaching, moaning, others in the corners against the walls. The oriental man moves around these groups gracefully like a shadow, like a breeze, and disappears down into the clusters of tall men with their high cheekbones and square jaws and pinkish-white flesh. And he emerges, shifts place, disappears again into another group, a bee from flower to flower, a cat chasing unravelling yarn.

On the other side of the room, I stand in the crowd, silent and stupid, watching him bob up and down in the waves, but never float on top, their jaws and lips locked on each other's mouths or chests, and him down below, negotiating the undertow. People enter and leave, the crowd ebbs and flows.

I walk around this party. I do not stoop my back. I look people in their eyes. No one returns my glance.

9. THE WAITING GAME
Steam for about ten to fifteen minutes. Hopefully, you'll be able to tell when it's cooked.

My parents chase a good Chinese restaurant until it closes or the cooks leave. They follow leads on the next one to go to: honourable grasshopper, a family of Charlie Chans.

Father orders a bowl of house soup from the back of the kitchen. It's communist soup, he explains, for anyone who wants it; it is always on the stove to be shared. I go through a whole childhood eating this soup, a clear broth with huge pieces of carrots swimming around, a piece of fatty beef. It becomes my motif to eat a bowl before the meal, and one after. The sun rises, it sets, then it is called a day.

We eat with all of their friends from the city, our relatives, and all visitors from out of town. If it is a special occasion, the owner puts a tablecloth over the shiny brown formica. The room smells of honey and garlic.

That restaurant closes. The next one as well. And another. And again. New ones open. Father orders dishes in Cantonese; they arrive, sizzling in earthenware pots. A clatter of plates, steam rising to the ceiling.

I am afraid I will never get my special soup again and I will never receive something I know exists but cannot describe.

10. DON'T PEEK
Resist the temptation to open the lid before the cooking process is done. All the steam will escape.

The subway leaves me on Yonge Street, only a block away from Church. My steps lift me higher and higher like the tall apartment buildings on each side of me.

I spend the day here, moving from restaurant to cafe, grocery store to boutique. I read the gay newspaper: comic strips first, then front page, skip to the events section, scan the personals. My eyes wander to the muscular ads for gay phone lines. I look up, see a man in tight jeans walking a bike spray-painted yellow; I wonder about his secret lives. My eyes follow his footsteps all the way up Church Street to that distant point on the horizon where all the lines of telephone poles, pavement, buildings, electricity wires intersect.

Then I cross the street. I move so quickly I'm sure no one can ever catch up. Maybe the hummingbird's wings are only beautiful in flight, and motion feeds desire but can't stop. Can't stop.

I am afraid that I'll never find my way in anything but action. I am required to move like this. If I halt for even one faltering second, the whirring of a thousand maple keys pulling downwards and the roar of a million angry bees will tear me apart.

11. READY?
Serve it any way you want. Thank my mother for the recipe.

Ian Stephens Wounds: Valentine's Day

Some guy stuck a lit cigarette into my shoulder in your storeroom. That was in October, my first time in Montréal.

When I was released back into the city I had five separate burns in an ugly arc on my shoulder, so when I got back to McGill I thought about you for months, even in Rochester, my home town; it was always sore; I never really healed, always somebody scraping them open, making me bleed.

And Winnipeg, the sadistic Indian with whom I thought I was in love, soft-skinned, soft-spoken, he too made me bleed, chewing my shoulder as he shot.

But when I left him I came back to you. St. Valentine's Day, empty-hearted at last, on a perfect day, perfect for you, with the wind blowing ash off the hood of your Buick, with another boy auditioning onstage in your empty club.

I used to think that your eyes were blue.

I used to worry about love, where it hid when the fires tore off the door, when the rubber hands squeezed the pale thin throat.

I watched him jerk and look sexy to the disco beat and the mirrors, but he took off his g-string with shaking hands, his half-hard cock escaping into light, squeezed at the base by a red suede strap. I knew that within a week you'd beat him and make him do anything for you just like you had done to me.

You lowered the music. Putting the cigarette in your mouth, you stepped over the braid onto the stage. You held the boy's elbow, instructing him, pouting at him, telling him to pose a little longer, take it easy. This went on for a few minutes until you laughed charmingly.

Without being seen I ducked into the toilet.

Waiting for you to come back was like waiting for the drug to kick in, knowing I'd be somewhere else, would be someone else and I could watch it all.

Finally, you showed up. I was waiting in a cubicle and I saw you pull out your cock and spray the back of the urinal. You saw me and grunted, almost laughing. I followed you into the alley. I took off my boots, jeans and shirt and threw them into the back of your car and waited.

Like I had the first time.

After putting on your gloves you told me to get in.

I don't know this city and I don't want to. We drove through a tunnel and soon we were through the suburbs and into an industrial park on the edge of the country.

Near a river, under a bridge you taped my ankles together and my wrists behind my back, wound tape over my eyes so I couldn't see you.

You pushed me down. The ground was wet, cold but clean.

The only thing you said was, "The Lord is my Shepherd I do not want...."

I didn't care. Even then I knew he was going to kill me; I could smell the knife as clearly as I could smell his ass. He put his cock in my mouth and knew he was going to slit my throat as he came because that is what I wanted him to do.

Roughly he shoved and lifted my legs so that he was over me with his smile poised and ready over my hole; he licked it, hit it, pulled his fist back and slugged it, then bit into my skin. I was numb when he shoved his cock into my ass. He had no trouble ripping my hole and pushing it in all the way. He fucked me for a minute then took it out, put on a condom, and started again.

I could feel warm liquid dribbling through my crotch. I heard ice floes on the river cracking under each other. Gradually, I forgot what was happening. The tape started to come off my eyes and I could see lights, some buildings in the dark distance.

After he came, he emptied the condom on my head and kissed me, his thin lips wired with nicotine, sharp nicotine, tongue so warm....I could feel his juice sliding down my neck, over my throat.

He took out the knife. He cut the tape off my ankles and hands.

But I don't care about freedom. Not when I'm with him.

Without a word, I knew he knew but it wasn't going to be easy. He shoved me towards the car. "You can work in the basement tonight."

He wouldn't let me touch my dick even though it was dark red and harder than cement. He gave me a blanket and told me to be quiet.

I started shaking as the street lights slid over my shoulders. I could feel the salt burning where you had scraped me. I knew that my arc was now bleeding and probably wouldn't heal. Ever.

You put on a tape—ChemLab. The music tore through my ears as we tore through the tunnel. I mouthed the words as Jared, the singer, shouted, "I still bleed, I still bleed," over and over. I knew that song, it was our song, darling, our song.

I looked down and pulled the blanket away from my groin. I slid forward and my cock throbbed like a fat fish on a plate. I knew that you'd like to cut it off and eat it. I knew that you were going to shave my crotch and make me lie in the shower in the basement on a leash and drink a hundred men. As a special treat for all the members. And at dawn you'd let me be fucked by twelve men, friends or rich ugly bastards and when it was over, when even the young boy who auditioned this afternoon had shot his thick load over my back and screamed, slamming his balls over my wide open hole, that you'd burn me, perhaps in the same place, perhaps on my face, perhaps when I was unconscious, perhaps when I was open-eyed and hungry.

I looked over your face as we emerged from the underground. Except for the scar, it was unlined and contented. At that moment you could have been my younger brother Jeff, the one working at Kodak as a mechanical designer, the shutter specialist.

I wonder what Jeff would think of his brother, the burn-freak, the queer. Or if he'd care. It is doubtful I've ever thought about what he does with his dick.

I'd rather hear slashing guitars and feel a cool orange butt on my flesh, the incense of flesh, flesh and smoke....

I don't want to ever shoot. I want to be hard for you always, naked, taped tight and burnt for you.

I still bleed, I still bleed.

Such is my love, my love, my love....

So my cock burned. At a traffic light, you looked at it and slapped it hard, hurting me. When it wouldn't go down, you squeezed my balls and it hurt too much, I almost passed out.

Almost. Almost.

On the edge.

Of Never.

I thought I was going to die until I didn't *think* at all. My brain was full of pain and there was nothing else.

As it was when you burned me, in an arc, five stars, on my shoulder.

Martin Stephens Coming Up For Air

Penetration is liberation.
—Affirmations

I remember hands. Big hands, strong and calloused. I remember being stroked. Fingers. Hair. Nails cut blunt.

Are you ok?

Of course.

I used to think that the more men I slept with, the further behind I could leave the past. Each sexual experience acted as padding, another bandage to wrap around the hurt. But now I see that the reverse is true, that each of my lovers has taken something from me, stripped another layer of my defences, peeling me like an onion. I want the armour back. I spent too much time constructing it to let it go so easily.

I've made a fatal mistake, seeking safety in the arms of other men. They've robbed me of my security, crumbled the walls I had put up against the world. I thought I had built the walls to keep others out, but instead they've served to keep something in, locked up: memories trapped deep inside, wrapped tight as the layers of a Chinese doll, each one neatly containing the next. Each experience claims another surface, leaving me smaller, closer to the core. Eventually the last shell will be reached. And when that is broken open, what will be waiting inside?

Are you ok?

Yes.

I'm pulling from sleep as if from water; any longer and I might have drowned. I come up gasping for air. My face is wet—have I been swimming? It's dark. Where am I? What am I doing in bed if I've just come out of the water?

It takes me a moment to recognize the hot wetness on my face. Of course this isn't the first time I've woken up crying. I curl the sheets around me, pulling away from one side of the bed as though someone were beside me. I rock back and forth, shuddering in spasms. My anus is inflamed, my penis firm though not fully erect. It throbs, in sync with my panicked heartbeat. I can't remember the dream. I can't remember anything. I want everything to go away. I want it all to stop.

Are you ok?

I think so.

The first time I slept with a man, he touched me down there and asked if he could do it. Of course I knew what he meant, despite his reluctance to name the act. The word itself makes it sound like a violation. Which of course it is.

At first I didn't answer. He asked again and I said no. He wanted to know why and I said it would hurt, which of course was true. That satisfied him for a while, and he busied himself with other things, caressing my skin as if moulding clay. Gently he asked if I'd ever done it before. I hesitated before saying no, which made it sound like a lie.

Soon he started stroking me down there again, ignoring what I'd said. His fingers probed my asshole, looking for an opening, a way in. Access to what's beneath the skin. I was ashamed to discover that I liked that. I didn't want to. The most damaging intrusions can be disguised as pleasurable.

I pushed his hand away, but he returned it, becoming more insistent. Why? he asked again, amused but determined. He couldn't understand my resistance; we'd done everything else. Don't, I pleaded weakly, moaning at his touch. He assumed I didn't mean it.

Eventually I let him. I don't know why—partly because he seemed to want to so much, partly because on some level I wanted to know what it was like.

I knew right away that I'd made a mistake.

Are you ok?

Am I ok.

I notice hands the way other people notice faces. They leave an impression.

I find myself looking at men's hands, looking for a particular pair. A prince with a glass slipper, searching for the appropriate foot. I'm looking for a pair of hands that will fit the impression I carry with me, a physical memory like indentations on my flesh. Seeking the body to which they must be attached, the body I can't quite remember. My recollection of those hands ends at the wrists, as though seen through dense fog.

Are you ok?

Maybe.

He turns me over and gets up on his knees, adjusting his position. His warm shaft presses against me. He lifts me up by the hips and spreads my legs apart, his hand returning to the crack where his finger probes me deeper, slipping hesitantly inside as though testing the water. I shut my eyes in anticipation, pressing my face into the pillow.

His first thrust slips to the side, failing to gain entry. He tries again, this time guiding himself in, steadying his balance with his other hand on my back. I feel a sharp pain as his penis slides past the sphincter's initial resistance. He shoves against me again, and this time enters deeper, sending a jolt through my rectum and up to my stomach. I shudder in response, grinding my teeth to hold back tears. I can smell smoke, woody and rich, like that from a pipe.

Am I hurting you? he asks, exhaling, his voice rigid. Before I can respond he's inside me all the way. I can feel it up to the back of my throat, it's like shitting in reverse. I think I'm going to be sick. The head of his penis is now deep within me, pushing against inner walls I didn't know were there. Now I can smell aftershave. Old Spice. I don't remember noticing it before. I didn't think he was wearing any.

Are you ok?

I'm not sure.

He begins to rock back and forth, sliding in and out with a rhythmic motion, his thighs smacking against my buttocks. Another jolt of pain rips through me, and I clench in reaction, tightening my asshole and nearly forcing him out. Gripping my hips with both hands, he pushes hard to maintain his position. He keeps his penis as deep inside me as it will go, waiting for my involuntary shudders to pass.

Something's wrong. I'm not sure what.

My vision blurs for a moment. I sense the light dimming briefly, like something passing over me. Passing through me.

With my crack shoved against the base of his shaft, I can feel his pubic hair tickling my ass, his balls slapping loosely against my own. The pain subsides and I almost begin to enjoy it. My anus relaxes, allowing his penis more mobility. His hands begin to caress me, circling my bum and rubbing up my back, calloused hands moving over my skin in waves. I moan deeply, lifting my back end to meet his thrusts. His legs clench around my hips. I can feel his hands on my flesh, smell his sweat on my skin. And yet I feel somehow detached; if I were to open my eyes I would be able to observe the scene from a distance, as though this were happening to someone else.

Are you ok?

I don't know.

Suddenly everything changes; the quality of light, the feel of fabric on my face. I'm in pain again; I'm not enjoying this. I'm being ripped apart from the ass up. I want it to stop. I let out a muffled cry, like a wounded animal. Like something being killed.

Are you all right? he grunts in my ear, pausing only slightly between thrusts. Of course I'm not all right. I want everything to stop. He shouldn't be doing this, I want him to stop, he shouldn't be doing this it's not my fault it's wrong it hurts oh god it hurts so much so much I want—

What's wrong? he groans, on the verge of climax. What's wrong is that it hurts it hurts so much oh god it's killing me I want my mother I want him to stop stop stop where's my mother? Where is she? Mommy make him stop make him stop make him *stop!* What's wrong is that this man is ripping me apart and I don't know where my mother is oh god I'm six years old again and I don't know where she is—

Are you ok?

No.

Now I remember:

This isn't the first time someone has done this to me. Nowhere near the first time. This is just the first time I gave consent.

I watch men's hands as if for clues, as though awaiting some signal.

I look at my father's hands. I look away.

The problem is I can't remember. Not much of it. Not consciously, anyway. In dreams, sometimes, though even then it's vague, like distant voices on a cheap radio. Words, but incomprehensible, another language perhaps.

I'm still not sure who did it to me. Some days I'm not even sure that it happened at all. I'm silenced by my own uncertainty. If I'm honest with myself, however, there is no doubt; it must have happened because I'm still recovering, always have been. It's like finding you have a cut or a bruise and not remembering how or where you got it. A missing limb, I know it by its absence. Gone but still hurting.

Are you ok?

No, but I will be.

There is of course no proof. I have to accept that there never will be. But I shouldn't need evidence in order to trust my own experience; or so I tell myself. I wish I had at least one clear, undeniable recollection that would dispel any doubt from my mind. That may come, eventually. Meanwhile, fragments of my own past continue to reveal themselves to me. Memories of a childhood I didn't know I had occasionally rise from the depths like bodies drowned at sea, seeking revenge. Bubbling up around me like air from a disturbed sea bed. I'd submerged the memories for a reason, cutting myself loose for my own preservation. Without their weight, I was able to keep swimming.

As yet I can't visualize a face, which is perhaps just as well. It's only a matter of time before that final detail floats to the surface, conjured up like a reflection in unstill water. It's coming, I can feel it. Then I will know; I will be certain.

Are you ok?

I'm still waiting.

John Timmins Red Bread

So I come out of the corner store with the bread and milk and down our alley I see there's this great big bug and it's eating Harry, and it's not the sound you'd think from watching TV, you know, shouting, cursing, broken glass, more a shiny high squeal like a middle-aged man coming for the first time. There are three, maybe four guys, eight shuttling legs not counting Harry's slumped down against the fence and they're pounding Harry so hard his blood splashes, little leaps of red landing on the pavement thirty feet away from where I stand turning the bread back into dough and I'm still getting this one thought: not get the cops or yell your head off so maybe they'll stop, just, what looks like this great big bug is eating Harry. So then me being small and quick (not from running but from running away, Harry used to laugh) I shoot in between and cover him somehow and in a couple of seconds it'll be my blood on Harry just like it's his blood all over me now and I get my arms around what's left of his face and bury it down next to my stomach like I'll probably be burying the rest of him later that is if I last out which I won't and they're going at my back like one man now really concentrating like I'm dough like there's a prize inside me when I realize I'm actually swallowing some of Harry's blood and Jesus you know what I'm thinking my last thought ever maybe you have to laugh My Sweet Harry

John Timmins Awkward Age

Now of course I don't mean like Alice, my head ludicrously shooting up through the roofboards into branches and birdnests, but I am apparently, at this late date, yes, growing larger. It's actually more like a slow, millimetrical distension, not entirely unpleasant. Time-lapse photography. What seem like expanding tunnels inside my skin feel airily hollow and my stomach has odd new pockets that food doesn't yet reach. I am gradually getting used to all of this, my bouncing off sudden door-frames, the tracing back of mauve bruise-blotches to their unremembered injuries, the gleeful skittering of tiny objects out of my fingers to a small accompanying flurry of quiet cursing—quiet because of course any shouting would wake him.

I suppose all of this could be just accumulated sleep-debt: he's often up until two or two-thirty, the coughing, the bloody phlegm, when I can finally collapse on the air-mattress beside his bed, only to lurch awake foggily the next morning, late with his meds which these strange big fingers regularly fumble and there now see how simple it is to concentrate on that one side of the fact that isn't true instead of on all those other sides of the facts that are, because of course it isn't I who am expanding but he who is contracting, subtracting, whose leached subtraction must remorse-lessly extend until more will have been taken than will have been left, until to hold him will be to hurt him, to touch, to tear.

Good afternoons on the couch he quietly dozes on me, scarcely dinting my pant-leg, a bony, big fuzzy bird nested and drooling on my hip. The new air inside me whirls and whines.

Jack Valiant A Fresh New Fair World

Charlie takes a left off Pacific Boulevard and drives onto the ramp leading to the Cambie Bridge. As his foot depresses the accelerator and we ascend toward the crest, we attain a height that affords an unobstructed view of the former site of the World's Fair sprawling below on the banks of False Creek.

"It's all just a memory now," I yell over the roar from our rusty tailpipe.

"Yup . . . it's all over, 'cept for the shouting!" replies Charlie, in his usual feisty tone. "The Great Exposition in Paris left that city a park and the Eiffel Tower. This fucking thing is built right on top of a toxic waste dump . . . left us a mess that'll take years to clean up . . . or cover up."

"Had some good times there," I muse.

"Great!" replies Charlie sarcastically. "Glad you could afford it, Jack!"

"Yeah, my parents bought me a season's pass. I mostly went there for rock concerts," I tell him. "I remember one really hot, really humid afternoon when a local band called Slow was playing for free. They were supposed to be kicking off a summer-long lineup of local music talent . . . but after *their* gig, the management cancelled everybody else local for the duration of the fair."

"I heard something about that," says Charlie. "Didn't that band strip onstage or something?"

"Well, y'know, that band was super high energy and they were sweating their bags off in front of a bunch of American tour-bus fogies. I guess they wanted to make some kind of anarchist statement, or maybe it was just a joke, but they dropped their drawers and shined their bare-ass moons at everybody and the management pulled the plug on them. *Everybody* was pissed off."

"Well, that backs up a theory of mine," says Charlie.

"What's that?"

Charlie smirks. "Society was in its oral stage of development during the sixties and seventies. That fair was the start of the anal stage."

I laugh. "Charlie, you've got some strange ideas."

"Gotta like those anarchists," he says. "My grampa went to the world's fair in Buffalo in 1901 and he had the privilege of witnessing the American president get assassinated by an anarchist. McKinley, I think it was . . . it didn't help to shoot him, though. They just swore in a new one right away."

Charlie is prone to wandering off the topic. "Didn't you go to the fair, even once?" I ask.

"Too rich for my blood," he says, spitting crisply out the window. "I didn't have a pot to piss in back then . . . lived right over there. . . . " He points toward the Downtown Eastside. From our cruising vantage we see the background outlines of the slummiest part of town, the rundown hotels and flophouses. "I was living down there while they were building the fair. There was a recession at the time. But it was worse than your run-of-the-mill recession. It was a world-wide Regression. Jobs were fuckin' scarce. I had to take what work I could get."

"What'd you do?" I ask.

"I got a job workin' for minimum wage as a dish pig in a gay restaurant, La Biche Riche . . . hated that fuckin' joint."

Charlie is getting a moody, irritated look about him and I can tell I must have knocked a chip off his shoulder, so I try to say something to pull him out of it. "C'mon, Charlie, I bet you met some hot young guys that summer, didn't you?"

Charlie doesn't answer right off. He just stares ahead into traffic. Then with a sigh he says, "I fell in love . . . but it didn't work out."

"Tell me about it, Charlie . . . I bet he was a cutie. What happened? How did you meet?"

Charlie glances at me for a moment and launches into his tale.

Like I said, I was working in a kitchen . . . and hey, I don't mind being out. But scraping the bottom of the gay workingman's ghetto was not exactly a fantasy come true. The place was full of clones and I had no ambition to work my way into becoming a waiter queen.

After slugging it out in a place like that all night, a person needs to unwind. I used to go to the bars once in a while, but y'know, the disco makes me want to puke and one-night stands leave me feeling more lonely than fulfilled. Most of the time I just went straight home to my dumpy hotel room, watched late-night movies and jerked off.

Then one restless night in the fall, instead of going straight home, I decided to go for a walk. I wasn't out to cruise for casual sex. I just felt like some fresh air, so I stayed away from the beach. I ended up walking along False Creek 'til I came to the chainlink fence surrounding the fairgrounds.

As I walked along the fence, I thought about the whole thing and it really galled me. There was so much bullshit propaganda built in with that show. Here the government was, spending hundreds of millions of dollars to build artsy pavillions and I was headed home to sleep in a rat's nest. The politicians kept saying that society was entering a new age of business. Times were going to get better, but work ethics were going to become very different. The way of the future would require workers with fresh new attitudes, fresh new haircuts, freshly lowered wages and lots of fresh clean new rules. Ordinary people like me were being forced to choose. If we were willing and able, we could jump onto the fresh new bandwagon. If we couldn't or wouldn't, we probably wouldn't even be able to afford the price of admission to the fresh new Fair World.

Charlie slaps his hand on the dashboard for emphasis. He's starting to sound bitter, so I try to lighten him up. "But Charlie, you were going to tell me about some fresh new dick and ass. . . . "

He cracks a smile. "I'm getting to that. . . . "

Y'know, no matter how wrong the idea of the fair seemed to me, I felt sort of a magnetic attraction to all that new improved plastic freshness. I guess it must have represented everything that wasn't in my own life. All that fantasy made me feel sort of hopeful.

Anyhow, I was walking around the perimeter of the site observing the march of progress and feeling like Chaplin's little tramp in Modern Times. *It was well after midnight when I got to the far end of the site, and that was were I first laid eyes on him.*

I noticed the uniform first. It was a blue security guard suit. There were lots of guards on the grounds. They looked like somebody's private army. But this one in particular was walking toward me along the dark inside perimeter of the fence. We were a long time approaching each other.

The closer we got, the more he piqued my interest. He was a younger guy, maybe eighteen or nineteen. He was tall and dark, with an attractive build. As his handsome face came into focus, our eyes met and lingered. He smiled and nodded. I said hi.

"Nice night," he replied. And we both continued walking in our separate directions. Of course, I looked back to check out his butt. And, aha—I caught him looking too. Anyway, we both kept walking.

When I got home and replayed the evening's events in the cutting room of my mind, I couldn't get that young guard out of my head. I jerked off thinking about him.

A couple of days later, after work, I took a cruise along the fence again. Sure enough, when I got down to the far end, I saw the same guy approaching. His handsome figure was unmistakable. I felt my cock getting hard. This time we both stopped.

"Nice night," he said, just like before. I replied that he was lucky to have such an easy job. The guy smiled. He told me he had no complaints and the money was good. Then he asked

me where I worked.

At first I told him it was just a little place in the West End and he probably wouldn't know about it. But the guy really wanted to know the name of the restaurant. He told me that he knew his way around pretty well, so I took a chance and told him I worked at La Biche Riche.

The guy laughed out loud. "That place?! That's a fag joint, isn't it? Y'know, a gay restaurant." He laughed and laughed.

Charlie winces at the memory. He asks for a cigarette and I light it for him while he drives. He glances at me. "It's a tough situation, y'know. When you want to come out to a stranger, and you do, but it happens in a way that makes you look like some kind of stereotype."

I tell him I guess it would have to depend on how experienced the stranger is. "Just because he's young, doesn't mean he's going to stereotype you."

"I know," says Charlie, continuing.

So I asked him how come he knew so much about the Biche. Had he ever been there? The guy laughed again. He was finding me pretty entertaining. He told me he'd been there once with his parents. They were supposed to meet someone for dinner and they got the name of the restaurant wrong. His parents freaked out when they sat down and noticed that the ladies at the next table were all drag queens. It didn't bother him, though. He said he thought the place was "kinda fun." Then he dropped me the big hint. He said he figured most people were bisexual anyhow and he couldn't relate to homophobia. But, of course, he would never hang out in a place like that.

I told him I was really bored with the job and the shitty pay and asked him how he got his job. He told me his dad pulled some strings. The old man owned a big forest products company, Mega Mills. He did a lot of business with the construction contractors. The young guy bragged shamelessly. He said if his rich daddy had his way they'd clearcut every good section in the country, even in the big rainforest parks. The kid said logging was the only thing keeping the economy running at all. In his way of thinking, all environmentalists were asshole hippie wanna-be's standing in the way of everybody who wanted a good job.

"Harsh!" I say to Charlie. "Did you tell the guy to eighty-six that bullshit?"

"No way," says Charlie. "He was too good-looking. I didn't care if he was rich. I wanted to fuck with his body, not his politics."

"So what happened?" I ask.

I asked the young guy if he thought I could get a job there too. He played it cute. "Why not? All you gotta do is put in an application at the cattle call! I doubt if you'll get hired, though. . . . "

I asked him why not and he told me I'd have to quit smoking, get rid of my earring, and get my hair cut. And then, hey, without any pull, I'd be lucky to get a janitor's job! I knew he was right so I didn't bother about it anymore. I asked him if he wanted to smoke a reefer and sure enough he said he'd love to. I guess his politics didn't extend to the 'War on Drugs.'

As we stood there passing the joint back and forth through the fence, he opened up to me. His name was Janus, same name as a Roman god or something. He went to private school and he had lots of rich friends, but most of them were too squeaky clean to smoke dope. He got turned on to pot by some older guy at a summer camp. I wondered what other pleasures that older guy might have turned him on to.

Janus told me he was only working parttime nights, to save some bucks because he was leaving in the spring to travel around Europe for the summer. He didn't care if he missed the fair. His parents were giving him the airline ticket as a grad present. He said he preferred real travel to sound and light shows.

When the toke was finished he said goodbye, and told me he'd look for me next time. I wandered home to my dumpy room dreaming big romance and big lust. I had to figure out some way to get around that fence.

As cool winter poured soaking rain over the grey city, the fair site became a thick, oozing mud bath. Sculpted steel-frame structures sprouted and grew outward in patches, as if the site was being nourished by some giant sprinkler in the sky. The main funding pipelines of government and business were definitely cracked wide open, pumping hundreds of millions into the construction. Nothing would be spared to ensure the success of the promised giant carnival. It was the golden dream of the moneyed classes. They were building a distraction big enough to make everybody forget the Regression. And they dreamed that, when enough people could forget, it would be as good as over.

By trial and error, I found out what nights Janus worked. I always carried a reefer just in case. Talking to that kid was like entering a different world. Some people go to movies to escape the drudgery of life, but all I had to do was listen to Janus. Being with him was like watching a commercial for the World's Fair on TV, the new clean fresh world of the future. Janus and the people he described in his life were all very pleased with themselves. On the inside, where he stood, there was affluence, influential connections, and certain success in the cards. Janus had it all: supportive parents and family, and lots of nice clean middle-class friends. I had nada.

Charlie is going on and on in his usual way, but he never seems to get to the meat of the story. "C'mon, Charlie," I say. "Enough of the hard-luck story. Did you get a date with him or what?"

"Not exactly," says Charlie.

I would have liked to meet with Janus outside of working hours, but where would we go?

1 2 3

There were social realities and constraints. I sure as hell didn't want him to come down to my dump and see how I lived. That would scare him away. On the other hand, he'd told me that he wasn't welcome to bring friends home to his parents' place unless they'd been properly introduced. So I kept trying to think of neutral places to meet other than at the fence.

Janus was a real tease and we both knew he enjoyed the sensation of control that the fence gave him. He would take a piss right in front of me and wave his dick at me before snaking it away with a flourish. It was getting into the colder winter months by then, but I would be sweating, standing there on the outside of the fence. His meat, such a beautiful cock. To me it surely seemed to be the most perfect, most potent penis in the universe. There it was, just beyond my grasp.

You guessed it, I had a huge crush on the guy. He had a talent for self-promotion and au courant trendiness that was at the same time both intimidating and fascinating to me. I gobbled up every word, admired every pose and facial expression. And Janus encouraged my adoration.

But y'know how it is, blinded by love's longing, I couldn't discriminate whether Janus encouraged me out of his own vanity, or whether there was any true potential for romance. I had no one else in my life at the time and I was going crazy with desire. I got to the point where finally one night I gave him an ultimatum. Either we got together somewhere, or I was going to stop coming to the fence. Janus was taken aback. Young princes are not used to being pressed. He said he'd have to think about it.

They say not to put your love to the test, but I couldn't take it anymore. I started to walk away from the fence. My heart felt heavier than my muddy boots.

I wandered along the fence for a while in the direction of home. Then from over my shoulder I heard him call, "Wait . . . Charlie . . . wait up!"

He ran along the inside of the fence to where I'd stopped. He was breathless and nervous. He told me he knew of a place where some heavy machinery had damaged the fence. I could sneak under it and we could go into one of the pavillions for our nightly toke.

I was stunned and amazed. He knew he was risking his job if we got caught. But even more exciting than that was the possibility of what might happen between us now. We could actually touch each other. I could jump his bones!

Charlie pulls the car over to the curb and parks. He gets out and goes into a convenience store to buy another pack of cigarettes. By the time he gets back to the car, I'm ready to jump him.

"All right, Charlie," I say. "Did you get him or not?"

Charlie shrugs. "Wouldn't you like to know! Do I detect a hint of jealousy?"

I reach over and gently squeeze his basket. "C'mon Charlie, get to the juicy part!"

Janus showed me the place where the fence was damaged and I snuck inside the grounds. He was very worried in case someone should see us. We ducked into the back door of an unfinished pavillion. This one was sponsored by some kind of world evangelical born-again group. It was God's pavillion on site. What an appropriate place for me to get better acquainted with my young pagan god!

Inside, Janus guided me up a stairwell. We climbed several stories 'til we got to the unfinished top floor. The area was enclosed on three sides. The other side opened onto a view of the entire site below us, gloriously lit with tiny lights. We sat together on a pile of fresh clean plywood, passing a reefer.

Janus told me he sometimes came up here to eat his lunch or to slack off when he didn't feel like working. I asked him if he ever jerked off here. "Hmm, I never thought about that," he replied. "Great place for an orgasm," I said. I rubbed his inner thigh.

He lay back on the woodpile, folded his arms behind his head and stared straight up at the ceiling. I rubbed his crotch. His cock grew hard at my touch. I wasted no time in unzipping his pants. I went down on him eagerly. He sighed and moaned and came very quickly.

While Janus sat up to pull up his pants, I stood before him jerking off. He looked at me shyly. "I won't suck it . . . I don't do that kind of thing." I didn't care, and I told him so. But I took his hand and placed it under my balls as I brought myself to an awesome climax. I was enraptured by his beauty.

"You sucker, Charlie!" I tell him. "You always go for those younger guys who won't reciprocate."

Charlie shrugs. "The actions may not have been exactly reciprocal, but I'm sure the feelings were. Anyhow, we got down more than once that winter."

"So you did become lovers?"

"I guess fuck buddies are some kind of lovers," says Charlie, continuing.

Janus and I had sex on a semi-regular basis over the winter. As he got more and more into it, he began playing with my cock a lot more. He would jerk me off and later even tried putting his lips to my dick head for a moment or two. The fair was due to open in the spring, and then Janus would be heading off to Europe. Our affair was quickly coming to an end and I was really bugged. I found myself ruminating about Janus every day at work. I compared him to this guy and that. But none came up to his standard. He was my god. In conversations with others, it was rare if I didn't mention his name. I was obsessed and my ego was cracking under the contrast between my own squalid existence and the beautiful, wealthy, carefree young man I'd come to idolize. The sex was plenty exciting enough, but I still wasn't having any luck in building any kind of relationship outside of the fair world. Thinking about him everyday, at work, at home, everywhere, all the time, sometimes I wondered if what I really wanted was to be him.

The night of our last meeting there was a full moon. All week I'd been prepping for that special encounter. I brought a bottle of wine and we drank together in our private eagles' nest. Janus was more aggressive than usual and began wrestling with me. We fell exhausted onto a pile of plywood. As we lay there panting, I asked him to give me something to remember him by. "Fuck me! Fuck me!" I begged him.

"Whoa, Charlie! Stop!" I yell. He sees the fast-approaching red light at the last minute and locks up the wheels. We screech to a halt.

"Sorry, Jack."

"Take it easy," I say. "Just 'cause you went crazy over this kid is no reason to kill me!"

"I don't want you to miss your flight," says Charlie. "But I want to finish this story before we get to the airport. . . . "

I lay belly down on the plywood with my face ground into a stamp that read 'Mega Mills' while he rammed his hard cock into my quivering butt. I turned my eyes upwards and all I could see was the dancing sparkling lights spread out below me like a fantasy come true. . . .

Charlie's story trails off, but I want to know if there's any more to it. "Didn't you ever try getting in touch with the guy again?"

Charlie smiles.

One day, I looked through the phone book and found Janus' address. The family home, in a neighbourhood of old-money, long-established prestige, was on a prime hill overlooking the city. In a fit of compulsion, I got on a bus to go there. I didn't really know why I was going or what I would do there. On the way I watched the cityscape transforming from filthy grey to lush green, tree-lined residential streets. I silently worked myself into a frenzied state. It was a confusing combination of embarrassment and excitement.

I was struck by a sharp memory from childhood. My grandmother had once taken me for a walk in the park on a Sunday afternoon. I must have been only four or five years old. There were artists set up on the path, painting canvasses with oils. Granny warned me not to touch. But one artist was doing a still life of a wonderful imaginary bowl of plums. The fruit in that painting looked so real. I'd never seen such a wonderful colour of purple. I wanted to touch the paint, to taste it, so badly. I'd felt the same confused thrill that day as I broke the rules, reached out, and scooped a fingerful of purple from the startled artist's canvas.

I got off at a stop several blocks from the address I was seeking. The contradictory impulses continued. I didn't want to see Janus in that neighbourhood. I mean, I always wanted to see him, but I didn't want him to see me there. He'd probably mistake my ardour for stalking. I just wanted to see the house where my idol lived, played and took his beauty sleeps.

I couldn't bring myself to actually walk down his street, so I took a circuitous route along an intersecting street and snuck down the lane behind the houses. I checked numbers on the garbage cans one by one 'til, heart pounding, at last I found the address. By now my armpits were soaked with nervous sweat. There it was, an enormous three-car garage, a landscaped yard with a swimming pool and tennis court, and beyond it a classic antebellum plantation house like in Gone with the Wind. *It was glorious, a deserted paradise, quiet except for a spotted owl or something hooting behind the tall thick oaks and laurel bushes. I stood in the lane burning with anxiety and awe.*

Suddenly I heard a whirring sound. It was the garage door opening. As it rose, I saw a pair of legs I knew very well. It was him, Janus, leaning on the sports car within, waiting. And there I was, nearly caught, a forbidden plebe invading the god's territory. I had to cut away fast. I ran for blocks and blocks, never stopping to look behind. I ran and ran 'til I was so winded I had to slow down for a smoke. I walked the rest of the way back downtown.

Charlie slows down as we approach the departure drop-off zone at the airport. He turns to me as I get ready to leave. "Be careful up there, Jack," he says with a chuckle.

"Whadyamean?" I ask him. "I'm not flying the plane!"

"Watch out for stray gods slumming in economy class."

David Watmough
Wedding Dress For A Greek Groom

He was both fat and hirsute and even though we were now well into a New Jersey fall, with frost-nipped mornings and foliage already rouged and ochred, he was still perspiring profusely the Saturday morning he offered me a podgy hand in the vestibule and invited me yet again to the apartment in back that he and his young wife had rented earlier that summer of 1961.

I could see beads of sweat shining on his neck where dark chest hair reached up from a pale throat. As I reluctantly accepted his moist palm against my dry one I felt guilty for not liking Aristides Georgiadis a little more, and for once more planning to avoid another visit.

Waiting for the elevator while he waddled back through the dim recess of the hall-way, I told myself that I was by no means anti-Greek and that I should not let Ango-Saxon prissiness over a sallow complexion and an oily skin feed my facile prejudice.

All the same, as I rode up the elevator (I would have walked the three stories had I not thought the elevator would deliver me from the plump pharmaceuticals sales-man more speedily), I couldn't help adding to my dislike of him the obsequious smile he felt he had to offer when he was bent on persuading me to see them again.

Alternatively, on his encounters with the two of us together, I certainly didn't like it when we provided a friendly greeting as fellow tenants, and he stared unpleasantly through us—as if Ken and I were somehow *detritus* that had been washed up from the Hudson and into that gimcrack building.

From the outset I thought I detected a suppressed homophobia waiting to surface from his hulk of Hellenic flesh. My lover was convinced of it—which was why he rarely accompanied me down to the Georgiadis' flat after the first time.

I never had a sense of concealed antipathy from his equally atramentous wife,

Maria, who was Italian and as slim as Aristides was obese, as timid and quiet as he was pushy and noisy.

Another cause of irritation from my side arose from his invariably addressing her as a mental-nurse might boss a dim-witted charge to whom everything had to be explained patiently in pedestrian detail. Only Aristides was *not* patient.

I knew all this because, in spite of Ken's warnings and my usual reluctance to socialize on my own, I found myself too often capitulating to Aristides' persistent phone invitations (or once by his large presence at our front door) to join them for a cup of tea—which apparently the newlyweds thought was only proper for an immigrant Englishman.

It was never quite clear whether Californian Ken was included—it was invariably my British background that Aristides stressed. After the first rebuff, when Ken had simply said 'no,' Aristides never again invited my roommate specifically by name.

When I first gave in to these subsequently regular entreaties, it was during a cruelly humid and hot August and I rationalized my weakness by reminding myself of the large and efficient air-conditioner which the couple had received as one of their more expensive wedding gifts.

Deep down I knew there was another attraction, a sort of fascination by repulsion. Or was it something about the Greek's huge and hairy self proving an erotic magnet to me, skinny and smooth-skinned?

Whether my motives were arcane or not, I was to quickly discover that the request for my presence involved no elaborate preparation. Tea, for instance, consisted of a bag dangled into a mug filled with tepid tap water. The huge television set was not only left on, but the volume wasn't even turned down.

That was okay for Aristides—who shouted anyway. And for me, too, who had a fairly penetrating voice. But it meant that I hardly ever understood a single word that escaped Maria's reluctant little Italian throat.

Not that conversation in a living room clogged with furniture and Venetian red glass on every conceivable surface needed a distaff contribution to illuminate it. Aristides saw to it that the 'talk' consisted of little else than itemizing and displaying the costly loot they'd received from the matrimonial alliance made between two prominent merchant families (his the classiest grocers, hers the most prestigious pastrymakers) in Fort Lee, New Jersey.

At first he was content to show me what gifts had been lavished on them by the Georgiadis family—such as the vulgar sofa we were sitting on and the wall-to-wall pale blue carpet at our feet. By my third visitation the *dowry* from the Menottis was also put out for my inspection and expected plaudits.

On that occasion I was shown the huge brass bed—a family heirloom, Aristides proudly explained—and a variety of kitsch vases and other vulgar artifacts showered on them by numerous siblings, cousins, uncles and aunts from their competitive Greek and Italian clans.

More than once, after having eaten huge portions of cakes smothered in sweet icing, which Maria had baked but which her husband paraded as if he had produced them himself, I came perilously close to dozing off. I would dimly hear my voluble host once more cataloguing every boring bit of Venetian glass he had acquired through betrothal, and vaguely watch him hold up dozens of other items for my bored inspection. I would then struggle to fix the proud owner of all that crap with a sickly grin before muttering thank-you's and staggering to my feet to escape to Ken and suffer his unsympathetic I-told-you-so's.

Until the crisp fall day of the vestibule encounter when I had come in off the street so laden with Saturday shopping, I couldn't escape Aristides's presence. He telephoned late that afternoon and persuaded me to come down briefly as there was something very special he wanted to show me.

It had been the best part of a month since I had risked my roommate's caustic comments and visited the 'Mediterranean Alliance'—as I unkindly referred to Maria and Aristides behind their backs. Nor was I minded to renew the dreary routine, for the truth was that there was another aspect of their menage which was increasingly troubling to me.

I have referred to Maria's shyness but, beyond a natural timidity, I'd grown to suspect a fear of her huge husband. Word on the newlyweds had reached Ken's ears when disposing of the garbage and being waylaid by gossipy Mrs. Eichelbaum from Apartment 2. Talk in Century Apartments was to the effect that our newlyweds were not beyond loud and lengthy quarrels.

On my last visit I had noticed a purple mark on Maria's throat which could have come from the grip of a man's clenched hand. Earlier in our acquaintance she had displayed a black eye but quickly explained it as the outcome of falling down the two steps leading to our utilities room while carrying a heavy basket of clothes to the washing machines.

I was not prepared to say, flatly, that Aristides was a wife-beater, but I had certainly witnessed his mental domination of her, which was unpleasant enough. A bullying thread ran through so much of his conversation and it did so again that evening. "Show Davey those cute salad forks I got you. The ones with the eagles as handles. . . . Don't just stand there looking at our guest. Go get the cake I had you bake this afternoon when I came in. . . . She can just about turn out a layer cake now, Dave, if I stand over her, but she sure can't manage angel food cake. The last one looked like Mount Etna erupting. Tasted like goddamn lava, come to that. . . . What can you expect from an Eye-talian baker's daughter, huh? Mamma's always been there waiting on her hand and foot, right?"

I turned on the gold-brocaded sofa to give the recipient of these demeaning remarks an encouraging smile, but her diminutive shape had already vanished from the room.

"You've upset her," I commented. "You've hurt her feelings."

Aristides laughed at me, black, bushy brows suddenly contracted. I thought he was about to tell me to mind my own business. If that had been his intention, he abruptly relented. Laughed instead.

"No way! She knows I'm just kidding. We do it all the time. Not just us—her family and mine. Greeks and Italians—we're always taking the Mickey out of each other. I go on about her big fat wop of a mother and she calls my old man a dirty Greek grocer. It's all in fun, Dave. Not to worry, kiddo—you're looking at the happiest couple in Fort Lee. That's Maria and me."

"I see," I said, wholly unconvinced.

"Hey, I got something to show you while she's out there in the kitchen."

He crossed the room with surprising agility, considering both his girth and the excess of bric-a-brac, and opened a closet door. He withdrew a large box, let the lid fall to the carpet and extracted from a nest of toilet paper a white velvet dress, which he held up to his neck to display. It hardly reached the curve of his belly.

I felt mischief overcome irritation. "It suits you perfectly," I said. "It just needs letting out."

He stared at me in a different fashion. "It's my taste—you're right there. I chose it for her, you see. It was her wedding dress. There's a train, too."

I knew I was playing with fire but I persisted in the banter. Something compelled me to push further; something to do with vague suspicions that had lurked in my further consciousness for some time. "I'd love to see you in the train. Wasn't there a hat as well?"

Aristides pranced away from me to the door to the kitchen where he quickly turned the lock before facing me again, the dress now stretched tightly across the front of his chest and held there by a handful of podgy extended fingers. His other hand had gone down to his waist where it rested daintily on a roll of fat.

"I've locked her out for a second. I'll explain to her later we were having men talk."

But what my host did next had nothing to do with men—at least not the type the world presumed Aristides to belong to. He was soon back at the closet and this time when he withdrew from his rummaging he was wearing a white bridal crown and veil which all but disappeared in the mass of his curly hair.

He looked so ludicrous that I clapped my hands in malicious glee. That, in turn, brought another unexpected result. The next minute he was pulling off his Hawaiian shirt and dropping his enormous jeans. I was still capable of awe at his blubber, perhaps even more at the profusion of chest and belly hair that covered the white flesh.

He was not vaunting his semi-nudity, though. He was just as quickly garbed again—only this time in an evening gown of bottle green taffeta and ornate flounces. I noted at once that it fit him, even if he did push the curves and eliminate any trace of creases.

"I bought this for her but she hasn't seen it yet. This, too." He reached into the closet for a matching felt hat with tiny white roses around the base of the crown. It would have done Garbo proud. He replaced the bridal headpiece with this much larger creation, carefully tilting it at an angle and looking over my head to the mantelpiece mirror to inspect the result.

"You play dress-ups, too?" he asked, breathing quickly and biting his lips—I imagined to stimulate blood and simulate lipstick.

"No," I said. "Should I?"

He was already pulling the dress over his head.

"I dunno. There's two of you guys up there. Neither of you's married, right? I just thought. Well. . . . " He broke off, obviously waiting for me to supplement his implication.

"Neither of us are transvestites, if that's what you're suggesting. Then I didn't know romantic young couples like you and Maria shared things to that extent."

"I'm not one of them *trans* guys—don't get me wrong. Just a little game, that's all." He airily tossed the hat back into the closet and threw the dress after it. I was pretty sure they would both be stowed away more neatly as soon as I'd departed.

"Pity you and Maria can't share sizes," I said casually, "particularly if you share sartorial tastes."

He scanned my face for clues: unsure whether I was mocking or making objective comment. "Maria doesn't have nothing to do with this. She knows I know more about clothes than she does and that's why she lets me dress her. But what I buy for *me* she doesn't know about. That's the way I intend to keep it. She's a nice little girl, is Maria. But not always bright. Specially about some things. Understand what I'm saying, Dave?"

I suddenly loathed the breathy, conspiratorial tone in his voice. I got to my feet. "Maybe Maria would like to come in before I have to leave? I came to see her, too."

Aristides shrugged. "Suits me. We're going out soon, anyways. Takes time to dress her—she panics if I don't tell her what to put on. Yeah, it's time we got her ready."

I was only too pleased to take a hint. "I promised Ken I'd only be a sec. Perhaps you'll give Maria my apologies when you let her out."

I stopped at the door, repenting a little. "Thank you for showing me your—your *things*, Aristides. I feel flattered."

But the conciliation didn't register. He was too nervous, too cross with himself for the rash revelation. "Yeah, well, give my regards to your near-invisible partner. I guess he doesn't think us peasants are worth a university prof's time."

I didn't bother with a retort to that. He went on anyway. "You might tell him we're liberals down here on the ground floor. You guys got nothing to worry about from me—and the little lady goes along with what I say."

"Thank you," I said heavily. "Those kind words will make his day. They've certainly made mine."

Outside I swore at the linoleum floor, swore I would never cross his fucking threshold again.

I didn't—and I suppose in the normal course of events my Mediterranean Alliance, however gloomily fascinating, would have retreated to the sidelines of interest and stayed there.

It *did* resolve along those lines—for almost four years, in fact. Until an April evening when I happened to be delayed in the office and was late getting back home. I was walking up from the bus depot when a woman approaching on the sidewalk looked up and smiled. It was Maria.

There was a youngish man with her, who, being short and dark, I first thought might be her brother. Only she introduced him as her husband. The name was either Marino or Fastino. Anyway, it was Italian. I guess I looked slightly bewildered, as indeed I was—naturally thinking of fat Aristides. But *this* Maria was assured and quick—not at all like the timid, bird-like creature I'd seen in Century Apartments.

"You don't know about Aristides and my divorce, then? It's all right, Davey, don't look startled. My husband knows all about poor Aristides." She shook her head and grimaced. "I guess everyone does now."

"Not exactly everyone. Ken and I didn't know you'd split up. Then, as commuters, we never do hear much about what's going on in Fort Lee."

"I wasn't thinking about the divorce so much—and it didn't happen in Fort Lee."

"I'm sorry," I said. "I don't think I follow."

Her husband smiled gently at her and then looked directly at me, the smile quite gone. "Aristides is dead. It wasn't very easy for Maria even though they'd been divorced for over eighteen months. It happened in Newark."

"I'm sorry," I said vaguely, feeling stupid in the very uttering of the clichéd response.

"He was mugged by teenage kids," Maria informed me. "In one of those parks. You know, where men go?"

I got the message and determined to say nothing. What was there to say?

Maria sensed my quandary, offering me a little smile to lighten the heavy knowledge suddenly between us. "Poor Aristides. He made such a mystery of things. As if no one knew what was going on! That was why my parents caused such a fuss when we got married. Only I thought I could help him. I guess it wasn't to be."

She put out a white-gloved hand. She was also wearing a small dark hat that perched jauntily on her dark waves. I was reminded of huge Aristides putting on her tiny wedding crown and veil.

"I hate to be the one to tell you about that horrible business. It was so sordid. You can imagine his parents. . . . I'm sorry we can't stay, Davey. We're off to Vespers and Benediction at St. Mary's and we're already late."

Her gloved fingers and my bare ones met tentatively. "Pleased to meet you," said her husband, preparing to move onwards.

"We must get together again and talk about nicer things," said Maria. "I'll give you a call. You still in Century? The same number in the phone book?"

"Same old address," I said, raising my voice as we began to move in opposite directions. "Same old number."

Dwayne Williams Behind Glass

These wards are a dreadful place where all crimes together grow and spread around them as by fermentation, a contagious atmosphere which those who live there breathe and which seems to become attached to them.

—*Musqinet de la Pagne, 1790*

10: The flame dances with his breath. He must write the letter quickly. In the hospital, candles are forbidden.

Dear Mother:

He touched me there. That was such a long time ago but I remember how it felt. The morning before he died, he made me promise never to tell anyone. Other people wouldn't understand, he said. He was right. After that night you never spoke of what you saw.

I was a boy. I didn't understand. I wonder if I do now. I do understand that he died to protect me and to protect

He stops writing, holding his breath as a streak of black smoke rises towards the ceiling. Somebody is there, beyond the candle's light.

"Mother? Is that you?"

"Time for your medication, Mr. James," the voice says. "It's that time again."

9: The receptionist scratched her pencil through his name.

"Take a seat, Mr. James. The doctor will be with you in a few minutes."

Ian headed for the men's room instead, stepping over the ashes of a young man's cigarette.

"C't'une maudite place ça icitte. J'attend d'puis de bonne heure à matin," the man complained, bouncing his heel up and down in a puddle of brown slush. "Hey, monsieur," he muttered behind a cloud of smoke, "J'espère que t'es pas trop pressé. Tu sortiras pas de c'te place de fou là avec ces Christ de docteurs là. Tabernac!"

Probably cancer, Ian decided as he closed the bathroom door. He locked it.

In the mirror his reflection squinted, imagining the hideous transformations—

dripping green flesh and putrid warts. He laughed. Maybe he was beautiful, in an unconventional way. "You have emerald eyes, my little boy," he whispered to himself in his mother's voice as he remembered it from the nights when she used to kiss his forehead and leave him alone in the dark to wonder if little boys could see with jewels. His eyes followed the reflection's finger as it traced the contours of his face. It slid down between the eyebrows and lingered on the bump. A broken nose gives a boy character, his mother had assured him. He was twelve then, still young enough to stand too close to a swinging baseball bat. It wasn't until much later, while eating seedless Moroccan oranges in bed with a stranger, that he was told that his nose made him irresistibly sexy.

"Mr. James. Ian James? Are you in there?" The receptionist was knocking on the door. He ripped a piece of toilet paper off the roll and tucked it in his pocket.

He didn't cry. Not a single tear. The doctor's reaction actually troubled him more than the diagnosis itself. Her incessant blinking and the way she bit her lip to deny its quivering challenged her professional composure. She was perspiring inside her lab coat, starched, buttoned to the very top, a stethoscope dangling from the breast pocket. In the cramped office there was no place for the luxury of optimism. She had spoken with the power of science, and he had listened. Now, as she shuffled through his file, he noticed her hands, the brown mottled skin clinging to her bones. She was an old woman.

"I'm sorry," she said with a sigh. "You're the first person I've diagnosed as having it." She cleared her throat and looked at him over the top of her bifocals. Ian could not bear to look at her; she needed, from his eyes, the acceptance of what she'd offered him as truth. He stared into the backs of the desktop portraits of her children, grandchildren, whoever they were who smiled at her from the other side.

That morning after he left the clinic, he called Sammy, his ex-lover, from a payphone at the Gare Centrale. The first thing that came out of his mouth was, "I've got it." He knew then from the long breathy silence. It was true. Long after they said goodbye, he continued to hold the receiver to his ear, mesmerized by the drone of disconnected lines.

He did not, could not, call his mother.

On the train he took a window seat furthest from a crying child.

8: His mother looked away. Her eyes sought a point of refuge beyond the kitchen window. The first traces of a winter sun drew shadows from the objects within the room, closing the spaces between the woman and the teapot, the bowl of sugar cubes, the black bananas (that surely she would have peeled, mashed, whipped into a flawless circularity of cake had she known that he was coming)—everything that witnessed on its surface the microscopic droplets of her anxiety—until they merged with her body and clotted the spaces within her. Then she was alone.

The light betrayed her face. It deepened the wrinkles and exaggerated the dusted pink intention of her cheeks. Her hair was not gray, but it should have been. She was no longer the woman in the black-and-white snapshot, who lay on a blanket on the beach, drinking Coca-Cola, rocking her bare foot to the portable melodies of Patsy Cline or Brenda Lee, tempting the camera with her smile.

That was the only photograph that showed his mother smiling. She'd kept it hidden amongst hundreds of yellowed photographs in a dusty suitcase, as though she'd planned to take them with her on a long voyage. Alone in the house, playing hooky from gym class, bored and horny, he found it while snooping through closets and under mattresses for his mother's dark secrets. Years later, when she disapproved of his *lifestyle* (as she called it), it was the only image that survived her distance. Eventually he could not control its appearance in his mind. It came back to him again and again until he was there, behind the camera, cajoling her with forgiveness to give him a smile.

In the suitcase there was a snapshot of his uncle.

He waited for the answer to his question. He'd been waiting for sixteen years, not for the answer, because by then he had discerned the truth about his uncle's death, but to hear her speak words that she had long since buried in silence, words that had taken root inside his body and grown, gnarled and thorny, against her. He watched her as she shifted her gaze towards a fly beating its wings against the pane.

"Stupid thing doesn't know it's nearly winter," she said, and coughed. She took the china cup with both hands and blew across the steaming surface of the tea. "Your uncle was a troubled man," she said, staring into the cup.

The fly buzzed around her head and she swatted it away.

"Mother, why didn't you—"

"Oh, for God's sake, Ian," she protested, slapping the table with her hand, tea splashing from the cup. "What does this have to do with your health? Now, exactly what did the doctor say? He can't be absolutely sure. . . . "

7: The hospital is dark. He listens—not a groan, not a cough, not even a snore. The ghosts of the nearly dead are silent. The muffled gossip of the graveyard shift drifts from the nurses' station, punctuated now and again by restrained laughter. One voice is recounting the scandal of a bridal shower. Something about crotchless panties. A male stripper. The sour-faced mother-in-law-to-be.

He turns a tiny blue sleeping pill between his fingers. Turning, turning, turning. If he could get to the bathroom on his own, he'd flush the thing down the toilet. There are too many mysteries moving within; he doesn't need another. Since he stopped hoping for a miracle, he'd been saving the sleeping pills. He hides tonight's with the others, in an empty box of chocolates. An extra one, for luck, he supposes. What else could there be at this point?

Sammy's dead. He had it too. At first Ian blamed him because he was the only man he'd ever allowed inside him. He imagined the virus escaping the ruins of Sammy's body, slithering quietly into his in search of new blood.

Ian scrutinized the past. He went through his calendar, trying desperately to reconstruct the events of each day, as though being able to pinpoint the moment of infection would make sense of what was happening to them. In the end he could only know that it must have been during some morning. That was the only time of day that they had sex after they moved into the four-and-a-half with parquet floors and stained glass windows on St-Joseph. They were both working too much in order to pay the rent, for brunches at La Tulipe Noire, for ties by Armani. Sammy worked evenings at the cafe while Ian endured the nine-to-five drudgery of unbalanced accounts at Fortier, Slade, Hoang and Associates. The period before he rushed off to work was the most convenient time to perform for each other's pleasure.

Ian was usually cranky and tired, his closed eyes concealing fantasies that lay outside the curves of Sammy's nakedness. Together they hurried through the flutter of kisses to the probing of tongues and penises into the estranged spaces of their bodies. By then, their love for one another had become a refuge, protecting them from their desires for other men. In that love and in the apartment that had become their home, they salvaged a reason to stay together—safety.

There had been warnings—in the death of the friend of a friend in Toronto; in the statistics that spelled SAFE SEX. One morning in January, a poster appeared, encased in the wall of a bus shelter—a pretty male face sharpened against a plane of grey that separated his female counterpart. The caption advised, *Better a Safe than a Sorry.* Ian despised the affected yearning of their faces captured behind glass that reflected his own sullen face.

As he waited inside the shelter, his fingers tingled inside his coat pockets. He knew where he had left his gloves. He'd set them on the dresser the night before so that he would remember to wear them but had forgotten them in his preoccupation with a phone call that had come just before he'd left the apartment. When he'd answered, the person had hung up. "Who called?" Sammy had asked, rather defensively, Ian thought.

Was Sammy alone now? He searched his memory for other shreds of evidence—a foreign hair on the pillowcase, a third mug in the sink, the stale punch of cigarette smoke. He could not recall any of these. As he hurried back to the apartment, Ian prepared himself for the discovery of another man. He rehearsed lines that he had vowed he would never speak. Straightspeak, he called it—*You've cheated. You don't love me. I want a divorce.*

In the bedroom, the blinds were closed. Sammy was snoring, face up, his underwear crumpled on the floor where he had tossed it earlier that morning. In the street, a semi rumbled by, and the whole apartment shook. Ian stood there, watching the rise and fall of Sammy's chest. Quietly he crawled into the warmth beneath the blankets, naked and pink still from the cold.

"Sammy," he whispered into his dark curls, tentatively, as if he wasn't sure that it was him. Sammy moaned something indistinguishable, his erection stirring beneath the blankets, then looked at Ian. "What are you doing home?"

"I wanted to be with you."

"What?" he yawned, rubbing his eye. "What about work?"

"I called already. I told them I've got the flu." Ian expected him to bitch or at least to question this explanation. They were broke and Sammy was the one who always received the overdue bills, leaving them in opened envelopes with notes written on the back—*We're going to get cut off, my dear,* or sometimes, *Pay up!* Instead, he pulled Ian into his arms and held him against his chest.

"Well," he grinned, "I'm glad you're back."

It was not supposed to happen this way. In bed with the only man he'd ever loved, Ian could not confront the issue of safety. At the bus stop he'd felt its fragility, so easily shattered by the possibility that Sammy was in bed with another man, one fitted tightly inside the other. But his suspicions had been wrong. Was it Sammy or himself that he could not trust? Without Sammy, he would be waiting in the cold, his fingers numb, his face trapped behind glass.

Safety. His tongue rolled back the word and he swallowed it.

Perhaps Sammy was afraid of dying alone, dreading the chance that only he was infected. Why did he never speak of safety? Ian is surprised at the return of this question.

While Sammy was dying, Ian was ashamed of his own resentment. He knew death, had known it even as a boy. But Sammy did not. He was afraid of it. Even as a baby his parents called him Samuel, but he preferred the diminutive form because, he said, it kept him young. If he'd been old perhaps he would have been prepared to go alone. Perhaps he needed Ian to die with him.

At night a nurse raises the bars on the sides of his bed.

On a distant shore a boy splashes naked through the waves, the moon sliding down his back. He calls to Ian but he doesn't go. The boy is beautiful, the colour of the sea at the moment before it surrenders to the nocturne, the light of a falling sun.

Even in the dream he will not escape an awareness of the inevitable awakening to sterility and isolation. That is what he cannot bear. So he lies inside the boat at the water's edge and waits.

6: He was hunting for an elephant in the clouds when crack, the world went black.

Ian waited outside the principal's office for his mother to arrive. Blood trickled down the back of his throat as he held an ice-pack against his nose. The baseball bat had broken it. He'd learned somewhere that bleeding to death was the slowest, most excruciating way to die. He gazed out the window as though he were blind. His free hand tapped out the theme song from *The Brady Bunch* which kept playing in his head. Finally his mother's yellow Bug turned into the driveway in front of the school and he could no longer hold back his tears.

5: "You got blood on your shirt, Mom."
"Yes, I know. I still have to get changed. I'm going to be late if—"
"Where you goin'?"
"Just out."
"Again!"
"Oh, Ian."
"With who?"
She didn't answer but drew the sheet to his chin, a linen chill tickling his feet. His father had been dead for six years but she still could not admit to having an interest in other men. Whenever one of them came for dinner she introduced him as *Mister* so-and-so. Before the man could get his shoes off she'd suggest that he play catch with her son in the backyard, which he always did until the meatloaf and scalloped potatoes were steaming on the kitchen table.
"I won't be late, honey," his mother reassured him.
"My nose still hurts," he complained. And it did too.
"It's going to take some time to heal. In the meantime, no more baseball for you, sport. Doctor's orders." Her fingers combed through his hair, snagging a knot.
"Ouch!"
"Oh, come on, that didn't hurt," she said. "Now you go to sleep and in the morning you'll be as good as new. I'll even make you some cocoa and toast for breakfast, okay?"
"O.J. too. Fresh-squeezed."
"All right," she conceded with half a smile. "Uncle John will be here so if you need anything—"
"I thought he was gonna leave tonight."

"No. He's decided to stay a few extra days."

"All right!" Ian liked his uncle, especially since he did things with him that his mother would never do, things like horseback riding and swimming at the park pool.

"But Uncle John needs to get some rest before he goes back to Vancouver," she whispered, glancing at the doorway.

"Can I go with you to the airport again?"

"Only if you promise to go to sleep. Right away."

"Promise."

"That's a good boy."

"Good night, Mom."

As she leaned over to kiss his forehead he smelled the perfumed sweetness on her neck. She whispered into his ear, "Good night, honey."

"And I'm not a boy anymore," he mumbled after she flipped off the light.

His mother laughed. "I'll try to remember that," she said, closing the door.

Monsters crawled out from under the bed, slid down the walls, leaped off the bookshelf. They'd been hiding in his room for too many years to scare him. Still, he could not stand to look at them. They had faces like the pale, withered face of the old lady next door who'd lost all her hair and who had, according to Chuckie Lowd, only one boob.

When he awoke, a man stood at his bedside. He saw in the nightlight's glow that it was his uncle, naked except for his underwear. He was smiling at Ian just like the day at the airport when he had spotted Ian in the crowd beside his mother and had ran towards them, a hug in his widespread arms, a present in his knapsack. His mother coughed when he hugged her. She was suddenly stiff in the presence of his uncle, holding a smile at the corner of her mouth. On the way home, in the backseat of the car, Ian could see in the rearview mirror that his mother was crying. She wasn't making a sound but there were tears rolling down her cheeks. He didn't dare say a word after that. He sat there, frowning at the killer whales on his new cap.

"Hi, Ian. It's just me. No need to be afraid."

"Hi," he yawned. "Where's my mom?"

"She's still out. You feeling any better now?"

"Yeah, I guess so."

"You need anything?"

"Umm . . . no."

"I brought you a glass of water."

Ian took the glass, touching his uncle's fingers. They were cold, like the water. He downed it all and set the glass on the nighttable.

"Would you like some more?"

"No, thanks," he said, averting his eyes from the heaviness of his uncle's crotch. He turned to face the wall. After a while, the springs in his bed creaked as his uncle sat down.

"Can I lie down beside you?" he asked, in a voice that lingered.

Ian didn't answer.

"Would you like a backrub?"

He shut his eyes and pretended to fall asleep. His uncle's body had a smell like the change room after gym class. Years might have passed, the house was that still. When he felt the breath through his pyjamas, he was trembling with desire and fear. When he felt the hand against the push of his cock . . .

Faces filled the room. A universe of hot-eyed stars. Every breath was the same question—*Can I lie down beside you?* Ian's own breath billowed, stuttered, clipped any sound that might have said no. Whenever Chuckie slept over, their sweaty hands stumbled under the blankets, only to flee at the slightest sound. But this hand was not afraid. It spread fire from the sparking jitters of his body. He held his eyes closed, opening them just in time to see a silhouette slip into the hallway outside his bedroom and disappear.

Years later he wondered how long his mother had been there, watching in the darkness.

4: Aliens will come someday to kidnap the world's population. That's what he'd heard on the television as he had been eating his breakfast earlier this morning, dipping toast into the huge mug of cocoa. Their spaceships had already landed on Earth, conducted secret tests on human beings to find out how our bodies worked, if we could survive a zillion light years away on a green-fogged planet. Maybe they wanted to use us as slaves, he wondered as he walked home from school. Or guinea pigs? Then he saw the flashing red light, but it was no spaceship, only an ambulance.

He ran towards the light. There was no siren. The street was wonderfully still and quiet, as if there had been a heavy snowfall. As he got nearer, his excitement receded into curiosity and finally into fear. The gaping mouth at the back of the ambulance warned him to go no closer.

Every neighbour seemed to be there, on the other side of the street, their greedy eyes focussed on his house. Was it his house? For the first time he noticed that all the houses looked the same. Maybe all the families were identical too and he could just walk into any of those houses and find a stuffed rabbit with a grape-juice-stained paw in his closet, after-school Oreos and milk waiting on the kitchen table, his mother vacuuming the jungles of plush carpets.

A cry hushed the eager whispers of the crowd. There was a body on the stretcher that came towards him. The face was covered. He wanted to run but he couldn't. His nose throbbed as he stared at the body beneath the sheet.

"Excuse us, son," an attendant said, his voice unnaturally calm. "You'll have to move out of the way."

He didn't move; he couldn't take his eyes off the body.

"Come on now. Run along inside, your momma's waiting on you."

Flashes of red bounced off his bedroom window. She was alive. The discovery of her face in the window prickled his cheeks. How long had she been watching? Why had she not knocked on the glass? Called out to him? Without expression or colour, a violence claimed her face. It was the face of the monsters, the face of the bald, old lady, the face that had lost something forever.

A hand flopped off the stretcher like a dying fish. One of the men in white—they looked like sailors—flipped it back over but it fell off again as they lifted the stretcher into the ambulance. He looked around on the sidewalk. There wasn't a single drop of blood anywhere. They'd said that that was the way aliens would take away bodies. Clean.

3: They placed a cross in his uncle's hand and rested it forever across his heart. It was Ian's first funeral. A woman in spiked heels—a third cousin from Kingston, he overheard—wiped away tears as she spoke about how handsome John looked. Men in long skinny ties argued over sports and the economy. Blue-haired women sat near the coffin, counting the bouquets of carnations, mums, roses. A man leaned over the body and kissed his uncle's lips. His mother did not say goodbye to the man when he left, a trace of powder on his mouth.

That night, as he lay awake, he hummed the organ's agonizing dirge, the only music that came to his mind as her sobs seeped through the bedroom walls. Her grief was uncanny, haunting, afflicted; he had never heard her cry before. He knew then that he wanted his body to leave this world in fire.

2: There are signs throughout the ward—a finger pressed against pursed lips— PLEASE BE QUIET. They aren't meant for visitors but for those who must stay here. Screams are forbidden.

Inside his head, Ian screams. The nurses jump, upsetting cups of black coffee across their charts. STAT! Virus attack! STAT! By the time they reach his room they are masked and gloved. Hundreds of them. And he's laughing at them with every goddamned bit of energy he has left in him. I'm alive! I'm alive! But they are laughing back at him—Yes, you are alive, Mr. James. You. Are. Alive. They toss their masks and gloves like roses at his feet. They do not insist that he calm down. They do not extinguish the thousands of candles that he has lit for the occasion. Their faces glow, a chorus of long-winged angels, ascending.

Silenced.

He no longer sees faces. Even the monsters have disappeared. What did Sammy look like? In his arms, Ian never thought a day would come when there would only be the memory of his face. And now he cannot remember. Is there still makeup on his uncle's face? How far into the earth is that knowledge? He is too weak to dig. Perhaps his mother's face has found its smile, buried in the suitcase.

He's been waiting for her to come. But he can wait no longer. The last sentences he will write in the dark.

Please, Mother, do not let them do to me what they did to Uncle John. I want to be cremated.

1: The boy walks towards him, his tanned skin glistening.

"You called for me?"

"Yes. Will you lie down beside me?"

His feet are wet. On his lips, he tastes the faintest trace of salt. His body surges, reducing the room to two.

Then one.

Then none.

Raymond John Woolfrey
Pages From My Window: Red Geraniums

Saturday, December 29, 1990 (3 p.m.), Montréal
A magazine I read said that this city is full of stories; you have only to look behind windows with calico cats or watchful dogs. There are none across the street from me, just some red geraniums at Alex's bedroom window. I see them today through a window coated by freezing rain, like the frosted glass used for bathrooms. The geraniums become a detail from a Seurat painting.

Alex bought his renovated little row house two years ago. Despite the modern windows with horizontal blinds, it's still as plain as any of the untouched flats on the street, their only ornaments a few scrollwork brackets on the cornices. Alex keeps the blinds in his bedroom raised just enough to let his geraniums soak up the sunlight at full strength. There's not too much of that on this rainy winter day.
The front of his house is flush against the sidewalk with two steep concrete steps protruding outward for the sidewalk snowplough to dodge. When Alex returned from the hospital after a bout of pneumonia last spring, it was hard for him to mount the steep risers so I offered to install a grab-handle on the door frame. He grips it firmly as he hauls his slender frame up to the door, one step at a time, and inserts his key. His mother, visiting from Toronto, uses it too.
"You've gained a lot of weight," I remarked when we met on the sidewalk last summer. His big, deeply set brown eyes stood still for a moment to apprehend me. He grinned—a string of small teeth set between thin lips. He couldn't work his mouth well enough to pronounce all his consonants perfectly, especially his T's. Slowly and quietly he said, "I hope I'll be able to ride my bicycle again soon."
He looked up at the front window of my greystone flat. "I like the flowers you set

out on your window sill. I'd put some out too, but my windows open outward."

"But you've got your beautiful garden in the back."

"Oh, I want to show you how it's come along."

As we passed through the house, Alex gestured at the bold abstract oil paintings hanging alongside his charcoal sketches of steam engines and railyards. "Those are Louis's. He just moved in, but he's not here right now." Dominating the large glass coffee table was a model of a modern passenger train from the railway for which Alex works as a mechanical engineer.

Once in the back I asked, "How did you manage to create such a beautiful garden with so little sunlight?"

Alex beamed.

(10 p.m.)

Tonight, dark-haired young men in black leather jackets go by with heads bowed under black umbrellas held before them against the blowing rain. As they pass by Alex and Louis's, they steal a glance into their living room through a window whose blind is stuck open.

Sometimes when I'm talking on the phone at my window, I too glance through that window and see them going about their daily lives: two frail, moustached men sitting on the sofa or at the table, often with friends. I've been enjoying the Christmas tree they set up in a corner of their living room. All I had done was lay some pine boughs and lights on my window sill, but Alex said he found them cheerful.

I wonder if the people who look into that little house as they pass by ever see what I see from my window, if they've noticed the grace and purpose with which Alex and Louis embrace what may be their last Christmas together. Do those other voyeurs ever wonder, as I do, whether the two travellers in that living room aren't the ones who are really living, that the rest of us are merely waiting for something? To die, maybe . . . or for life to begin?

Friday, March 1, 1991

Louis died the day before yesterday. When I was leaving my flat, an ambulance was waiting out front. Alex waved me over and explained, frantic with imagined guilt. "I got back from Toronto late last night and didn't want to disturb him. I only realized something was wrong when he slept way past his usual time, so I tried to wake him. He was burning up—incoherent, delirious. I should have noticed something last night."

I had met Louis before Alex moved in across the street. At the AIDS conference in

June of '89, we both wore sandwich-boards publicizing the Names Quilt. I hadn't seen much of Louis over the two months before his death. One airless, mid-winter day I performed an errand for Alex. "Would you like some homemade soup?" he entreated. I entered an overheated house that had that dry, medicinal smell old ladies' places have. Despite Alex's best intentions to create cheer, the atmosphere was dank with despair and frustration. He sometimes snapped and mumbled at Louis. Louis was remote and uninterested, even in the television he stared at. I felt uncomfortable sitting alone at their table with Alex serving me, as he insisted. I tried to make interesting chatter, but I was afraid I was intruding.

"Am I interrupting your show, Louis?"

"No," he replied, resurrecting his charming smile. "I don't really pay attention to what I'm watching. It's all the same." The magic that had sustained them over and beyond Christmas had dissipated, leaving them with the reality of their deteriorating bodies. Late in January, a Buddy had been to clean their house and the Christmas tree was finally put out for collection. It had no needles left at all. For two days, arctic gusts rolled the skeletal tree like a tumbleweed up and down the deserted street.

Calling on Alex one evening, I was dismayed to discover that I'd awakened Louis. Though no longer spending day after day on the sofa in front of the TV, he was still sick. It was minus twenty that evening, but he didn't ask me in to shut out the cold. He just stood there in his dressing gown with the door wide open and said, "Alex is in Toronto visiting his mother. He's coming back on tomorrow night's train." Astonished by his insouciance toward his health, I kept the exchange short. After Louis died, a friend of his told me that Louis had wanted to hasten death.

Sunday, April 1

Tonight the freezing rain is spraying my window in waves. It sounds like pieces of hard candy crumbs being hurled against the glass.

Alex is in the hospital for severe stomach pains. His mother, Maretta, is the sole occupant of his house. She must have gone to bed by now—the downstairs windows are all dark. I called on her earlier to see if she was okay all by herself. A thin smile formed at the bottom of a round, cherubic face. "It's all right. I'm used to being alone."

I called the hospital today from the big downtown church to which we both belong. It was only recently that Alex and I found out about each other (he'd been attending the early Sunday service and I sing at the ten o'clock one). The rector had assigned me as Alex's area steward, a position created to help the clergy of our parish with their work. I was surprised to find my neighbour from across the street on my list.

When I first went over with my area-steward kit in hand, Alex appeared to appreciate the gesture. I, however, felt like some kind of church lady running over once a month with propaganda, so instead I began to mail the information and would stop to chat with him on the street. I don't want to bother him; I only want to be there for him whenever he calls, and to take him to church when he wants to go.

I'm pleased when Alex goes with me. If I don't sing in the choir, I have no one in particular to sit with, and I feel I have a special bond with him that I don't have with anybody else. He always wears a tie and a brown tweed suit even though it's not easy for him to dress himself. And in spite of (or maybe because of) being so much thinner than when he had the suit fitted, he looks strong-willed and dignified with his neatly combed, grey-brown hair. He even manages to shave his bony cheeks.

His mother came with us once. Together we crept to and from the Communion rail, Alex's right arm on mine, the other driving down shakily on his cane. We each took our turn accepting the wafer and sipping the wine—first Alex, then Maretta, then me. Others followed. I couldn't help feeling proud of us all: Alex for daring to claim his right, and the rest of us communicants for being too enlightened to hurt him through groundless fears about a common chalice.

As we slowly made our way back to our pew near the rear where Alex could lie down if he needed to, I glanced up at the congregation. On one or two faces, I thought I caught the barely-perceptible flash of recognition—the sudden panic and horror when you realize that the skinny fellow you've been unconsciously examining is just a little too gaunt to be merely thin, that it's not just from stress or overwork, that there's another explanation.

I often feel helpless with those who aren't as healthy as I—guilty for my robustness, embarrassed by my sexual well-being. The only help I can offer is practical: driving someone somewhere, fetching things, installing grab-handles. Mostly I just keep an eye on Alex from my window, as though one day I'll see him collapsed on the sofa, call the paramedics, and feel like a hero. It's that part of me that fears I'm nothing more than a snoop and a busybody.

Saturday, April 13

I left Alex a little while ago. I helped Maretta get him upstairs and into bed where I stayed with him until he was ready to sleep.

He now uses what used to be Louis's room. He says it's quieter than his own room in the front, but the street side is only noisy when the windows are open, and of course it's not yet warm enough for him. Alex never speaks of Louis since he died, except when he invited me to the reception he had in Louis's memory two weeks ago.

I lay with him on his bed for about an hour, his head nestled in the crook of my arm as I stroked his thinning hair. He clutched my other arm with a hand dotted with lesions. They look to me just like chicken pox pimples when they dry up.

We could see his copy of Lawren Harris's *North Shore, Baffin Island* out in the hall. "In high school I painted in his style," I said. "I'll show you the one I did of the mountain across the lake from my cottage."

From his bed we thought of other places in his native Ontario where we'd both been: Shadow Lake in Toronto's cottage country, and Northern Ontario where the Polar Bear Express runs between Cochrane and Moosonee. I asked him about Chicoutimi where he worked for a few months.

"I didn't care for it—too wintery, and I was homesick the whole time."

Lying there on the bed with him, I felt as if we were lovers. I pressed my body against his. "I'd like to drive through Northern Ontario," he said dreamily.

"I could do the driving."

"You know, I don't think you should go away to Japan to teach English," he said. "You'll miss your cottage in the Laurentians, for one thing. Normally, I never tell people what to do, but this time, I feel I have to."

I was leaning towards staying anyway, and that was all I needed to convince me. If I'd gone, I would have missed this time with him; he might even have felt abandoned. He has many friends and Buddies, as well as his mother, to look after him, but I began to wonder whether he regarded my role in his life as something that needed to be played out to the end. I feel as though we're now floating along on a light beam together and soon I'll have to get off and leave Alex to ride on without me.

This afternoon Alex stared at a paint sample for a long time, as though meditating on it. It was the same colour of turquoise as in the Lake Superior print. "Would you paint the wall in the upstairs hallway this colour, to go with a portrait of my grandfather?" he asked.

When he finally broke away from the turquoise, a rich, bold green caught his attention. He looked up at me and exclaimed, "Green is the colour of life!" The April sun seeped through the blinds, daubing him with streaks of gold while his mother clanged pots in the kitchen.

Before supper Alex insisted on going for a walk to get some sunshine and air. As though he were a little boy, his mother and I bundled him up in clothing suitable for mid-winter. It was a mild day in April, but he feels the cold so. We got out just in time to stroll through the pale light of the early evening sun. Arm in arm, the three of us crept along toward the dépanneur. Thinking of how Alex loved his country and its beauty, I said, "It's so Canadian, this light." Until then he'd been vacantly concentrating on the sand-strewn sidewalk before him, but he looked up, as though startled, and contemplated the fronts of the houses glowing from the amber light. "Yes." Behind him the sky loomed electric blue.

As we approached his house, Alex remembered that the outdoor light was burnt out. Inside, he asked for the plastic bag full of light bulbs and pawed through it until he found a sixty. I cleaned the globe, replaced the bulb and switched the fixture on. I see it glowing brightly now as I write.

The concept of light seemed to come up everywhere today. It reminds me of that 'white light' that people say they see when they die and come back, the one I'd glimpsed in guided meditations. It occurs to me that part of my job is to help him toward that light. I pray I'm doing this right.

Wednesday, May 1
Tonight, like every night since Maretta returned to Toronto, a single lamp glows in the living room. Just now, another one came on in the front bedroom above. Timers, like ghosts, turn them on every evening and someone comes each day to take in the mail, water the plants and occasionally alter the lighting sequence. A large sign fixed to the brick reads 'For Sale' in French.

Alex had been growing steadily weaker since his return. It came down to a choice between the disease and the short-term cure, and he chose to stop the chemo. Though he needed help just to get to the bathroom, no one but Maretta felt he should be in the hospital. "I want to stay home, where my friends can come," he said. But the strain on his mother and his Buddies was really too much and patience was wearing thin.

Last Sunday was very wet and windy. Inside the hospital room the rector stood smiling on the opposite side of the bed, and Maretta sat in the corner, chatting with Alex and the priest. The side I was on was crowded with Alex's friends, mostly men dressed up in suits. We were all ready for the Holy Communion Alex had asked for.

The tube that yesterday was running to Alex's nose had been replaced by a mask. His breathing was laboured but he was conscious and aware. I held a prayer book for him as he read aloud with the rest of us. Alex shared his last Eucharist with those who wished to do so and then the rector anointed him with oil. Toward the end I asked him if he wanted a hymn. Yes, he nodded. Would he like 'Holy, Holy, Holy' (his favourite)? Yes, he nodded again. He sang all four verses with as much vigour as he could raise. When it ended, we gathered outside his room to let him rest, and voices previously known only over the telephone were matched with faces and bodies.

The storm worsened throughout the rest of the day and into the evening. At ten the phone rang. "The hospital called and they think I should go back. Could you drive me?" Maretta's small voice implored.

"Sure."

"But I just got back from there and I'm soaking wet. I need to change first."

"Turn on a light downstairs when you're ready. I'll see it from here."

The wind rocked my little car as we sped through the wet night and climbed the mountain to the hospital. Mercifully, the lights were green and the streets empty of traffic. I didn't know what to say. All I could do was listen, though she didn't say much. In a small, thin voice she said, "I didn't expect this to happen so quickly."

After we parked the car, we tried to skirt the lakes that had formed in the hospital parking lot. The rain lashed at us; umbrellas were useless. I thought of all that Maretta had already been through this day, how tough even the weather was treating her, just so she could see her son die.

The hospital guard, when I told him we had been summoned, nodded us on. We waited for the elevator in silence. What can you say to a mother who's about to lose her only child? She had already buried a husband who was ill most of his life, and had to support her small family. She had taken care of two other family members until their deaths. I asked her if any relatives were coming from Toronto for her. Panic seized her features with the awareness that the only one left was six floors above and about to leave her.

We found Alex shaking, convulsing, eyes rolling back into his head. The nurse gave him morphine. As Maretta held his hand and spoke to him softly, the drug quickly took effect and Alex became calm. Soon all he did was breathe deeply as we watched. This tiny, gentle woman held onto his hand—watching, incredulous, wishing she could stop it, knowing she couldn't. Alex breathed at longer and longer intervals. Within a half hour of our arrival, there was an endless break through which we kept watch, wondering if there'd be more. Even when the nurse checked his pulse, even when the doctor did it.

Alex had gone. The exact moment had been imperceptible, at least to me. It was all orderly, planned almost, as though he knew exactly what he was doing. His body had been failing him, he received his final Communion that day as he had requested, and he died with his hand in his mother's. Then he moved on, confident he was ready.

For a few moments afterward, it was just Maretta and me, her eyes fixed on her son, mine on them both. She looked like an old James Thurber lady, with her little-old-lady hat still on her head as she peered at him, not wanting to believe, but knowing all too well. We sat there, waiting for the official word, until a family friend arrived to meet Maretta. I stood up so he could sit next to her. As he took her hand, Maretta turned to me and said in a still voice, "Thank you very much, John. You can go home now."

I knew I couldn't sleep right away after that, so I went out to a bar I like. Luckily I ran into a friend who was a priest from another church.

"Where are you coming from?" asked David.

"I just saw somebody die."

Before him I unbound the night's events: the utter sadness of a mother's loss; the steadfastness of Alex's last steps; my perplexity at the dual experience of death and rebirth, and the miracle of the parting of soul and body.

Somehow this friend swept it all back into this world for me. It no longer felt bizarre, alien or unreal. I had been present at the mystical transition of a soul from this mortal paradox of joy and suffering to a mystery beyond. I'm glad David was there. Otherwise, I might have gone on to live as though it had all been a dream that had nothing to do with this world or this dance floor with its everyday, pleasure-seeking lives.

I left him to have a dance for Alex. As I danced, I thought of one of the hymns he'd requested for his memorial service, Lord of the Dance, about dancing through it all: love, pain, fear, crucifixion. And as I danced, the music pounding through my body, I felt intensely aware of my feet and the simple joy they were giving me. I was tremendously aware and appreciative of having a live, healthy body to dance with.

Friday, November 1

The house was finally sold last month and the new people moved in: two guys, just friends I think, friends of one of the brothers next door. The façade looks just as dull as before, with all the blinds still the same. When the new inhabitants want to close the one that's stuck, they run their fingers up across the vanes as though playing an arpeggio. I saw one of their visitors use the grab-handle as he sprinted up the steps and through the open door.

As I look at the house in its umpteenth new life, I realize that, during the whole time that the place was empty this past summer, as its timer-ghosts operated the lights, and the geraniums grew bigger and pushed out more red blooms, I never once saw a passer-by glance into the living room windows. Maybe they only looked in before because they sensed something warm and magical happening there.

The geraniums left the house with the rest of Alex's furnishings. On a few occasions, I've seen a calico cat on the window ledge. This seems so contrived that I almost wonder if I've imagined it, just to make the story come full circle, to show that it has ended and that the house is now just like any other, death no longer within.

I wonder if this is a happy ending.

Wayne Yung Brad: December 19, 1992

Grazing through electric blue fields of late-night television, Jack's eyes glowed neon. Soft, milky flesh sagged into the beige velour of the recliner. In the cool aurora, his briefs glowed like polar ice, and fine blond hair sparked like static on his skin. His palm cradled a sleek remote control, the thumb pulsing against the buttons with a movement as subtle as the dreaming eye.

The phone began to purr, like a kitten. Absently, his fingers rooted under an inky nest of newspapers.

"Hello?"

"Hi. Is this Jack?"

"Yeah." His eyes remained locked on the far blue horizon.

"This is Brad Wong, from Calgary. I replied to your ad."

"Uh-huh."

"I've just arrived at the bus depot." There was a hiss of static. "In the ad you said I could spend the night. I was wondering—is the offer still open?"

With a blink, his vision snapped back from the distance. "Sure," he said. They arranged to meet in twenty minutes, at a nearby hotel lobby.

He turned off the television and drifted through the velvet darkness of the hallway. Like a sleepwalker, he tracked his footprints by memory.

The bedroom was dim with starlight. His fingers traced the carved relief of the wardrobe and skimmed across the mirror, seeking the door seam. The double doors opened with a gentle push. By touch, he chose a pair of faded jeans, hollowed to the contours of his flesh. Over his pale, icy skin, he pulled a dark cableknit sweater, bearded and torn with age.

Pale blue digital numbers floated in the dim recesses of the top shelf of the wardrobe. Reaching overhead, his fingers scanned the braille of machine buttons. He pressed one, and a tiny pair of eyes flared in the shadows above, one red, one green. Satisfied, he closed the doors.

The hotel lobby was worn red carpets and polished wood. Brad sat in a tapestried armchair, his face suffused with the glow from a yellow silk lampshade. A warm pool of light spread beneath the lamp's fringes and fell on the plaid carpetbag that slouched by his knee.

"Hi," said Jack, offering a handshake. Brad's long, fine fingers were wet and cold, but the grip was surprisingly strong. "Have you waited long?"

"No."

"Good." Jack hefted the bag and slung it over his shoulder. "Then let's go."

He led Brad through the cold tunnel of streetlight, overarched by naked, iron trees and concrete towers. Snow fell, lightly. Quietly, they spoke of minor things, and soon were at the apartment.

"Can I make you some coffee?"

"Tea."

Jack filled a copper kettle and set it on the stove. The boy crossed the sand-coloured linoleum to warm his fingers by the burner. Stepping behind him, Jack began massaging his shoulders and felt them sag with relief. "So tense," he said.

"Long bus ride. Sixteen hours."

His hands circled around Brad's chest, drawing him close. "How old are you?"

"Twenty-one."

"You look much younger."

Brad shrugged. Jack rested his chin on a shoulder as the two men kept vigil over the steady blue flames under the kettle.

"You must be tired. Why don't we sit in the living room?" He led Brad to the floral beige chesterfield. They sank into its padded cushions, sliding on the sleek velour. Casually, Jack draped one arm around Brad's shoulders and stretched his legs onto the glass-topped coffee table.

Brad's eyes studied the room, avoiding Jack's steady gaze. After a moment, the man gently kissed his neck. He shrugged with surprise and pushed Jack away.

"You don't waste any time, do you?"

"I'm overcome by your beauty."

Brad smiled, unbelieving. The kettle whistled and Jack rose.

When he returned with the tea, he found Brad by the tall pine bookcases, head cocked, reading the titles.

"You like to travel?"

"Yes," replied Jack.

"You've been to all these places?" Fingers fanned the titles.

"No. But I like to read about them." He poured the tea. "How do you take it?"

"Black." He accepted the bone china cup. It clattered slightly on the saucer, then was still.

"You travel much?"

"No," replied Brad. "But I want to." He turned away, and sipped his tea. "I like it here, in Vancouver. There are men, like you . . . who like Chinese."

"But not in Calgary?"

"No. They like cowboys with moustaches and big muscles." With a wry smile, he produced the small hard lump of his bicep. Impulsively, Jack bent to kiss it. He laid his hands on Brad's waist, and then sank his lips into the boy's neck.

Abruptly, Brad pulled back. "Not so fast, okay?"

Jack shrugged. He turned and gestured at the television. "Do you want to watch some movies?"

"What do you have?"

"I've got some porn: some straight, some gay."

Brad was silent. "Do you have any with Asians?"

"Just one. From Thailand. It's kinda boring though."

He paused. "I want to see it."

Jack turned on the television and turned off the lamp. The movie opened in a men's shower. One young man knelt before another, water dripping down his brown chest. There were no voices, just sixties rock guitar.

"I've never seen Orientals have sex before."

"It's hard to find."

"Does this one have any white guys?"

"No."

After a few minutes, Brad picked up the remote and the sex abruptly sped by. The quiet darkness was warmed by the hum of the spinning motor.

"What is it you like about Chinese guys?"

Jack thought for a moment. "The skin," he said. "It's so smooth and golden. And I like black hair, and brown eyes." He ran his fingers through Brad's hair.

"I'm not attracted to Oriental men."

"No? Why not?"

"I don't know. I've only been with white men."

The video shifted to three young men in a daisy chain.

"Do you sleep with white men too?" Brad asked.

"Not often." He reached over and took a sip from Brad's teacup. "I don't like them. Too heavy and crude, especially in the face. I sleep with them only if they're young and thin and absolutely hairless." He stroked Brad's cheek. "Even then, I don't like pale skin, blond hair, blue eyes."

Brad turned to face him. "Even yourself? You're blond, blue-eyed."

"Me?" He considered this for a moment, as the boys on screen sped to orgasm. "I've never really thought about it before. Men have always been attracted to me." He turned to Brad with a sly grin. "Especially Asians. They like blonds."

Brad smiled. "But you don't."

Jack twisted the black hair with his fingers. "I don't mind being blond. But I like sleeping with men who have black hair. Maybe it's like salt and pepper shakers." He kissed the boy on the cheek, gently. "I'm happy with who I am. I just happen to prefer making love with Orientals. And, hopefully, they like to make love with me."

Brad lowered his eyes and smiled before turning back to the television. Two boys were necking in the back room of a grocery store.

"When I was a kid, I always wanted to be white."

Jack kissed his ear. "I'm glad you're not." He nuzzled his nose into the soft neck, breathing in the moist heat. "I like the way you smell. Like Chinese food."

Brad laughed. "You'll be hungry again in an hour."

"I hope so."

Abruptly, the video cut to snow.

Jack stood and turned off the TV. In the darkness, Brad saw Jack's silent black silhouette stretch and yawn against the deep indigo sky.

"How about a massage?" asked the man quietly.

"Okay."

He offered his hand and led Brad down the darkened hallway.

The wide bed was wrinkled with white cotton sheets. As they undressed, Jack admired the graceful arc of Brad's figure. The boy stretched out on his stomach across the bed, and Jack crouched naked astride the boy's thighs. His warm, dry hands kneaded Brad's shoulders firmly. His strokes were deep, slow, and deliberate. Gently, he traced the length of the spine with his fingertips, each pass punctuated with a warm, dry kiss, one below the other, in a path that led to the crack.

Jack inched his body onto the calves. Stretching like a cat, he milked the buns, then spread them, and nuzzled his nose and tongue deep into the groove. Brad moaned. His hips bucked as his spine arched. The pelvis ground slowly into Jack's face. He reached under and gripped the hard, stiff snake that lay there.

He crawled up Brad's body and embraced him. His lips sought a kiss, but the boy turned his face and offered his neck. Jack's sandpaper cheeks rasped against the tender flesh.

His kisses drifted down the boy's body as the torso squirmed and writhed like a snared eel. Jack took the cock in his mouth, but Brad withdrew. His hands pulled at the man's scalp, mashing his cheeks into the inner thighs.

Jack nudged the boy's head down to his own crotch, but the mouth would not cross the edge of his bush. The lips dragged across his belly, with no trace of tongue. Finally Jack took the slender fingers and wrapped them around his cock. Cupping the boy's hand with his own, he brought his fever to peak, then relief.

The boy lay still under the weight of the other man's semen. After a moment, Jack moved to take the boy's rocky erection into his own mouth.

"No." Brad gripped Jack's hair, restraining him like a cat by its tail. "Not tonight."

Jack looked into the boy's hooded almond eyes, shadowed by the moonlight, and could read nothing there. He shrugged.

They showered together, Jack's lathered hands slithering down the smooth yellow body. Brad finished first, and Jack followed a few minutes later. When he returned to the bedroom, the boy was already asleep. He slid under the sheets and spooned Brad from behind, wrapping his arm around so that his palm lay over the sleeping heart.

The next night, they went to a nightclub. Amidst the thunderous glamour and steaming smoke, Brad was silent, watchful as a child at the edge of a playground. Friends came to greet Jack but faded away as Jack's mute shadow became apparent. He made no mention of Brad, no introductions. They barely acknowledged each other's presence but, even without contact, their connection was palpable, an invisible string that connected hand to hand, foot to foot.

Without a word, Brad pulled Jack into the sweaty crush of hard bodies. He raised his arms and they swayed overhead like golden cobras while his narrow waist writhed and twisted under the circle of Jack's grip. A musky sweat rose from the boy's flesh. Jack felt the distant eyes watching, dark with smoky envy. Lost in dance, dreaming, the boy was blind to cruising glances.

That night their sex was harder, stronger, driven by a rhythm deeper and more urgent than their beating hearts. Jack stared into the hooded depths of Brad's eyes with a silent appeal. With a nod, the boy assented. As he watched the latex being rolled down the man's shaft, his fingers stroked the thighs, idly, as if waiting for the bass beat to resume.

The thrusts began slow and deep, and the boy sounded each new depth with a moan. Jack's rhythm became more and more jerky until, with a silent shout, his body exploded and collapsed. His sphincter clenched with every pulse of the boy's heart and Jack twitched with the memory of agony. After an eternal silence, he kissed Brad's neck, and cheek, and lips.

"I love you," he said.

Brad smiled and pulled Jack's torso down onto his own so that his face was hidden.

Hours later he woke to find Jack slouched against a pillow, a cigarette in his fingers, a can of beer on his belly. A television sat in the corner like Buddha, alive but silent. Brad's shoulder nestled into Jack's armpit, his cheek against the heart. It was enough to touch, and to hear the hidden drum that pulsed under the thin layer of moist heat.

Brad's attention shifted to the tall dark wardrobe that faced the foot of the bed. The doors were ornate with carved relief. Two large mirrors, half-circles, were set in the centre. The glass reflected snowy peaks of cotton sheets from which rose two breathing mountains, the raven-peaked one leaning against the fair.

"It's bad luck to put a mirror in front of a marriage bed," said Brad.

"Who says?"

"My grandmother. She says that love is reversed in the mirror, and comes back as hate."

Jack took a long drag on his cigarette and held it. As he spoke again, his words appeared smoke-coloured.

"Do you love me?"

Brad paused. "No."

"Good. Then there's nothing to worry about."

The next evening, Brad returned at dusk. Jack welcomed him with a kiss and led him to the candle-lit dining room. Two solemn flames were matched by their reflections, suspended in the mellow depths of the lacquered mahogany table.

They shared a salad of butter lettuce and nasturtium, with a slender bottle of herbal wine. Jack fed asparagus to Brad with his fingers before unwrapping the salmon baked in foil. Afterwards, there was a pot of chrysanthemum tea with white petals floating on the amber liquid.

That evening, they made love quietly and tenderly. They spoke little and, afterwards, Brad showered alone. When they parted, he didn't offer his phone number, and Jack didn't ask. His bus left at midnight.

Weeks later, Jack was at home, alone. In the bedroom, he undressed slowly and deliberately by the cool light of the streetlight below and the starlight above. From the wardrobe, he took a new pair of briefs, crisp and white inside the crackling cellophane. He tore the package open and breathed in its clean fragrance, smothering his muzzle in the crisp cotton. He slid it up over his ankles, dragging it over his thighs to finally stretch and cling to his pelvis.

Overhead, in the darkness of the top shelf, his fingertips skimmed across the spines of videotapes. Groping blindly, his finger found the last tape and retrieved it. On the matte plastic was a stark white label: BRAD: DECEMBER 19, 1992.

As if sleepwalking, he drifted through the darkened hallway to the living room. With a touch of his fingertip, the video machine awoke, and the television screen ignited with a crackle of static. The padded velour recliner sagged as it received the weight of his milky flesh. As the video played, Jack's eyes focused on the horizon far beyond the ghostly image of two bodies making love in a starlit field of white cotton sheets.

Somewhere, under a light cover of newspaper, the phone softly purred.

Writers' Statements

Joshua Berkovič

I've always loved 'culture,' both for its inherent beauty and for its embodiment of the society represented. As a gay man, I have always found it paradoxical that, so often, homosexual artists have made great contributions to Western culture, yet these artists are usually not accepted as members of that society.

Does society need to develop a 'fringe' in order to define its parameters? Does the artist need to be on the 'outside' in order to chronicle society, or is the artist's perspective distorted by a focus on 'difference'? Does the ability of homosexuals to 'pass' in society give an element of irony and ambiguity to their work that reflects more upon the artist than the society chronicled?

I myself could 'pass' as straight while writing. I was taught in school to admire in awe the tragic men: the Hamlets, Lears, and Agamemnons; I was trained by society to understand that men do not respond emotionally to art—hell, we're not supposed to go to the opera, read poetry, or see "Dark Victory" unless it's to feel up the girl we're consoling; and if a man's gonna write, he should write like a man, a Hemingway: ballsy characters, potent conflicts, seminal language, and a hard-driving linear plot that climaxes quickly then concludes, leaving the reader still aroused. (Looking back, we realize that the climaxes were never as explosive as the jacket covers promised.) 'Real men' read and write tragedies about other 'real men'. Everything else is just 'women's stuff'.

I like the 'women's stuff', the melodramas, because they also represent a gay aesthetic. Melodrama is a shared and understood voice of the less powerful in society, those without the privilege required to achieve heroic status.

I prefer the bravery of everyday gay life. It is harder to act bravely when one is conscious of the difficulties, the inequalities of daily living, the constant oppression. I'm interested in the strategies and energies needed in order to wake up every day knowing someone is living with AIDS, may be bashed, has come out at work, is in love with the person next door but isn't sure if s/he is a) homosexual, b) available, c) into Johnny Mathis.

In tragedy, the hero challenges the natural/social order, and loses. Melodrama may have victims rather than heroes, but it is also about people who resist, who fight, who demand change. Often they suffer, but sometimes they also win. Melodrama inspires, while tragedy only provides vicarious nobility. Tragedy makes us think, "I'll never be so great, nor suffer so much"; melodrama makes us respond, "I've suffered that much, I can be that great. Into the streets, girlfriend!"

As gays and lesbians, we have had to (re)define life, create our own society while struggling within the larger one, try to make sense of it all and, hopefully, emerge with a proud identity, commitment and humour.

The characters in my stories go through the same shit as you and me, and are as melodramatic as you and me, so don't read my work expecting a classic hero to appear. I've never met a classic hero. I do, however, know some great fags and dykes whose stories I'd like to tell.

I'm interested in recounting the rituals we've developed to celebrate our culture: the coming-out stories, the gay pride marches, the memorial quilts, the coded drag, the reclaiming of our history.

No longer are we just chronicling the society from which we are excluded. Now our stories are also about our lives, our cultural renaissance, our pride.

Stuart Blackley

Three years ago I began working on a writing project that I hoped would permit gay men to speak for themselves in the homophobic, AIDS-besieged eighties. It seemed such a simple project at the time. I wanted to gather an anthology of writing in various genres and find a progressive publisher who would consent to publish the project. Now, three years later, the project will never be finished. I offer my experience as an explanation to those who have been involved and maybe as a lesson to others who would attempt any similar action.

This is how Gerry began his letter to me four years ago, and I think it will always disturb me. What does it mean to write and, more to the point, get published as an openly gay man now, in the still-homophobic, still-AIDS-besieged nineties? Gerry's anthology did not fall apart because he didn't receive enough worthy submissions, or because he failed to find a progressive publisher, or even because Gerry resigned as editor. In the end, as Gerry wrote, "I was seized by panic about the possible homophobia that such a book would generate and I phoned the publisher to cancel the project." In the end, Gerry tore up the poetry and short stories of the contributors.

In Gerry's last letter to me, written during his mental breakdown and perhaps, as he wanted his readers to believe, from the beginning of his recovery, Gerry suggested a number of motives for his act: "Poisoned by self-doubt and not trusting anyone around me, I made the decision to withdraw the manuscript." Gerry's letter is filled with both paranoia and concern about the homophobic reprisals that the publication of such an anthology might create. Are they separable, the real from the delusional homophobia? Before we dismiss Gerry's bleak lesson, I think it's worth considering the aspects peculiar to what we might call gay fiction in Canada.

First of all, where is it? Nothing until Scott Symon's *Place d'Armes* in 1967, and his *Helmet of Flesh* two decades later. In the eighties, Scott Watson's *Platonic Love* and David Watmough's Davey Bryant series. Then, in the last three years, Peter McGehee's *Boys like Us* and *Sweetheart*, Patrick Roscoe's *Birthmarks* and *God's Peculiar Care*, Stan Persky's *Buddy's*, and Dennis Denisoff's *Dog Years*. This year,

Doug Wilson's posthumous novel, *Labour of Love*, will complete the trilogy his lover Peter McGehee had projected. Both are now dead from AIDS. A handful of dustjackets.

This scarcity of openly gay fiction is unsurprising, since fiction published in Canada is so overwhelmingly traditional in forms and values. B.W. Powe identifies this as the influence of the Academy of CanLit, where virtually every author elevated to the canon has been a teacher, frequently of the other canonical CanLit authors: "With a few notable exceptions, the university poets and authors, writers-in-residence and creative composition teachers have created a literature of narcissistic self-contemplation and mandarin staleness, of conventionality and acceptance."

It is only because gay writing has become a booming business in the U.S., and been promoted by huge publishers like Penguin and Random House, that a tiny leakage of Canadian works can take advantage of that overflow. The core market of gay writers and their audience is a real achievement in difficult times, and now very attractive as a source of potential profit. This readership is as close to a real sense of community as exists in our maelstrom of deviancy, the notwithstanding clause being, always, the gravitational pull of AIDS.

Within Canada, however, access to any gay and lesbian writing has been systematically blocked by our government for as long as bookstores have provided it. Glad Day Bookshop in Toronto has been involved in debilitating and expensive lawsuits for over a decade. For years, the seizure of books and magazines in Canadian gay and lesbian stores has been a commonplace, daily experience, but in the last year, for the first time, our 'suspect' material has been detained from more mainstream stores such as Toronto's Pages and the Toronto Women's Bookstore. Previously unheard-of attacks on individual writers have materialized as well. Robin Metcalfe in Halifax had his own books, sent from his American publisher, stopped at the Canadian border, and Robert Lally in Edmonton faced the police in his home, where they removed the only available manuscript of his unpublished novel. The official apology coincided with the news that his book had been destroyed.

The Crown, in its most recent foray against Little Sister's Book and Art Emporium in Vancouver, attempted to deny the store's owners of even the right to present their case, and accused them of trying to "create an enclave for homosexual pornography of unknowable parameters." As visionary and sexy as that sounds, the store's goal is much more banal—to continue to operate, and to connect gay and lesbian writers and readers. The latest prediction is that their day in court will finally arrive about the time *Queeries* is launched and, in case anyone is worried that this statement is too time-specific, I can assure you that the harassment will not cease with either the victory or failure of this particular court case, and that these battles will continue into the numerous editions of this book, and well after it is out of print.

Gerry eventually moved to Vancouver, and had what seemed a pretty normal life: studying at UBC, working at Little Sister's. I was a regular customer there, and we would chat about books. I only knew him as Gerry, someone I had never met previously. One day he invited me out to lunch and, as we sat down, he asked, "Do you know who I am? I'm the one who wrote you that letter." But he did not resemble the person I had constructed in my mind years before. During that lunch, we talked enthusiastically about the project, happy even at how close it had come to being pulled off, how much support it had turned out there had been, as if all those stories and poems from across Canada were now momentarily reassembled, and the torn pieces of paper made whole. Within a year, after a close friend that Gerry had helped through his final illness had died of AIDS, Gerry jumped off the Lion's Gate Bridge, and was gone.

It has been done differently now, and in what ways, we will never know, for there is only silence where so many of us imagined a book.

Speak its name.

Gordon Bradley

I started keeping a journal in Toronto in 1987 to stop from going insane. I was living in a boarding house, in a walk-in closet, with eight zebra finches and a dwarf rabbit named Coco. In that city, then, I was on the margins: living on St. Clair West, *really* West—almost Calgary.

When I couldn't stand the whining of my journal any longer, I started writing fiction. At first I could only write about lounge singers, detectives and bitchy old ladies—ridiculously glamourous people strolling through a carwash of overwrought prose. (My first-year English prof said: yes, but at least it's consistently overwrought.) I felt my prose was in some secret code, and I wondered about its origins. I entered a story in a Halifax newspaper's short story contest and, to my humble shock, won first runner-up. For me, the literary equivalent of 'coming out' was starting to believe that my voice had some authority.

I don't know how I feel now about margins. 'Outside' is a great place to be, if you can speak from where you live and occupy the space proudly. Outside, you write the 'not-straight'—you're 'Other.' Why always self-definition in negatives?

I didn't initially write much about gay men. I had an advanced case of Virginia Woolf's 'you can't say that' syndrome. I thought I would 'weird people out,' that it was like airing dirty laundry. Woolf uses the illustration of a girl fishing in a lake, and every time the hook hit something submerged, murky, dark or interesting, she hauled the line back up. Reader, I was that fisher-girl.

This is certainly not to say that I'm now one hundred percent together and outspoken. My mother's on the phone talking about 'empowerment,' which is nice work if you can get it. I happen to write a lot more now about gay people. I don't know what happened, but I know it's slow and ongoing. Two years ago, I would have told you that I'm not political. I was wrong, but I insisted on it. I still feel that fiction has, at its heart, only its own agenda. But fiction starts in someone's head before it moves onto paper. I'm dual-minded about this.

"Brennan's Eyes" is about an almost-universal gay experience: accidentally/

purposely falling in lust/love with a straight/unavailable man. It's a story about stories—every reader becomes Brennan as their eyes 'cross (the) text, left to right and slowly down.' It's also about 1,993 words.

I'm unqualified to speak about gay fiction at large, but I hope *my* gay fiction is banal and lyrical, strange and unsettling, lush and vulgar, fragmentary, evasive, self-conscious. It should start with tart citrus and fruity top-notes, and evaporate down to mellow spices and musk. And it should undermine itself constantly.

Lawrence Braithwaite

In a culture of consumption, the demand for reproduction is necessitated w/ a fren-
zic immediacy that renders someone/thing a commodity. The influence of media
technology operates when a constructed environment, such as the gay community,
submits the inhabitants to search and accept any form of well-marketed/madison
avenue identity:

gay meta pornstar Marky Mark,
nazi skinhead drag,
drag,
orientalism,
negrophilia,
herb ritts,
fascist leather imagery. . . .

The result is the commodification of all aspects of existence—sex, politics and culture.

It is therefore reasonable to say that the further marginalized cultures who choose
to dwell w/in a constructed marginalized community are sought out to be repro-
duced and represented, thus becoming a commodity and being subjugated by the
ruling factions—who are inevitably white men, whose sole disenfranchisement is
often homosexuality. The sexual preference, viewed as an unacceptable form of
expression, serves as the only block to the white man's full entrance into the privi-
leged class. A rational desire amongst white gay males is to seek entrance into this
mainstream arena and cease being counted among the number of blacks and
women. This creates both a power dynamic which remains unquestioned and an
increasing danger to the self-actualization of a decentred people, causing the being
to come to the fore and the becoming to be sent back into the shadows of repro-
duced puppetry = product/user/imitator.

A control over these understood lower classes is necessary, therefore, in order to maintain an image of the white gay male which would, eventually, be acceptable to the status quo. Within the homosexual arena, the subjugation of sexuality and gender is imposed through youth, race, ethnicity and the misogyny inherent in drag, in replacement of the heterosexual male subjugation of the same.

The running theme in, and influence on, my stories is the police murder of, and violence towards, blacks in Montréal, namely, Marcelus Francois. My stories are designed to explore these power dynamics—namely, gay/Queer culture and sexuality as a form of colonization—community as stratification, especially when it involves interracial relationships. The text's contruction is postliterate in layout and sentence structure: paratactic—clipped and short to allow for immediacy of access to information, and visual—to emphasize the hyperreal. Literature can be as addictive and skewed as television; therefore, hypertext is used as a dialectic on stream of consciousness—even in fake thought there are intrusions from the surrounding media.

Daniel Cunningham

People often ask me why I write the things that I do. The questions vary, but usually fall into two categories. The first involves my characters—why are they gay? The second, my stories themselves—why are they so violent? Questions concerning the first issue, usually asked by straight people, are easily answered. I write about gay men because I am a gay man. Enough said. Gay men and lesbians often ask me questions about the violence, and these questions are much more difficult to answer.

Why *are* my stories so violent?

Not because my life has been touched by violence. I had a very ordinary middle-class childhood, filled with typical youthful experiences. My first forays into sexuality were all positive and I had no problem accepting the fact that I was a gay teenager. When I started entering into relationships with other men, my family accepted my lovers in the same manner that they would accept my brother's wife or my sister's husband. Indeed, when Arthur, my lover of eleven years, was dying of AIDS, my mother took care of him. It was a kind and gracious gesture that gave me peace of mind and to which I am deeply indebted. Like my family, my straight friends and my employers have no problems dealing with my homosexuality. In short, I have surrounded myself with understanding and compassionate people who accept my lifestyle. Why, then, the violence?

Although I believe that individuals may be accepting of homosexuality, I also believe that society as a whole is not. This lack of acceptance pervades every aspect of life and, as a result, homosexuals are treated in a manner that would be totally unacceptable if they were heterosexual. Consequently, we end up with a federal Minister of Justice, now Prime Minister, redefining the term 'family' to exclude same-sex couples, or a provincial Minister of Culture who equates homosexuality with criminality. Double standards abound, so it becomes acceptable for police to raid public parks that homosexuals frequent, while they turn a blind eye to the heterosexual equivalent just down the block. When the institutions of society sanction such behaviour, it becomes easy for the lunatic fringe to take matters into its own hands and assault, maim or even kill. Although such behaviour is not condoned by society at present, it is not difficult to imagine a future in which it could be. It is far too easy to envision a world in which everything that we have achieved could be taken away from us because we are members of a minority. Such things have happened too often in human history; they could just as easily happen again. Given that such thoughts possess me, is it any wonder that my stories are violent?

At present, I have a bet going with another writer who challenged me to write a love story—something that does not contain violence. Failure to meet this challenge will result in my taking her out to dinner at the restaurant of her choice. I have a feeling I'm going to lose this bet. Sometimes, though, I wish I could win it.

David Dakar

I'm not an angry young writer, but I can and do get angry over mainstream gay writing. I mean the 'big' books, the well-known stories, the commercial novels from commercial publishers that could easily be transposed into pulp romances, mysteries and other popular genres, by simply changing the gays to straights, the sodomy to coitus, and the Noguchi lamps to Ethan Allen straight-back chairs. Actually, what I'm really trying to say is that I don't like reading David Leavitt. And I don't like to come out and say such a thing, because I don't want to alienate all the literate queers who might otherwise read my writing—but it's the truth, and it's better to tell the truth here and save the lies for characters in novels stuck in awkward situations. I don't want to alienate literate queers because literacy is a good thing (right?) and so many literate queers love David Leavitt—he makes them cry, for godsakes. He moves literate people. The overwhelming desirability and intangibility of Cocteau's Dargelos in *Les Enfants Terribles* isn't gay enough for gay readers—whereas David Leavitt writes about really, really gay people leading really, really gay lives; likewise, the scrappy, unsentimental hustler in Luis Zapata's brilliant *Adonis Garcia* isn't artificial enough: the story is too concerned with basic survival and a world outside of the urban, politically correct domesticity of gay life in domestic, urban gay novels. And Zapata writes with a surprising lack of punctuation.

David Leavitt's writing is like the porridge in the middle, it's not too hot and it's not too cold, and I don't ever want to write like the porridge in the middle. When I say I don't like David Leavitt you may think this is an entirely personal sentiment. It's not. What really gets me about his prose is that it reads like a really tidy apartment right after a cleaning person has come in and made it even tidier. All the gay characters live immaculate, respectable, intellectually stimulating, concise urban lives. They're gay, they've come out, they grapple with modern ills, they find out their parents are gay, they grapple with gay parents, they get VD, they grapple with gay doctors, they're culturally elite, they grapple with homoerotic art in the Met, and so on. It makes for good reading, I know, but by trying so hard to represent gay life Leavitt seems, to me, so removed from queer life. Has he ever had anal sex (I daren't say sodomy)? Did he ever have it in the pre-condom days when you had to shit out come afterwards? Has he ever been in a bar at three a.m. when they turn the fluorescent lights on? What would he look like if he was, who would he be with, and how much would he have had to drink? Has he ever had a passionate affair with someone who didn't know who Jacques Derrida was? All I'm saying is that so much gay writing is about precise gay statements, it's based on the literary clout that is inherent in 'technical' accomplishment, and it thrives on rising above the idiosyncrasies and eccentricities of everyday life. Nowhere is this more blatant than in the fabricated, idyllic relationships characteristic of the wave of mainstream gay 'classics' that swamped us in the eighties, like the 'serious love' in *The Lost Language of Cranes* or Andrew Holleran's *Dancer from the Dance*. If only Leavitt's writing was a little less perfect, I'm sure I could embrace him, quirky ice-cream suit and all; I'm sure, as a child (a queer child), his schoolwork always came back to him with coloured stars on it.

I'm not saying I'm a slob. Well, actually, I am a slob. So my writing is sort of slobby—which is not to imply that I'm a careless writer. I'm certainly as caught up in how words present themselves to the reader as any writer is. (Words and their presentation are my preoccupation.) But at the same time I have no intention, nor make any attempt, to frame gay life in the scope of what I write; rather, that's just the basis of the writing itself. I happen to be queer and so too is the writing. Hopefully, queer writing, in general, as it becomes more relaxed, less pretentious, less 'on about being queer,' will become a little more meaningful in the transition, a little more powerful—as queer writing. As Bernard Herrmann noted, "When the audience says 'the orchestra is playing,' the music director has failed in his purpose." Ideally, I would write music as effective and powerful as Herrmann's magnificent film scores. Unfortunately, piano lessons were a childhood torment. Come to think of it, so were all the English reports returned to me without coloured stars. I guess David Levitt knows something I don't know. Whatever it is, it's unlikely to ever turn up in my writing.

Peter Dickinson

So here I am walking down Burrard Street, on my way to St. Paul's Hospital, listening to my Walkman and lip-synching to "Freedom '90." And I'm thinking, I've been down this road before. Okay, so it was a different road, and a different hospital, in a different city. But the song is the same. And so is the disease that is killing my friend.

In the summer of 1990, George Michael's song had just been released (as its title so obviously indicates). I used to listen to it over and over again on my way to Toronto General to visit Mark. Now, almost three years later, I am re-discovering its cathartic capabilities while visiting David at St. Paul's. Strange, how a seemingly innocuous pop song can act as such a powerful mnemonic device. But then, I was only beginning to understand that dealing with the vicissitudes of memory was a necessary condition of what Maurice Blanchot has called "the inexperience of dying."

A narrative of identity cannot be written evangelically; that is, a narrative of identity cannot exist *a priori*. Rather, it can only be endlessly re-written, making visible in the process all of the discontinuities that compose it. Certainly this is true of any 'gay' narrative. For me, gay experience cannot be narrated in the patriarchal/heterosexist tradition of a unified subject telling a story linearly from beginning to end with no breaks, unidentified fragments or temporal jumps. As such, my writing tends not to be chronological, but rather a non-sequential re-ordering of apparently uncon-nected thoughts, ideas, impressions and events—all of which seem to share the same proximity in time and place—by emotional resonance. Re-membering gay desire, as it were. Some critics might see this as a postmodern rejection of master narratives; others, a post-structuralist deconstruction of my own text. While I do not discount these readings, I also see my writing as part of a post-Stonewall project of developing a queer poetic/politic.

And yet, we are not past the last post. We are not post-AIDS. As a member of 'Generation X-tasy,' that is, as a twentysomething gay male who has never known sex without the association of death, part of my identity has necessarily been informed by AIDS—the pandemic, as well as the social responses to it. During a recent trip to San Francisco, I came across an article by Gregg Taylor, in which he counselled younger queers like myself to practice "naughty pro-active hooliganism" in the name of social advancement and change, to be "contentious rather than content" (*San Francisco Bay Times*, 13.24, 13 August 1992: 36). Sound rhetorical advice for the practice/praxis of queer activism on the ACT UP frontlines. But how does this "naughty pro-active hooliganism" translate into the situation of queer agency at the microcosmic and micropolitical level of my own text? At a theoretical level, it translates into an examination of the collision/elision of different codes of representation and experience that change historically and contextually, as well as an admission that I can only accede to representation through my own historical and experiential context. In other words, I am constantly exploring the degree to which the emergence of a queer poetics within my writing is co-extensive with my subject-positional politics as a gay man.

At a more immediate creative level, however, my desire to be "contentious rather than content" within my fiction manifests itself in a literalization of the personal as political. Thus, while my story "Home" is an attempt, in part, to come to terms with the deaths of two friends from AIDS, it is also a political statement about the neoconservative right's repeated efforts to legislate morality and re-define the concept of family in the wake of AIDS. Gay men's double gesture of disclosure—naming the disease as well as our dis-ease with the murderously slow responses to it from dominant groups—is a measure of the extent to which gay men have channeled personal grief around AIDS into political action.

David died in February, just as I was finishing "Home." As George Michael so aptly put it, in "Waiting for That Day," "my memory serves me far too well." With memory, I have discovered, there is always the look backward (especially into the face of bereavement), but also the gaze forward, into the rarely glimpsed order of things.

Charles Dobie

Besides this story, I've had one poem published, so to say very much about my writing would be pretentious. There are several boxes of floppy disks in my desk holding a jumble of short stories, children's stories, more navy stories, part of a murder mystery—almost nothing ready for publication.

Last year we moved from Toronto to a farm, so gardening, wood cutting, snow clearing and huddling around the stove in winter have all taken precedence over writing. And by the time this is published, we will be in the process of moving again.

With my creative work, as with my approach to most things in life, I basically wing it; when I start to write, I rarely know how the story will end. The characters seem to take control; they usually don't do what I expect them to do or they refuse to do anything interesting at all. There are many literary forms and genres that I would like to explore, but I don't have the patience to fully develop them on paper. This reminds me of the successful writer who was told by a cab driver that writing was so easy that he had written several novels; they were all there in his head and he just hadn't gotten around to typing them out.

So what are these stories in my head? Like the floppy disks in my desk, they are a jumble of everything I've experienced. Once they are written, perhaps I'll find out from their characters what it really means to be queer and what it really means to be a writer.

Peter Dubé
Eccentric Pleasures

I write. I am queer. Although I am certain of both of these statements, I am far from certain that their correctness qualifies my work as 'queer writing,' a category I find both vague and theoretically suspect. Having said this, I am sure that being both a queer and a writer has made me a far different writer than I might have been had I been a straight man, and a far different queer than I might have been had I been less inclined to believe that my text held some interest for any number of people I may never meet.

Looking back, I cannot say for sure whether I started writing or looking at handsome strangers first, or whether it really matters; both of these things have been crucial elements in the person I wanted, and still want, to become. You see, I want to find some of the same things in writing and in queerness, although I'm not sure I can.

Queerness asserts itself through a resolute heterogeneity, a refusal to conform to a totalizing culture. Call it a near-cult of difference, a self-congratulatory excessiveness, a wide-awake artificiality standing at the margins of the canonical and the quotidian. The queer is stubborn, often caustic, impossible to ignore and always fabulous. Queer is the frame of mind that lets us take vegetable shortening out of the kitchen and into the bedroom, *with style*. It demands attention and can be more than a little intimidating. Of course, standing as we do in the middle of spectacular capitalism, this sort of queerness means thinking on your feet. Queer means a perpetual self-reinvention that is not reactionary, but is a creative and active force of imagination and a cultivation of pleasure.

The unapologetic joy in this pleasure is another quality of queerness. Queerness knows that pleasure is important. It values sensation, delight, the moment. And, more importantly, it knows *why* pleasure is important. In the totalizing culture around us, work is valued at the expense of play, and an underlying assumption that these two categories are mutually exclusive is busily operating. Queerness recognizes what couldn't be more apparent, but too often passes unnoticed or uncommented on—that working hard doesn't make you happy. That takes a little something else, a little something different. Queerness recognizes that pleasure is self-justifying, that it doesn't need to be rationalized away or abandoned, because feeling good is a positive thing, and that play is also productive.

The writing I care about operates in some of these ways. My favourite texts, by Oscar Wilde, Jean Genet, Arthur Rimbaud, Angela Carter and so many others, resist the categorization and celebrate their own pleasures. They deny the discourse of common sense, naturalness and realism, preferring instead to play with their position as artifact, happily turning themselves upside-down when it seems like that might be interesting or fun. Their concern is not for cleaning up the complexity of language or representation but for enriching and troubling it. These stories, novels and poems foreground their metaphors and embrace nuance, plurality and ambiguity. They play shamelessly, but never carelessly. They are writings that knew they had to go out into the world and decided they might as well dress for the occasion. It is a literature that cares less about working and more about working it. Whether this makes them 'queer writings' is something I am uncertain about, but it does make them wonderful so, frankly, I can live with the uncertainty. That too is a little queer.

Sky Gilbert

I think it's important to use the incidents surrounding the original non-publication of "Censored" as a starting point for a discussion of my work. As a playwright (which is what I am, as opposed to a novelist or poet, primarily), one's work is constantly in the public spotlight; one is constantly confronted with the 'philistine' reaction. People watch plays, review them, discuss them, attack them, dismiss them, etc. The reaction to queer work (when it is deigned to be reacted to) is often swift and virulent.

But beginning with my experiences with "Censored": I wrote the piece in 1988. The piece was requested by a gay editor (he was an acquaintance of mine, having served on the board of my theatre company). I was asked to submit a short piece for an art magazine. The criterion was that the piece would fit onto one page, for each contributor was to get one page only for their work. I decided, as a queer writer, constantly censored, banned and ignored, to see the page limitation as the censor's rigorous knife, to imagine that my poem/story had been cut off at the edges of the page. I submitted the piece and the editor called me months later. He was tortured. The conversation was obviously a difficult one for him. Should he or should he not include my piece? For me, the question was astounding, not necessarily because I thought so much of my own work, but because I had (and still have) a reputation as a queer writer, a drag queen, an outrageous personality who writes on sexual subjects such as sadomasochism and drag. In other words, I assumed that this man would know what to expect from a 'Sky Gilbert piece.' He claimed that he was going through enormous angst. Then he asked me if he could censor "Censored." I was astounded. I explained to him what I saw as the irony of his request: here was a piece entitled "Censored" which I had 'pre-censored' in order to make a point. The irony was lost on him. The piece was never to appear in the magazine.

All of this should give you an indication of what kind of pressures a queer writer is under, not only from the straight world, but from uptight pillars of his or her own community. Frankly, I would not be a writer or have a body of work if I had not started my own gay/lesbian/innovative theatre company (Buddies in Bad Times Theatre). No producer in Toronto, or Canada for that matter, was ever interested in my work, or ever will be. When I first started the company, I wasn't gay. But even then, when I was writing about Baudelaire, I would take my work to producers and they would ask, "Why do you want to write about this?" Confronted with such a question, an artist is powerless. One can only answer, "Because it is there; because it interests me." I get the same sort of questions today: "Why do you always have to write about gay things? Why do you have to write about sex?" The answer is because 'gay things' and 'sex' are the most important things in my life. Of course, such an answer immediately makes one superficial. Gay art is defined by straight culture as being superficial (all surface, humour, grace and style, no content . . . flamingoes that we are!). Sex is, of course, in the context of straight culture, an inappropriate subject matter for art. Never mind Henry Miller or Kathy Acker or Georges Bataille; it is just . . . not done.

As a gay playwright, I am constantly under pressure to write and direct pieces on straight subjects, non-sexual subjects. When I do so, I am praised and given awards. When I write about my life—about promiscuity, sadomasochism, hookers, a sex-driven life—my work is censored, or what is worse, ignored.

Which brings us to writing about sadomasochism. My only other experience besides "Censored" with writing about S&M came with my play "Ban This Show," a theatrical exploration of the life and work of Robert Mapplethorpe. The play, which ran in Toronto in the fall of 1991, was reviled and ignored. The piece, in fact, moved the critic Ray Conlogue to rhapsodize about how I had refused to deal with the 'violence' of a fist plunging into an asshole, a 'violence' which he, of course, could never forget. Conlogue's review led me to the unmistakable conclusion that human stupidity (racism, sexism, homophobia) is directly related to the limitations of one's human experience. In other words, humans seem naturally inclined to the 'Tower of Babel' syndrome; when cultures collide, there is fear and revulsion, due to lack of experience. I have no doubt that racism comes simply from the fact that many white persons simply know nothing *about* blacks, that misogyny comes from the fact that many men simply know nothing *about* women. So for Conlogue, fisting was an alien experience; for me, it was (though not out of the ordinary) pleasurable. An ode to fisting was not only objectionable to Mr. Conlogue (let's face it, any image of men as submissive is politically threatening to straight men), but he quite simply had no idea how much fun it could be.

Perhaps that's what queer writing is all about—somehow making the foreign experience not quite so remote. That doesn't mean, however, that the queer experience is not often presented in a language or style which is alienating. It does not mean softening the presentation, or making it palatable to 'normal' people. It means simply that 'foreign' subjects (the black experience, the Native experience, the woman's experience, the queer experience) are proper subjects for art. In fact, no experience is improper. Experience is that which we endure; it is neither good nor bad, though it may be pleasurable or not. What is wrong is not to have experienced at all.

George K. Ilsley

I find it difficult to write about my writing. I am too inexperienced to talk about myself. Self-awareness has its limitations in the creative process. Others read my stories and say, "Oh, it is about this," or "Oh, it's about that," and they ask, "Did you intend this or that?"; well, maybe it is and maybe I did but I was not aware of it, and what can this mean? Analysis is one thing and creation another.

I find it equally difficult to speak with sincerity about queer issues and sensibilities—might as well presume to discuss human issues and sensibilities in a few sentences. There is no 'outsider' or 'queer sensibility' when that experience is accepted as part of the natural spectrum of human experience. To talk of 'queer issues' is to construct intellectual or cultural ghettoes, inviting the politics of exclusion. Yet I would be the first to deny that We Are Just Like Them; then again, neither are we all like each other. *Homo*sexual does not mean *homo*geneous. The only safe ground in the shifting sands of the politically correct quagmire is to describe an individual (for each individual must be valid even if she or he appears to be a stereotype) or to confess to a romantic vision.

My romantic vision for queer issues involves historical speculation and the integration of homosexuals into the fabric of society where their 'special gifts' are recognized and appreciated. A model for this would be traditional Native American cultures where 'two-spirited' ones were recognized as gifted and, as such, were often healers, diplomats or shamans. As shamans, the two-spirited ones were able to mediate between the physical and spiritual realms as a parallel to their ability to straddle both male and female experiences.

My novel-in-progress features a dream therapist and his subjects—an attempt to reclaim the (romanticized) traditional spirituality of homosexuals. This novel is a combination of new age mysticism and age-old cynicism and tends to be quite funny. That's the gay male sensibility, if I must have one, a cultural value I share with many of my fellows—humour.

Mark Kershaw

As a gay writer, I perceive and choose to explore alienation not only from dominant heterosexual society, but also from the so-called mainstream of gay culture. Some might call this the plight and desire of the artist: to be removed from his/her culture. Marginalization is partially fulfilled by the marginalized, due to the knowledge that the integration of minority cultures with a dominant culture may be folly born of major compromise. Such is the nature of the contemporary debate on *mainstreaming* and *assimilating* gay lifestyles with those of heterosexual society. Though empathetic with regard to the daily struggle for more than the mere tolerance of homosexuality and lesbianism, I interrogate, in my work, not only how gay sensibility is articulated in, and marginalized by, heterosexual patterns, but also the marginalization and segmentation internal to gay culture itself.

Much of my early poetry and short fiction concerned with gay issues centers around releasing the voice of young gay men, seventeen to twenty-five, who have often been depicted as purely sexual beings burning from a confidence in the apparent invincibility of youth. They are presented as vain boys exploring fully yet blindly the possibilities of getting off, of playing the club scene, and of providing pouty, willing mouths, rock-hard, peach-fuzzed torsos and yearning assholes for the satiation of the over-thirty, often middle-class narrators. This is a generalization, to be sure, but so much serious gay literature does objectify the young male entity to the point of divesting him of any essence other than that of a machine to thwart or accommodate desire.

If we, as gay men in this decade of 'generation hyper-consciousness,' are to understand our relation to the world in general, we must first account for the social dynamics amongst ourselves and create a body of work displaying patterns found in reality. A twenty-year-old man who has lived his entire gay life under the sign of AIDS can devise his own philosophical take on his abuses of, and devotions to, a forty-seven-year-old lover who berates him for his ignorance of life before the plague. Likewise, a seventy-year-old man can articulate that he remains a sensual being beyond the bland structures of youth-rich photo-erotica.

"We Two Boys Together" is part of a series of pieces which provide a variety of perspectives on gay culture, in relation to itself and the outer world, through the personal inventories of several young men. It reflects the poetry of Walt Whitman, particularly the homoerotic verse of the "Calamus" section of *Leaves of Grass*. It also reflects on the organic need for gay men to develop a language that is not only historically conscious, but mythological and open-ended. In this work, Whitman's style and intent are appropriated in an attempt to give both language to the culturally silenced entity of gay cruising trails in urban parks, and a voice to the narrator, who goes beyond the anonymous nature of the trails to reveal not only his own weaknesses and desires in the face of contemporary culture, but also both his need to devise some kind of historical literary continuity for gay men, and his attempt to redefine the clandestine act of public sex as a quasi-mythological and political act.

Jeff Kirby

When I have something to say, I write. It's my voice. For a long time, having a voice for me has literally meant survival. Fortunately, I learned this very young, writing poems about my love for a man named Jesus. He was my first love, although at the time I wasn't able to recognize him as my first gay love. At seventeen, I fell in love at Bible school with a boy named Howard who killed himself because he had no home in the church. If I didn't have a voice, I might have chosen the same.

Mostly I write from my observations of ignorance and injustice—what I, as a gay man, see and experience as the 'obvious'. I like to poke fun, take things to their extreme, get everyone on 'our side' and ridicule those 'others'. More appalling to me than 'accepting liberals' are 'gay assimilationists'. Why try to be in the world when I'm here already? People can either meet me or not. I don't want to do the work for them.

I especially like writing about sex. It sort of puts me on the map. Early on, in my teens, I was so fucking self-loathing, sex was just another put-down. Now, my self revels in man sex. So do my stories.

The best comment I've heard about my work is that I give voice to what most gay men only think about. Isolation is a killer in gay men's lives. It's vital for us to give voice to our selves.

I write my self, taking generous yet truthful liberties, but that's what gay life's about, taking liberties, until it becomes a given for everyone.

Mike Murphy

For me, writing is most importantly a means of communicating, of connecting with other people, of initiating some sort of dialogue.

History. Identity. Subversion. For a number of years I didn't talk much about my history. I had become acutely aware of the limitations of the dominant discourse, of inequalities, of oppression based on definitions of race, class, gender, sex, sexuality, etc. And while often able to transgress such constructs, while working towards *whatever* in my relationships, I found that I, as an individual, felt nonetheless uniquely dis-placed, still too different.

Writing is a context for expression and exploration. As a gay male, it is also a space for subversion. I believe it is necessary to express the spectrum of similarities and differences that comprise our identities in order to break down stereotypes, in order to (un)define ourselves.

I must admit to feeling somewhat strange about having "Something Makes a Difference" included in *Queeries*. Prior to this point in time, I had written strictly poetry; this is how "Something Makes a Difference" began, as a poem. Yet, as I realized that the subject matter I wanted to deal with didn't fit this format, the lines shifted, becoming what is essentially my first piece of prose. In some respects, "Something Makes a Difference" is still very much a poem. It is also perhaps atypical, the most modernist piece of prose I have written. Yet it occupies an important place in the process of my development. Although I didn't realize it at the time, there is much that is autobiographical in this story. (Waving, "Hi-Mom-I'm-on-television!": suffice it to say, I grew up in Windsor/Detroit.)

The works which followed this piece became progressively more personal, poetic and theoretical (perhaps intensely so). Now I find myself again re-evaluating such approaches, wondering where to position them and how explicitly. But where does one draw lines? After all, it isn't a matter of isolating aspects and placing them in certain limiting boxes.

Perhaps all writing is fiction and all fiction part of a process of living. It should be noted then that the work included here necessarily fails to tell us the whole story. This writing is more a means to an end, and my desire to use language to provoke you (reader/writer/lover) to respond.

I believe that as members of queer culture, we should not merely posit ourselves as inside or outside dominant culture; rather, we should be aware of our abilities to blur the lines between (so-called) truths and fictions, to continually question them through our experiences. And so, in whatever ways we can, we must speak out. We must act up.

Christopher Paw

History will record the devastation AIDS wrought on society through the loss of lives and talent. There will be monuments and perhaps legal holidays to mark the memory of Western civilization's greatest and most widespread holocaust. But historians will forget (as historians sometimes do) to record the prejudice, segregation, moral judgments and apathy of that era . . . our era.

But historians document events; the writer pens the social conscience of the times. "5 a Day" is an attempt to explore not the issue, but the impact the issue has on the individual. Despite compassionate rhetoric and political posturing, the individual suffers or enjoys a genuine existence that is the human edge to our present reality. I seek to find that human edge, to put a face to the issues and document the emotions that historians inevitably omit.

I don't believe in a contrived 'positive portrayal' of my subculture. To me, asking the artist to present gay life as 'honourable' or 'decent' by design is paramount to requesting that we lie. Honour and decency are defined by the measure of honesty with which we examine ourselves. And honesty, as the saying goes, is brutal.

For me, honesty means not only extolling the virtues of my culture, but also exploring its pitfalls. I try to provide an alternative viewpoint that the reader may not have previously considered.

In chronicling the gay experience in contemporary Canadian society, I see no reason to pretend that we are a happy, homogeneous family of quirky misfits with the same value systems and morality as the dominant culture. Nor are we immune to the social maladies that afflict that culture. We are, however, responsible to ourselves.

I do identify myself as a gay writer and as such try to examine the sensibilities of my culture. I take great pride in our differences and do not try to 'package' that diversity into a generically palatable format.

So much of the current trend of gay literature focuses on either 'coming out' or 'dying' that I feel we are ignoring the very real aspects of life and living. Living means making mistakes. It means being wrong. It means challenging our own beliefs even while confronting those of others. It is a constant re-evaluation.

Whether writing a *comedie noire* or a darker piece like "5 a Day," I try to tap into the learning experiences that make us who we are. I want my work to reflect the emotional rather than the practical. The gut is a more accurate barometer of self than is rational thought.

Stan Persky
Negative Findings

As far as I can determine, my bisexuality (boys and young men are two of the available for possible sexual preference, aren't they? Or am I simply an *adultophobe?*) only seems to come into play in my writing when I happen to be writing autobiographically about sexual preferences (i.e., it's tautological), or when I'm writing about some form of constraint or freedom that evokes political consequences I've had by virtue of being identified or self-identifying as *homo*, gay, queer, whatever.

I'm playful about my identifications (of which, like almost everyone else, I have many), including the above tongue-in-cheek satirization of what a label might be good for—i.e., I'd rather imagine boys for a second as a separate sex, distinct from males, than enter into any other agreement about how to categorize myself; only if it turns out that someone politically has something against 'homosexuals' (etc.) am I willing to be one. (For example, the original publication of "It's What's Inside," in the Vancouver magazine *Sodomite Invasion*, occasioned a couple of columns by an op-ed writer of the *Vancouver Sun*, who was attempting to get me fired from my job at the college where I teach philosophy.) This sort of Wittgensteinian nominalism has led to all kinds of difficulties with lesbigay leftists (to say nothing of right-wingers), as you might well imagine. Well, of course, no one likes to be accused of failing to *think*, and I can be pretty irritating, I guess.

My concerns in "It's What's Inside," insofar as I'm considering it as writing (and not, say, as an effort to work out my life or solve the world's problems—neither of which I've any objection to doing), are mostly writerly concerns. I don't see myself as a *gay* (etc.) writer; I see myself as a writer. When I'm writing about, say, the current debate over the nature of the welfare state, my experiences of sexuality seem to me less useful than when I'm, say, writing about getting fucked by 'Greg.' I guess, by definition, a gay writer would be someone who wrote either mostly for gay writers or mostly about gay experiences. As it happens, I don't.

In "It's What's Inside," I was concerned with several problems. The most obvious one is how to write about a commercial advertisement and about a masturbatory fantasy accurately, and to interweave them so that the result will be interesting to readers. More substantially, one issue I'm exploring is the relation of commodities and the power of the marketplace to the sense we have of ourselves (identities), and I attempt to 'deconstruct' or, really, abstract that from the instance of a core sample item in the culture, namely, a commercial that infected my consciousness for a few weeks. Much of that concern finds its origins in conversations over a number of years with poet George Stanley and, in particular, reading his "Teenage Boredom Poem."

Conversely, I took the reductionism involved in pornographic production (both the commercial and home-brew varieties) as an issue. And here, I should say, that I indeed view pornography as 1) particularly a gay political issue insofar as images of homosexual desire and practice are systematically denied to people identified as gay, and 2) as a particular writing issue for writers dealing with homosexual desire insofar as it's the case that all accounts of such desire are viewed by some portion of society as a kind of pornography in and of itself. The solution, for me in this piece, was to explore the biographical complexity involved in a given sexual fantasy in as much detail as possible. That is, in insisting on the reality of such mental productions, I could regard it as an opportunity to develop an auto-critique of my own desire.

Finally, in terms of genre, "It's What's Inside" is a further exploration (within 'literary non-fiction' or 'non-fiction fiction') of what I think of as the 'narrative essay,' and syntactically (since that piece of writing appears to employ unusual lengths, rhythms and grammatical devices), I'm interested in registering some of the *paratactic*, as it's known, disgressional quality of my mental phenomenology to see how much of that can be included in writing, and whether there's any point to doing so; I have game-like technical concerns (for some reason, this reminds me of Elliott Goldman, with whom I was friends at about age eleven or so, explaining to me how he built radios; I suspect writers' technical obsessions are of as little interest to non-writers as Elliott's utterances were opaque to me).

Andy Quan

Difference powers my creativity, my need to express myself and my personal politics. This is where I write from. I view the world through my blessed and cursed identities, as an Asian Canadian, as a gay man, as a gay Asian. This affects not only the themes in my writing but also the act of moving my writing into the public eye. Friends of mine who write are not always as driven as I am to make submissions to magazines and publications, and to write articles for newsletters and newspapers. Because I believe that diversity should be recognized and celebrated, I also believe that I have something important to say.

Therefore writing, and sharing that writing, is a political act. In performing this, I speak with my own voice and attempt to do so on my own terms. My words on a page prove to myself, and others, that I exist, that I am not invisible. At the same time, my voice must not be reduced to dialectic, and my person reduced to precise, correct labels and identities. "How to Cook Chinese Rice" reflects my perplexity about who I am, and my efforts to find out more.

I assume that, if I am confused by the implications and subtleties of my identities, others will be challenged. The question of audience is a difficult one for me: will the reader be familiar with the themes I present? How much can I assume that they already know? It's easy to slip into a confessional voice when talking about experiences so different from the mainstream and marked by so much hurt and violence. Even if I've managed to avoid this tone, I can't avoid a very self-conscious voice. Part of the gay identity involves constantly querying what family, friends and strangers think about homosexuality, what they would think if they *knew*, what they think after they know. Though my self-confidence nowadays means I'm not crippled by other people's opinions, I am still very aware of an audience when I write.

The self-consciousness of my writing relates to my sexuality. "It's not easy being green," said Kermit the Frog, "you have to blend in with the colours of the trees." Growing up gay, always aware of a different perspective and reality, I learned to move between contention and subversion. Have I learned to use this to advantage?

If I share my search to understand this world with others in a relatively conventional writing style, aiming for clarity and accessibility so a reader will be drawn in rather than alienated, maybe I can more easily sneak in thematic and political subversion. My most important creative aim, though, is simply to write well. I don't believe in an absolute power in art, but good writing does stand out: it gathers people around it like a campfire glowing with warmth in the middle of a dark forest. I want to be able to fit words together like a living jigsaw puzzle, ready to jump from the page into breathing air, to sparkle with sudden truths, to draw the world in with grace and beauty.

Queer writing, and any writing from a marginal site, is at an interesting point in our history. Lesbians, gay men and bisexuals often face the same hostility as in the past, and we face daily instances where we can shake our heads and think "nothing changes." At the same time, there seems to be real progress being made, and gaps opening in the mainstream to new and diverse voices. Queers are more open and visible, especially in the artistic world.

Whether we are coming out to the mainstream or coming in from the margins, I think it's a good time to be writing. I hope that the world of art continues to open its strange-coloured doors. Roque Dalton, the Salvadorean poet, wrote, "I believe the world is beautiful / and that poetry, like bread, is for everyone." I feel the same about writing, and I hope that literature will reflect each one of us, and all of our diverse voices.

Ian Stephens

I slithered from the womb crying and wet into his hands.

I'll slither out the same way.

It all makes sense, the jagged cycle—the faces, flesh and barking cum scenes, the hard boys soaking the raw sky.

No, no, no, there's an *intellectual* way of putting things, this relationship between writing and being queer; I'm suffused with it, marinated with being a fag, righteous, outlandish, jaded and wise to a scum society that hates me, that gives me the death we suffer, faithful to the faith that no one will care even as I dare to be decent to my fair brothers, my ugly hearts, the days that are past, the little time I regret, the timidity I became—skulking around the orgy lightly caressing the butcher's flesh, kneeling for another silver cock that won't stop; I became a shadow and wrote it all down; I did it for you and sulked like a tiger watching the gorgeous sluts, waiting for a call from Sweet Terror, the loser with a hard-on, the guy possessed, the dead ones who glitter, the glowing dancer, Ulysses Dove of the Alvin Ailey Dance Co., with love, with love, I usher the heart to the altar.

In the can I suck off the mechanic with the tribe of coroners oiling off Valiants and Cougars; porno jets jerk in the Pope's face . . .

Queers aren't any truer than others, no more prone to kindness than the dear nurse who pulls the blood, politicians and power queens, ready to do but not to *feel*, as petrified of this age as anybody else—I write for this; I don't think the initial need to write had much to do with being a fag, I don't care about that except that *what* I write smells of being fucked, that's all, and if sensuality or male cum is queer then I am sperm, too.

I sing in bands and even there I don't like to rehearse much or cart around equipment from cheap bars to pool halls; same as with the music—I write, that's all. Just to get the tape rolling . . .

"Wounds: Valentine's Day" is typical of my style: a true emotion (obsession & the wounds thereof) spilled onto the highways and spread by blind monkeys to the dirty flesh of buildings on fire.

And I don't know *exactly* what I'm doing. And I don't wanna know his name and the history of it all; if it's dark, that's better, if the leather's good and you have a nice cock and know how to hurt me right, get me wrong, spoil it and shut up, shut up for once in your fucking life. If I can write as the soldier slowly turns away and you shoot it out as I kiss the shoulder of a bastard in front of my wasted life and keep it forever while the Skins arch their backs and say, "His poems have a rare expressiveness. With his loose style and intense vision, his exuberance and thick sense of irony, he provides unending enthusiasms—I'm coming, I'm shooting, shit. Ah . . . Fuck . . ."

And beyond this, there is a quieter love, the vibrant, steady life-long affair with one; slower, less dramatic, yet as important as blood, this love endures and heals and to this I rejoice, to him whom I haven't written but would if will was time.

Martin Stephens

The man who used to rape me is dead. I learn of this in a letter from my mother, who mentions it after updating me on the inclement weather and the declining health of her dogs. "I'm sure you'll be sorry to hear that V. has died. He was killed in a boating accident on the weekend." Further details follow, but I've stopped reading. The news sinks in quickly like a stone dropped in still water. He is dead. The man I have wanted to kill is now dead.

I can't decide which disturbs me more: the news of his death, or my mother's presumption that I would be sorry to hear of it.

The man who used to rape me is dead. There will be no trial, no investigation, no interrogation. Nothing more will ever come of this. There will be no public acknowledgement that a crime ever took place. Nor will I receive any kind of apology.

I am at once both disappointed and relieved. There was never any evidence to begin with. It would only have been my word against his. And now his words have run out, his voiced drowned. Only one version of the truth remains. I may never be proven right, but at least now I can never be proven wrong.

I am free. Free at last. But free from what?

None of this is true, of course.

I am eight years old. I am with my family, walking up Mount Royal. Beside me is my mother; slightly ahead is V. with my brother and sister. We're walking up the path towards the stairs which lead to the lookout at the top of the hill. The leaves are turning colour, so it must be early autumn. I've slowed my step to keep pace with my mother, waiting for V. to walk far enough ahead so as to be out of earshot.

"V. is mean to me," I tell her.

"What?" she asks.

"He's mean to me. He hurts me."

"Nonsense," she says. "How does he hurt you?"

"I don't know. But it hurts." This is the best I can do. I don't have the words for what he does to me. All I know is that it hurts and I want it to stop.

She considers what I've said for a moment, then brings the conversation to an abrupt halt. "Don't be ridiculous," she tells me. "Stop making up stories."

So I do. I stop making up stories. For fifteen years I tell no one else about the abuse. I tell no one about much of anything at all.

None of this actually happened.

I am ten years old. I am sitting on the top landing of the stairs leading to the basement. My mother is below me, standing beside the washing machine. She is bent over the cement laundry sink, oblivious to my presence at the top of the stairs, scrubbing at a piece of fabric. Her elbows are in furious motion, like the wings of a bird. What she has in her hands is a pair of my underwear, from which she is desperately trying to remove the bloodstains.

She looks up suddenly and realizes I've been watching. For a moment our eyes meet, and I recognize in her face a reflection of my own experience. Behind the fierce denial her eyes betray the damage that she herself has withstood, the abuse she suffered at the hands of her uncle. Abuse which has been passed down from generation to generation like a defective gene.

I think that she might actually have believed it, too, believed that she could wash the entire incident down the drain along with the blood. As long as it all came out in the wash, there would be no reason to make an issue of it.

Mother. How can I ever forgive you for this? Your complicity hurts me more deeply than the abuse itself. You knew. And did nothing. And put me back in this man's care.

You're making all of this up.

I have something to say to the ghost of the man who used to rape me. And to my mother. And to her uncle. And to anyone, in fact, who will listen.

Here is what I have to say, what must be said over and over again until it is heard, until it is believed, until I believe it myself.

This cycle of abuse ends with me. It stops here. It goes no further.

Stop making up stories.
Stop.

It ends as it began: with a dream. The man who used to rape me comes back for me one last time. He is wearing a uniform; at his waist hangs a gun. He is a customs clerk at a border gate. I have just stepped off a plane and am trying to get through. He makes me empty my pockets, to show him what I have with me. I offer him my passport, my wallet. My map. Still he glares at me with his hand out, insistent, dissatisfied, demanding something which I am unwilling to give. What is it he wants from me? I have nothing left to give him. I have nothing left. I am spent.

He reaches out for me and I feel something stir inside, the slow burn of a dormant longing. I want him to touch me. I want to be held by him, to be held down. I want him to wrap his arms around me and whisper in my ear. I want him to tell me that everything will be all right, that it won't hurt for much longer, that it will all be over soon.

Guilt washes over me in waves of recognition. This longing is what I have tried so hard to forget, this is what has kept the memories so deeply buried all these years. The truth is that along with the blood and the lies, what took place between us occasionally resembled intimacy. Not only did I allow the abuse to continue, but parts of it I almost enjoyed. This is the true source of my shame: that there was some pleasure mixed in with the pain.

I have never admitted this to anyone. I have scarcely begun to admit it to myself. But only the dead keep their secrets forever.

There. I have named it. Are you satisfied? Now will you let me go?

I reach out to touch him and my hand passes through his flesh as easily as through air. He is gone. Dead and now gone. The border is open. I walk past the gate. I have no map and no currency, uncertain even if I speak the language. Nonetheless I step forward, into an unknown country.

John Timmins

I would hazard a guess that in the recent prevalence of the postcard story, or 'flash fiction,' critic and novelist Annie Dillard could find yet further exemplification of the thesis she details in *Living by Fiction*. Postmodern fiction, she argues, has jettisoned the felicities as well as the excrescences of conventional narrative and character construction, replacing them with intense, bizarre and internalized distortions, angles, voices and patterns. The sea-shell intricacy of the postcard story which, in its brevity, frustrates our impetus to go forward, our hunger for more of this world in which a tantalizing crack has momentarily opened, is a fine example of this refracting tendency in contemporary modernism. Ideal instances of this genre, however, like Kent Thompson's "Ponderosa" or Allan Gurganus' "A Public Denial," make this small world so large, so vividly peopled, that we can often draw, from that one ray of the prism, all the colours in a trilogy of novels.

In her study of contemporary fiction, Dillard repeatedly shows how postmodernist forms and devices are most apposite to marginal characters and situations: in fact, postmodernism is seen as virtually consubstantial with marginality. Few members of society have a richer, longer litany of subordination (calumny, misrepresentation and assault) than homosexuals or, as some earlier epochs referred to them, the partisans of Greek love.

Looking again at my two postcard stories, I find that they are linked not only by genre and gender, but also by my attempt to dramatize perplexing, crisis-cracked states of mind, consciousnesses squeezed out of shape by catastrophes whose urgency is reinforced, not diluted, by the short duration of the stories. In "Awkward Age," the obsession with size, with the physical shrinking of the beloved, also implies a fear of his abstract shrinking, after death or separation, in the heart and mind of the narrator. One of our most common, unspoken fears, uncovered when the emotional fumes rise, is that the loved one is not really as large, as capable of filling all the chambers of the mind, as we had once thought. A man travelling away from me dwindles just as palpably as a man physically reduced day by day right in front of me by the ever-growing resources of a hideous affliction.

The speaker in "Red Bread" also confronts a plague, but more with viscera than with abstraction, and a plague different in kind, but not degree. With his body as transformer, he attempts to switch the current, from violence horrifically, passively witnessed to violence ecstatically, sacrificially embraced. In *Chris and His Kind*, Christopher Isherwood refers to the "heterosexual dictatorship"; with the swollen water table of bloodletting that continues encroaching upon gays everywhere, I now see that he was being neither radical nor florid nor allusive, but only precise, literal and prophetic.

Jack Valiant

"A Fresh New Fair World" is meant to illuminate aspects of marginalization experienced by some young gay males in Vancouver in the 1980s. The backdrop of Expo '86 serves as an ironic and starkly contrasting example of the lifestyle ideals presented by the ruling elites in that period. The protagonist's lover shows some of the suffocating homosexual repression and covert quests for affection that accompany the politics of power. The structure of the story presents two narratives simultaneously to encourage an atmosphere of movement, integration with history and potential for change.

David Watmough

I started writing professionally as a teenager, before I publicly acknowledged my homosexuality, but I didn't embark upon my gay fiction until over twenty years later, in 1969. The question of why I began to address gay themes when I did is not too difficult to answer. I'd written a succession of plays for both the theatre and the electronic media and, although they were gratifyingly received, their creation left me with a curious emptiness. By then I was aggressively out as an individual and felt a corresponding compulsion to be equally candid in print. This was the era of the counter-culture, and an urge to level with my readers and affirm an uninhibited honesty over sexual experience and gay sensibility became paramount whenever I took up my pen.

I wrote a couple of short stories based upon mildly homoerotic experiences in the Cornwall of my childhood, and subsequently read them to an Australian-born writer friend who was thus also an immigrant to this country. Although straight, he felt the echo of shared experience, and immediately suggested I perform them on stage because of their strong histrionic content. That suggestion of his led to my compiling enough of these early stories about homosexual childhood and adolescence (I originally called them 'monodramas') to start performing them on radio and TV, and in venues across Canada, the U.S. and Europe. In 1972, a collection of them was published under the title *Ashes for Easter*, which turned out to be the first of eleven short story collections and novels featuring my homo-hero Davey Bryant and the various adventures he experienced from childhood to middle age in the three countries that have most shaped him—namely, Britain, the U.S. and, for half of his life, Canada.

Because I am chronicling the personal life of one gay person rather than working as an author dedicated to evoking the gay scene, the degree of gay subject matter varies from book to book, although I ensure that none is without homosexual content with usually enough to upset the purist and the prude. As my first half-dozen titles draw substantially from Davey Bryant's youth and early manhood, I think they include a substantial degree of what one fan has described as my "randy pages." Certainly there are more evocations of fellatio, cruising of public johns and parks, and erotic encounters between Davey and black studs in earlier collections than more recent works. But I am not trustworthy in these matters, and do not intend to be in the future.

AIDS doesn't cast its dour shadow over these events, as they belong to a gay history of twenty and thirty years ago, when uninhibited gay sex was more extensive and exuberant and its price tag less devastating.

A progressive factor in my fiction has been the concept of the gay family. The notion of family is prominent in *Vibrations in Time* and *Thy Mother's Glass* and even more so in my upcoming book *The Time of the Kingfishers*, which, significantly, began life with the working title *Families*. A distinct impetus to this family theme in the gay environment was provided for me when my partner and I celebrated our first forty years together back in 1991. But my background as a Cornish Celt, the sense of clinging to kin as an immigrant utilizing the twentieth century technology of travel and communications, has been a contributing factor to my fiction from the outset. This family theme highlights the link between David Watmough and Davey Bryant. They have much in common but there is substantive difference, too. As a gay author, I need the freedom to fabricate and distort experience—in other words, to write fiction. I do not write autobiography, distancing myself by fictional event from the roughly parallel life-experience of my character, who always appears in the first-person. So although my own life—and, by extension, the lives of those I've met in the course of it—provide the motherlode of material for my fiction, it doesn't provide a mirror for it.

The story in this anthology is one of a series about occupants of an apartment house in Fort Lee, New Jersey, which faces Manhattan from the west bank of the Hudson River. It roughly derives from an experience I had when living with my lover in New Brunswick, N.J. shortly before we moved to British Columbia in the early '60s. Yet it is recent vintage, as I return to this apartment series whenever the mood takes me. Then that's how I write. I sometimes imagine I am sitting before a gigantic and incomplete jigsaw puzzle and, depending on the mood of the moment, decide which part of the puzzle I will tackle next: young Davey or old, in San Francisco or Vancouver, via story or novel.

My literary goal is eventually to provide the completed fictional biography of a gay everyman of the twentieth century through an unfolding series of novels and stories. It has taken—still takes—my own life experience to feed that goal. But a word of warning. Woe betide those who blithely confuse David with Davey or search for inner consistency over details in book after book. The inconsistencies strewn deliberately within my pages provide a path at the end of which lies a reader's madness.

Dwayne Williams

Someone once asked me, "Did your sexuality make you become a writer?" "I don't know," I answered. "Does it matter? I am not exclusively compelled to write about gay characters, gay themes, gay this or that, but I do know that my work is so deeply connected to my body and psyche that being gay largely influences what I write and how I write it."

Queerdom, then, is an inevitable and wonderful aspect of my sensibility as a writer. I write not from a political agenda (I'd get on a soapbox if I wanted to incite revolution), but from the desire to free the language of my body. The story is a gesture, psychological but also physical, that tries to make sense of the body-in-the-world. What goes on within the story must also be going on within the body—the same concert of movement and desire. I write not with my hand but with my tongue. I strive for a physicality in my writing that will allow the reader not only to hear, but also to taste and feel, every word.

Salman Rushdie, in internal exile, wrote, "Literature is the one place in any society where, within the secrecy of our own heads, we can hear voices talking about everything in every possible way." Gay men know the toll that silence, censorship and denial can exact on human lives. I wrote "Behind Glass" in response to a sort of exile that came to typify the lives of many gay men throughout the '80s. AIDS, of course, exacerbated that exile. I suspect, however, that estrangement was there long before AIDS came along and will continue for some time into the future. It is an odd condition of this exile that it is enforced and perpetuated not only by the homophobia of the 'evil oppressor' (whoever that might be) but by the secrecy of gay lives. Many gay men continue to live within the exile of the closet, sacrificing their voices for a degree of safety. They live not private but secret lives. Such secrecy, I believe, isolates the individual and starves the imagination. Maybe literature is that place where we can have our secrecy and eat it too—eat it and eat it until it liberates gay lives, rather than confines them.

Raymond John Woolfrey

I find gay culture fascinating—I love observing it and being a part of it. People, especially gays, love to point out its weaknesses. Of course it has weaknesses—what could anybody expect of a people who are treated as the scum of the universe? It is important to remember that. We're lucky we survived at all—so many didn't: suicide, drug and alcohol abuse, now AIDS.

But despite our hardness on each other, we need each other. As we meet to have fun, sex or build something together, we learn each other's stories. I love the stories I hear from gay men and see unfold—extraordinary tales of coping, hoping, loving, lusting and losing. I see boys come to the city to forget the families that have forgotten them. They come with nothing and they make their friends, eke out a living somehow, get into trouble, and dance. Always dance.

Gay writer Ethan Mordden said that it is men who are the romantic ones, always looking for adventure and love. I believe that. Buddy Cole said a three-month gay relationship equals six straight years; we love hard, live multiple lives, and are now dying hard.

I mean for "Red Geraniums" to speak to two groups of people. I wanted to show gays something about spirituality. Alex had already embraced spirituality long before he got AIDS—he was a church warden in Toronto, for example. Many people with AIDS, like others seeing their death approaching, start to look at spirituality; some embrace it. Friends have come with me to my church to see what it's about. Once they let down their barriers and listen to the teachings and reflections of the clergy and congregation, they find a good deal of sense in it that is relevant and helpful to them. Remember, faith is purely a matter of believing, believing in more than just our petty, puffy ego and its drive for self-gratification.

Organized religion has hurt and damaged so many people, but Christ's message was simple: Love one another. If we can go beyond the wrongdoings that have been perpetrated against us by poor, misguided members of the Church, and consider rather what Christ said—or the teachings of other faiths that speak of love, peace and the higher self—what do you think will happen?

I also wanted to speak, in my story, to spiritually motivated people—Christians, New Age Aquarians, Hindus—about gays: our love for life, our sorrows, our need to be loved by the world that has despised us for so long. We've all heard stories of people dying alone of AIDS because others have rejected them. I've seen gays gather around their dying friends. I challenge spiritual people—especially those who claim to follow Christ—to "love the lepers." We're here today. And we continue to dance.

Wayne Yung

"Brad: December 22, 1992" is a snapshot from my pilgrimage in search of my sexual and racial identity. As a gay Canadian, I lust for the snow-skinned Adonis; yet as a gay Chinese, I stand outside the forbidden city of "gay white male seeks same." If beauty and love are the white man, can I be beautiful and beloved? Growing up gay and Asian in Edmonton, it has been a struggle to discover the romantic potential in myself and my brothers.

For a gay man alone among straights, it can be difficult to imagine the romantic potential of same-gender love. Gay writing is often the spark that inflames the romantic imagination. Homoerotic fiction is rich with fantasy lovers, from English aristocrats to Midwestern farmboys to Fire Island disco queens. The promise of cruising blue eyes and sweaty blond hair beckons. In a world of love liberated, there is a place for each of us.

Unless, of course, you're not a sweaty, blue-eyed blond. There is no place for Asian men in the romantic imaginations of most Canadians, straight or gay. There is no Chinese lover in the rose garden, the hayloft, the tea dance. He belongs in the laundry, not the bar; in the restaurant, not the bedroom.

His one apparent refuge is in the arms of a rice queen. Then, the stone-faced eunuch becomes a dark-smiling geisha, arms swaying to the flute and drum. After standing outside the bedroom door, the dancing feels good. Eventually, however, the kimono becomes a straitjacket. The burden of exotic stereotyping can be just as painful as sexual invisibility.

My writing today explores the struggle to establish a gay Asian identity that is somewhere between the emasculate and the exotic. It shifts the focus, from "gay white male seeks same" to "gay Asian male seeks other." As gay writers honour the unique beauty of men loving men, I honour the distinct beauty of the Asian lover.

In the end, queer writing is not about any sexual preference in particular, but about the diversity of preference. It is the affirmation and celebration of the varieties of love. Asian sexuality is a vital part of the larger sexual community, and love and sex are alive and well among those of the 'Asian persuasion.'